Richly Deserved

Brenda Margriet

RICHLY DESERVED

First edition published March 2021
Copyright © 2021 Brenda Margriet Clotildes
Print ISBN 978-1-7773513-2-8
Digital ISBN 978-1-7773513-3-5

Cover Art by Steven Cote

"I'm going to draw you," Titus said.

"Don't be silly." Claudia shifted as if to stand, and he held her down. Even in his furor to get a pencil and paper, he kept his touch gentle.

"I have to. I've been thinking about it for days. And now, with the light streaming in..." He gestured to the nearly full moon glowing outside the window and she lifted her chin to look where he pointed. "Don't move!" he said urgently. He wanted that exact tilt of her jaw, the angle of her head over her shoulder.

She ignored him and turned to look at him again. "I am not going to model for you, Titus."

Desperation to create welled up inside of him, fierce and strong in a way he rarely experienced. He didn't have time to argue.

So, he kissed her.

His palms on her cheeks, he pressed his mouth softly to hers, doing his best to wordlessly convey his need. She gripped his wrists but as he deepened the kiss her touch grew slack. Her mouth opened, welcoming him in, and her hands slid up his arms to his chest, and then wrapped around his neck.

He'd wanted to distract her, bewilder her so she'd sit for him without complaint. Instead, the heat of her passion was like a backdraft, the fire he'd set roaring out to consume him.

He dragged his mouth away reluctantly. Her eyelids fluttered open, and raw satisfaction filled his chest. Her gaze was dreamy and dazed. She didn't resist when he took her chin in his fingertips and placed her exactly where he wanted her.

"Look at the moon," he said. "And think about me."

He went to get his sketchpad.

To all the Inspiring Women in my life -
Family, Friends, Colleagues, and Readers.

CHAPTER ONE

It is a truth universally acknowledged that a businesswoman acting as her own general contractor must be in need of a large hammer.

With which to hit recalcitrant sub-contractors on the head.

Unfortunately, bastardizing Jane Austen wasn't going to fix the current situation.

Claudia Aronson bared her teeth. The grizzled man in front of her jerked a shoulder toward his ear and looked away.

"Tell me again, Cecil, why the paint on that wall is *not* the colour I chose?"

Cecil spun the roller in his hand. Claudia took a step back to avoid the drops flicking off the fuzzy head and almost stumbled, her heel catching in the drop cloth protecting the floor. Her temper flared and she clamped down on it.

"You said you wanted white," Cecil said, waving a hand at the wall behind him. "This is white."

"I chose Dove Wing in a matte finish," Claudia said with what she thought was admirable patience. "This is Super White in glossy."

Cecil squinted at the wall. "Well, sure. But they're both white. And this was on sale."

"I don't care. It is *not* the white I chose." She nudged the paint can with the toe of her shoe. "Return this, get

Dove Wing, and redo the wall. And if there is no refund, you'll have to absorb the cost of the correct colour. I did not order Super White, so I am not paying for Super White."

Without waiting for a reply, she sailed through the door and down the hall leading to the main room. Thank goodness she had caught Cecil's error before he'd finished more than one of the smaller walls in the rear of the gallery.

The main exhibition area was still in the throes of renovation, but Claudia could already see the finished space in her imagination. She stood in the middle of the room with her hands on her hips and let the vision that had been dancing in her head for months erase the tension of the last few minutes.

The entire front of the building was a wide expanse of glass protected by an awning that allowed muted daylight in—enough to give the room a natural glow but not enough to cause issues with potentially fragile artwork. Of course, it would be supplemented by discreet, appropriate lighting where necessary. Half the space soared two storeys high, while the other half had a twelve-foot ceiling that didn't detract from the lofty, airy feel. The walls, now a bedraggled canvas of unfinished Gyproc and drywall mud, would be the soothing, classy shade of white she'd lost sleep deciding on, now that she'd sorted that issue out. Drawing a deep breath through her nose, she reminded herself there were still four weeks until her soft opening, and that was plenty of time to correct Cecil's mistake.

He wasn't all bad, after all. While he might have rebelled over her choice of paint colour, he had followed her instructions exactly when it came to the false walls she'd had him construct. These were currently lined up like dominoes, waiting for their own coats of paint, but when completed she'd be able to place them in various locations throughout the space, giving her the ability to customize traffic patterns and displays. She'd even gone to the considerable cost of having an electrician run wiring under the floor—being careful to preserve the original hardwood as much as possible—and installing discreet outlets in several places so that the portable panels, each wired internally, would have proper lighting.

She heard the backdoor slam shut and deduced that Cecil had left to get the correct paint. Stepping carefully around the piles of construction paraphernalia, she manoeuvred toward the folding banquet table placed near the front windows that was serving as her desk until her office—in the back, next to the smaller gallery that was also going to be a client lounge—was completed. Her heels clicked on the floor, which still needed to be sanded and refinished, but that would be one of the last steps to avoid any potential damage. The deep honey colour she'd chosen for the stain would soften the white of the walls even further and warm the space from industrial to natural.

Flipping open the lid of her laptop, she began reading and replying to emails. While the gallery was taking up a lot of her time and energy, she still had her framing business to run. Its decades of success were the foundation on which she was building this new venture and it deserved her attention.

Dreams were all well and good, but they needed to be rooted in practicality.

She had worked her way well into her to-do list when a shadow crossed her desk—and stayed. Assuming it was a lookie-loo wondering about the work going on in the long-abandoned space, she ignored it. After several moments, when it didn't move, she looked up.

Silhouetted against the sharp June sunlight was a man. A large, broad-shouldered man with a shaved head, heavy eyebrows, and a short dark beard. He wore stained, ripped jeans and a slouchy black hoodie, and stood with his hands in the pockets, staring intently past her into the interior of the gallery.

Still expecting him to move on, she waited. He didn't appear to have noticed her, tucked into the corner against the wall, and his gaze swept the room, sharp and assessing. An uneasy feeling trickled down her spine. No artwork was stored in the building yet, but the tools and supplies visible were worth hundreds if not thousands of dollars.

She reached slowly for her phone, before remembering with relief the front door was locked. The movement must have caught the man's attention, though, as he turned his head toward her.

The glass did nothing to dim the concentrated focus in his eyes. Claudia blinked, frozen with one hand on her phone and the other gripping the edge of the table.

"Can I come in?" he asked, his voice muffled but audible, and moved to the door.

Not on your life, Claudia thought, and remained in her seat.

He grasped the handle and tugged firmly, rattling the frame. "It's locked," he said. He raised his eyebrows and smiled, gesturing her to approach.

Cautiously, she rose, circled round the table, and stood in front of the door. Now she was no longer seated, she realized he wasn't quite as tall as she'd thought, probably only a couple inches taller than herself. But since she was wearing two-inch heels and was five-eleven in her socks, that still put him well over six feet.

"What do you want?" she said.

"Are you Claudia?" he said. "Claudia Aronson?"

Most of the tension leaked out of her shoulders. "Yes. And you are?"

He held a small, square card flat against the glass. The stylized rendition of a mountain framed three words forming two lines of text.

Titus Wilcox. Artist.

She unlocked the door.

Titus was used to being regarded with caution. His size made many women—and some men—step warily around him. He didn't mind. He wasn't one for small talk, didn't enjoy meeting strangers, and was happiest on his own. If others preferred to keep him at a distance, he was fine with that.

Once he'd decided to interact with someone, he wanted to get it over and done with. Claudia Aronson had initiated the contact, so now she'd have to deal with him on his terms.

As he waited for her to release the deadbolt, he scanned the small, professionally printed sign fastened to the glass beside the door. *Future home of FAUNA,* it read in large font, and below, in smaller type, *Art Gallery Opening Soon.* He liked the name. It gave him a good vibe.

Claudia swung the door open, stepping back to allow him in. "Thanks." He moved past her, deeper into the large room. The multi-level ceiling gave it character, made it feel less warehouse-redone chic. "Nice," he said. "Versatile. Location's out of the way, though."

"Prince George isn't a big city. Nothing's *that* out of the way," she said with a faint bite that hinted he should mind his own business. "We're only a few blocks from the downtown core."

"In a light industrial area."

"It's changing. There's a craft beer pub just down the street and a communal artists workshop one block over."

He'd obviously poked a sore spot given the blue fire in her eyes and the faint flush rising to her pale cheeks. He liked the vigour of her response. If he was going to allow her to show his work, he'd need her to tap into that passion to make sure it sold.

"You never replied to my emails," she said.

"I read them. That's why I'm here."

"I appreciate that," she said. He was unbothered by

the undercurrent of sarcasm he detected. He didn't need her to like him. If she wanted him badly enough, she'd have to take him as he was.

She hadn't moved from her position near the door. She stood straight spined with her hands clasped at her waist like a nun in a medieval painting. An Amazonian nun, he thought, one confident in her height and voluptuousness. An electric blue skirt clung tightly to generous hips and her white blouse was unbuttoned at the neck, not indiscreetly low but enough to hint at abundant breasts. Her shoes were an eye-catching blend of colours with slender heels high enough to emphasize the strong curve of her calves.

"I rarely do exhibitions," he said, wandering around a pile of supplies to get a closer look at a row of unfinished, free-standing panels. They were placed like books on a shelf, spines facing out, each about ten feet square and fifteen inches wide.

"I know. But you've just moved to town. I'm opening a new gallery. It would benefit us both."

"I've been here ten months." And would be moving on in two more. A year was the most he stayed in one place. "I hate schmoozing."

"Ten months is new to town. I'm good at schmoozing. And making sales."

"I don't need the money."

"*Everyone* needs money. But I agree, it's not about the money. It's about sharing your art."

He shot her a glance over his shoulder. Did she really understand that was the basis of all creativity? Or was she that good at her job?

She had left her sentry post and now stood a few feet away, neat and pristine in the middle of the renovation rubble. Her blonde hair was textured and wavy, just longer than chin length, and if it was coloured to hide the grey a woman of her age might be expected to show it looked natural and flattering. Her blue eyes met his with calm assurance.

Before he could say anything further, the front door opened, reflecting light like a sword stroke across the room. Claudia turned her back on him.

"Mae," she said, striding toward the young woman standing uncertainly in the entrance. "Is it that time already? I'll be ready for you in a moment."

Titus noted the thin, rectangular, paper-wrapped package clutched in Mae's right hand. Was she another artist Claudia was courting? The young woman had straight dark hair and, next to Claudia's vibrant persona, appeared slight and frail. Tiny arms and legs dangled from a baby-carrier strapped to her front and a pink cap peeped out under her chin.

Claudia took her arm and escorted the younger woman toward the table in the corner, before hurrying across the dusty floor back to him. "I'm sorry, I have another appointment."

"That's okay, I can wait."

"But—"

"I want to get a feel for the space," he said. "It will help me decide about the show."

"It's a construction zone."

"I'll use my imagination. I am an artist, after all." He nodded at the panels. "Movable walls?"

She nodded. "Yes. Almost any configuration you want."

"Excellent."

She hovered, a frown creasing between her brows.

"Go." He shooed her away with one hand, and she went, giving him one last puzzled glance over her shoulder.

Artists, **Claudia thought,** torn between indulgence and irritation. *Totally oblivious to normal social niceties.*

Titus had disconcerted her from the moment she'd seen him looming outside the gallery, but she didn't have time to deal with that now.

"I'm sorry," Mae said the moment Claudia drew close again. "I can come back if you're busy."

"No, it's fine. But I will ask him to leave if he makes you uncomfortable." She studied Mae, trying not to be obvious about it. The younger woman stood beside the table, darting nervous glances at Titus.

"It's okay," she said. "He's just...very...big, isn't he?"

"Yes, he is," Claudia said gently. "But he seems quite pleasant." Domineering and arrogant, but pleasant with all that.

The baby gave a tiny squawk and Mae automatically started swaying. "I hope it's okay I brought Jasmine. I didn't think we'd be long, and I didn't want to leave her at the shelter's daycare. She's been fussy today, and I thought the walk would do us both good."

"Of course it's okay. I suppose I should start getting used to having a little one around."

"Your daughter is due soon, isn't she?" Mae's face lit up. Talking about babies, either her own or others, brought out a loving spirit that made her glow.

"Still eight weeks. She says it feels like she'll be pregnant forever."

Mae laughed. "I remember thinking the same thing."

The contrast between the person Mae was now and the battered, downtrodden being who had appeared at the women's shelter four months ago was indescribable. Memories of the heavily pregnant woman, face bruised and reddened by blows, who had shown up during one of Claudia's all-night volunteer shifts had her blinking back tears. She said briskly, "So, what have you brought me?"

"It's probably nothing," Mae said, placing the package on the table. She leaned over awkwardly, the happily gurgling baby kicking in the carrier as she tipped forward on her mother's chest, and Claudia hurried to help unfasten the paper. "And I would hate to sell it, but Jasmine and I need to move out of the shelter, and I need all the money I can get to do that and set up my daycare business."

Claudia didn't bother mentioning Mae's soon-to-be ex-husband. She and the younger woman had had that discussion many times. Mae was refusing to take anything from him, although Claudia had convinced her to accept the court-enforced child support and put it in a savings account for her daughter's future. She could sympathize with Mae's need to cut off all contact with her abuser—understood it with her heart, as well as her head—but also knew that life would be hard enough without undercutting the financial support she deserved. Mae would come to be grateful for the money. She just wasn't there yet.

Mae pulled back the last fold of paper and Claudia studied the painting she revealed.

CHAPTER TWO

Titus watched the two women out of the corner of his eye while he wandered through the gallery. They were deep in discussion about the painting the younger woman had brought. He caught a glimpse of it as they unwrapped it, and it reinforced his earlier belief she was also an artist, although why she would have brought a single original and not a portfolio with more samples was a question. Instead of growing impatient as the conversation went on, he found himself curious about what could be causing that look of concentrated focus on Claudia's face.

When he'd exhausted the limited attractions of the front room, he glanced at Claudia, made sure she was too engrossed to notice, and then stepped into the back hall.

Faint bangings and clangings had started up a few minutes ago, and he followed the noises into another room about one quarter the size of the front. Inside was more construction debris, and an older man with a faded ball cap, paint-stained coveralls, and a disgruntled expression on his not-recently shaven face.

"Who are you?" he said, eyeing Titus, a flat-headed screwdriver poised over a five-gallon bucket of paint.

"Waiting to talk to Claudia," he said vaguely. "Is she planning on displaying art in here? The white on that wall is blinding. It doesn't work at all."

"Not you, too," the man said in disgust. "White's white, I say. But, no, she wants something called Dove Wing. And what Claudia wants, she gets." He bent over and pried the lid off the bucket. Even without seeing it spread on the wall, Titus knew it was a much more suitable colour.

"I'm Titus."

"Cecil." He slopped paint into a roller tray and hammered the lid back on the bucket.

Titus waited for him to stop pounding. "Are you the general contractor?"

"Nah. She doesn't have one. Just hiring people as she needs them."

He wasn't surprised Claudia was leading the renovation herself. Nothing in his minimal interactions with her had indicated she preferred to be anything but in control. "Have you worked for her before?"

"Done some carpentry for her over the years at Four Winds. Built those fancy floating walls in the other room, too. Don't usually do painting, but the guy she hired backed out a few days ago, so she asked me." Cecil began rolling the new paint over the bright white. Titus felt tension ease in his shoulders. Colour was a language to him, and that wall had been shouting obscenities.

"Four Winds?" He hitched a hip onto a metal sawhorse and settled in. Despite his professed aversion to people in general, individuals were interesting. And he was still unresolved about the exhibition. Maybe Cecil could tell him more about Claudia, help him decide.

"Four Winds Framing. You know, a place you can bring Gramma's doily or a sports jersey, get it all fancied up. She used to work there, then bought it about fifteen years ago. Few months back, got a bee in her bonnet about starting a gallery. Signed for this place the moment she saw it, started things rolling within weeks. Don't do things by halves, Claudia."

"She's going to keep running the frame shop?"

"Far as I know." Cecil loaded more paint onto the roller, made a large W on the wall and began to fill it in. Despite his surly attitude he appeared a brisk and efficient worker.

"Does she have art for sale there?"

"Sure does. Says she's going to have different stuff here." Cecil shrugged. "Don't know much about it, myself."

Titus sighed. Now he would have to visit Four Winds, too, but he had reached his peopling limit for the day. He said goodbye to Cecil and received a grunt in return then headed back to the front. His timing was good. Claudia was waving Mae out. The painting still lay on the table and without hesitation he strode toward it. Always good to know what the competition was up to.

Claudia turned to him. "Where did you get to?" she demanded.

He was struck anew by her presence. Her snapping blue eyes and the confident set of her shoulders challenged him, but the wariness she'd exhibited before letting him into the gallery hinted at a well-hidden vulnerability. He'd sensed the same in her emails—a determined demand couched in language that could be read as conciliatory and accommodating. The contradiction was intriguing.

A thrill, faint but recognizable, trickled through his gut. The same thrill he felt when inspiration for a new painting struck.

Changing direction a few degrees, he stopped an inch closer to her than politeness suggested. She straightened her spine but didn't step away. "Talking with Cecil," he said.

"Is he back?" She shot a glance past him and stepped to the side. "I'd better make sure he brought the right paint this time."

He touched her elbow and she stopped. "Dove Wing?"

She nodded.

"He's got it. Good call on that. Much better than what he had before." With a gentle grip on her wrist, he drew her toward the table and the painting. "Did that young woman do this?" He released her and touched the carved wooden frame. "It looks older than she does."

"No, she didn't. And it is. At least, I think so." Claudia remained beside him, the closest she'd been. She needlessly tucked her cropped hair behind her ear and her shoulder brushed his. She shifted away. He caught a whiff of scent, subtle but seductive.

"What's the story, then?" he asked.

"According to family legend, the painting holds the secret to a great treasure." Claudia looked at him, a small smile curving her lips.

"Really?" Even more curious now, he placed his hands on either side of the frame and studied the image.

The canvas was about twelve by eighteen inches, and on closer inspection he could see the grime of years had dulled the colours of the oils. Despite that, the scene was easily visible. Two men sat around a campfire, one tending a frying pan set on the flames, the other leaning against a rock, tendrils of smoke rising from a cigarette in his mouth. A third man crouched next to a nearby stream, gold pan in hand. They were surrounded by a dense evergreen forest, and behind them mountains rose, tips white and tinted with the orange and pink of a gorgeously painted sunset.

"It's good," he said.

"I know. I was surprised, too." Claudia shared another quick grin. "When Mae said she wanted me to look at a family heirloom, I was prepared to be polite but realistic. But this isn't the usual run of the mill amateur effort."

"Who painted it? I don't see a signature."

"That's one of the mysteries. According to Mae, her

parents gave it to her as a wedding gift." Claudia's eyelids flickered. What in that innocuous sentence bothered her? Titus filed the observation away to think about later. "It has been handed down from oldest son to oldest son for at least three generations. She was an only child, so her father broke the patriarchal tradition and gave it to her."

"Where do you come in?"

"She wants me to value it. Or find someone who can." Claudia frowned and stroked the frame of the painting. Her nails were neatly rounded, painted a deep burgundy, and long enough to hide the tips of her fingers, but not the talons he'd seen other women sporting.

"For insurance?"

"No."

When she didn't expand on her bald answer, he said, "It needs to be cleaned. Do you have someone you use?"

"No. It's never come up before."

"I can do it," he found himself saying. "I've had some practice."

"I'm sure that won't be necessary." Claudia squared to face him and said, "Well? What about the exhibition?"

He folded his arms, still rather startled at his uncharacteristic offer of help. Something about the painting had his fingers tingling. "I'm still thinking about it," he said.

"I can give you a few more days, but that's all. I have approached other artists, and I need to start making plans. Fauna's opening is four weeks out, and I intend to host the exhibition two weeks after that. Your art is exactly what I want to showcase—contemporary yet rustic, thought-provoking yet livable. But I have other options if you feel we don't fit."

He decided not to call her out on that bit of fantasy, though her bravado made him smile. Maybe she had other choices lined up, but he doubted they were of his calibre. That wasn't bragging, it was self-awareness.

"You'll hear from me soon," he said, and headed out onto the sidewalk.

Two days later, Titus still hadn't called, and Claudia was beginning to panic. Despite her tough words, if he didn't agree to do the exhibition, she would be hard-pressed to find another artist that suited her needs so perfectly.

Thinking of *Titus* and *needs* in the same sentence had her shifting uncomfortably. He was so different from what she had pictured. His website had one photo of him, and that was a long distance shot with him at the edge of a lake. It had given no sense of his sheer size, no hint he was built like an MMA fighter. And his eyes— Claudia closed her own against the memory of the intensity in their grey depths.

Thank goodness she was no longer attracted to men with such excessive physicality.

She was reaching to turn off her desk lamp when Patsy popped into her doorway.

"Are you still here?" The woman swept into the office, energy unflagged despite a ten-hour workday. "It's Friday. Isn't this your usual drinks-with-Frederick night?"

"Leaving now. Everything closed up?"

"Lock, stock, and barrel."

Claudia had spent the afternoon at Four Winds Framing, and she had to admit working without the distractions and noise of the renovations going on at the gallery had been a relief. But soon Fauna would be her focus.

It was time to let her staff in on the changes she had planned.

"Actually, before we head out, do you have a minute?" she said.

"Sure." Patsy dropped into a chair on the other side

of the desk. "What's on your mind?"

Claudia studied the other woman with satisfaction. She'd hired Patsy more than five years ago, selecting her from out of a clutch of qualified candidates. The then thirty-year-old woman had stood out with her experience, references, and attitude, but it had been a risk taking her on, as her full sleeve tattoos, pierced nose and spiked, bright blue hair had contrasted sharply with Claudia's usual clientele—suits that could afford to drop a thousand dollars to frame a signed Wayne Gretzky jersey or a classic Robert Bateman print.

She had never regretted her decision. The tats, piercing and vivid hair—pink now—had camouflaged a bright, artistic mind and a work ethic second to none.

"You know I couldn't run this place without you, right?" she said.

"Well, that's a lie, but a nice one." Patsy leaned forward and patted Claudia's hand. "If there's one thing you've taught me, it's that anyone can do anything. If you can't do it yourself, you find someone who can. In the end, it's the same thing."

"I know I haven't been as focused on the frame shop as I should be lately," she said. "And it's going to get worse and worse the closer we get to the gallery opening. Then afterward, I'm going to have to spend most of my energy there to make sure it achieves what I know it can."

"We got your back," Patsy said confidently. "You leave Four Winds to me and the other girls."

"I will. And I know you'll do an excellent job. That's why I'm naming you manager and giving you a fifteen percent pay raise, retroactive to the beginning of this month."

Patsy's mouth dropped open. "Me? Manager?"

Claudia nodded. "Don't think I haven't noticed you've been picking up my slack without even being asked. You deserve it. We can work out the details later, and I'll always be here for you, if you have questions or concerns. But in effect, I'm giving this baby to you."

"I can't believe it." Patsy's eyes brimmed and she blinked.

"No one deserves it more." A bite of panic clutched Claudia's gut. "You will accept, won't you? I never even thought—"

"I accept!" Patsy rocketed around the desk and pulled Claudia out of her chair into a vigorous hug. "You're the best boss ever. You won't regret this. Thank you!"

"You're welcome." She squeezed Patsy tight one more time. "All right. Let's get out of here before we get too mushy. I'm already running behind, and you know Frederick. If he's not fifteen minutes early, he's late."

Titus wasn't deliberately avoiding giving Claudia his decision.

Well, he was, but it wasn't malicious. It was necessary.

When he'd left the gallery, he'd taken a step back from everything he'd experienced that day. He put aside his impressions of Claudia, tried to forget about Mae's painting, dodged thinking about the show. He'd come perilously close to forming new relationships in the short time he'd spent there, what with chatting with Cecil and offering to help clean the painting, and he needed some space.

Opening the wood-framed, black-stained French doors, he stepped onto the deck of his house, whiskey glass in hand. When he'd decided to make Prince George his next transient headquarters, he hadn't expected to find a home that suited his needs so perfectly, so easily. His art required the inspiration of wilderness and isolation—but his career needed the sophistication of internet and business networking. To find it all less than a half hour drive from the largest city in Northern British Columbia had been more than he'd hoped for.

It was as if it had been meant to be. Except he didn't believe in fate.

The house was far too large for one man, but that hadn't mattered once he'd seen the view. He would have rented a palace—as long as it had a decent space for his studio—in order to call the sight before him *his*, even if only temporarily. He'd happily signed the one-year lease, though that was on the outside edge of his usual length of stay in any one place. The husband and wife who owned the house were doing a stint with Doctors Without Borders and wanted the security of the twelve-month rental.

Now that term was coming to an end, and he had to admit the thought of leaving was causing a pang or two. He would miss watching the lake change with the seasons, creating in the excellent studio, and working out in the well-equipped gym. But most of all he would miss the sense of home that enveloped him when he walked in the door.

Maybe he was getting old, but picking up and moving on no longer held the exciting appeal it once did.

Setting his glass down, he leaned his elbows on the deck rail and looked over the edge. A cliff dropped precipitously at his feet, slashing thirty feet before cleaving into water that in certain lights appeared amber, but in the dimness of dusk was a gleaming ebony. To his right, a small bay swooped around in a gentle curve, dark green spruce and pine marshalled along the edge of the rocky beach that rimmed the shore. From this vantage point, he could see no other sign of habitation, though he knew there were numerous cabins and houses out of his sight beyond the opposite point.

An annoying tinkling noise came from inside, and with a sigh he went to answer the video call from his agent.

CHAPTER THREE

"Hello, Yvette," Titus said, carrying his laptop to the living area and folding onto the couch, stretching his legs out on the white leather and propping a pillow between his back and the chrome armrest. The house had come furnished—he would have chosen something much more comfortable and far less trendy.

"Titus. How are you?"

"Had a couple productive days," he said. "I finished those two pieces I told you about and even managed to update my website."

"Good boy."

Despite the facetious tone of the compliment, Titus accepted it with a smile. During their long, tumultuous relationship, the one thing that hadn't changed was Yvette's refusal to pander to his temperament. She continually brushed aside his successes, challenged him to do better, refused to fawn over him. He needed to keep his head grounded, she insisted, and it was part of her job to make sure he did.

She was right, of course. Not that he'd ever admit it.

"So, what's on the agenda today?" he asked. "You know I love these weekly get-togethers, but I've got things to do." Nothing pressing, but Yvette didn't need to know that.

They spent an hour discussing which images to include in next year's calendar (always a big seller) and new sales opportunities (Germany was emerging as a solid market for his work). The last topic was Claudia's proposal (he couldn't avoid it forever, after all).

"I know you hate schmoozing," Yvette said, "and we definitely don't need another incident like what happened in Edmonton, but you agreed long ago you would do at least one public appearance a year. My recommendation is the one in Vancouver. You'd be wasting your annual trip off your figurative mountain if you used it to attend a new, untried gallery in a substantially smaller market."

An unexpected surge of defensiveness made Titus bristle. "You're always telling me I have to expand my horizons. Claudia Aronson has run a successful frame and art shop for several years, so she knows business. She has a degree in Art History from the University of Toronto, so she knows art. Prince George itself has a thriving artistic community, including a well-respected public gallery, and its per capita personal income is above the provincial average."

On screen, Yvette's eyebrows lifted. "You've been doing your homework."

He was not going to admit he'd done some stalking of Claudia since their meeting, mostly to reassure himself he was making his decision for business, not personal, reasons.

"I'm doing the local show," he said firmly.

Yvette sighed, but she knew better than to waste energy trying to change his mind. "She wants a new piece from you?"

"That's what her email said."

"I can negotiate that out if you like. The event is what, six weeks away? I don't want you to feel any pressure."

"I can handle it. I'll flip through my sketch book.

Something will pop."

"Great. I'll send her an email."

"You know what?" Titus said, "I'll let her know."

"You will?"

He wasn't sure he appreciated the note of amazement in Yvette's tone or the speculative gleam in her eyes. "Yes, I will."

"All right. Make sure you send me the contract *before* you sign it."

"I'm a big boy, you know. I can even read."

"What do you pay me for?" she demanded. "Send it before you sign it."

"Fine. Is that all?" he asked hopefully. The business side of his art always gave him a headache.

"Not quite." Yvette bit her lip and Titus' attention sharpened. It was her tell when she knew he wasn't going to like something.

"Out with it. What's the bad news?" he said.

"It's not exactly bad news. Well, not for me at least."

Now Titus was *very* suspicious. "Yvette…"

"I'm moving to Toronto," she said in a rush. "I was headhunted to manage one of the most prestigious private art galleries in the city." She mentioned the name, but Titus was so flabbergasted by her news he didn't absorb it. "I won't be an agent anymore. My clients will need to find other agents to assist them."

"Except for me," he said automatically.

"*All* my clients," she said softly. "No exceptions."

"But I'm not a *client*," Titus said. Dizzying déjà vu swept through him. Yvette had left him once before, when he'd been young and stupid and had put his art ahead of everyone and everything.

"I love being your agent," she said. "But I need to do this."

Titus knew he could be blind when it came to interpersonal relationships. It was as if he put all his powers of observation into his art, with none left over for the people in his life. Pushing aside his anger and dismay for a moment, he studied Yvette's familiar face.

She had gamine, delicate features that had reminded him of Audrey Hepburn from the moment he'd met her. Not that it was her face that had initially captured his attention. On his first day in the Visual Arts Program at the University of British Columbia, she had taken the seat in front of him in the Approaches to Media course. Her dark hair had been piled in a knot on top of her head, and he hadn't been able to take his gaze from the nape of her neck. The almost-ebony strands had silvered over the years, and she'd recently taken to enhancing the look with platinum colouring. Now that he was paying attention, he noted the lines at the corners of her eyes and lips, the softening of the skin of her throat. She was a few months older than him, which he realized with a shock meant she had already turned fifty.

"Say something, Titus."

"Why did you agree to become my agent in the first place?" he asked abruptly. "You left me because I couldn't balance my work and our life. So why did you take me on as a client when I came knocking on your door five years later?"

"Why did you ask me, instead of finding another agent?" Yvette countered.

"Because..." He paused, gathering his thoughts, trying to remember those heady, whirlwind years when his art was gaining recognition. "Because I trusted you," he said.

"I took you on because I'd accepted I would never be a great artist, but *you* would be. I wanted to be a part of that."

"You can't leave me again," Titus said. It wasn't a plea, it was a demand.

"You didn't get to make that decision the first time," Yvette replied, "and you don't get to make that decision this time either, Titus."

Usually, Friday drinks with Frederick meant they would go to one of the local restaurants or bars. They had made a conscious decision long ago not to get in a rut, to make sure they sampled all the new and different places that were constantly popping up. Tonight, though, Claudia had suggested they stay in, and Frederick, amenable as always, had agreed to come to her apartment.

She was uncorking the red to give it a chance to breathe when she heard a discreet knock. Smiling, she opened the door. Frederick stood on the small landing outside.

She'd been convinced to lease this building for Fauna, despite its slightly out-of-the-way location—yes, Titus was right, damn him—partly because of the apartment that came with it. As soon as she'd seen the compact one-bedroom unit on the second floor, she'd recognized it as another cost-effective revenue opportunity. It hadn't taken long to find renters for the home where she'd raised her two daughters, and she'd moved into the apartment even before renovations had started below.

"Hello," she said, dipping her head to give Frederick a kiss in greeting. "I'm glad you're okay with this. I really needed a night in."

"No problem." Unlike the suit and tie he would normally don for their nights out, he wore a sport jacket with a shirt striped in blue and yellow unbuttoned at the neck and khaki pants. He smiled back at her, his brown eyes warm, and followed her inside.

"Thanks for understanding." She handed him a glass of merlot and he took a seat on the sofa in the living room. Bringing her own glass, she sank down next to him with a sigh. "It's been a week. I just want to put my feet up and relax." She inhaled the rich, chocolatey scent of the wine and took an appreciative sip.

"This is a nice change." He laid his arm along the

back of the couch and tasted his wine. The usual comfortable silence grew between them.

That's what she thought of, whenever she thought of Frederick. Comfort. When her marriage had ended about twenty-five years ago, it had taken her a long, long time to even consider dating again. But then she'd taken over Four Winds, and she'd started attending more and more social events for business reasons. She had no problem going alone—still did on occasion—but it had left her feeling a little out of place.

Frederick Colbert was her accountant. She'd inherited him from the previous owners, as he'd been doing the books for the frame shop long before she purchased it. When his own marriage dissolved several months after she'd taken over, she'd impulsively invited him to attend a Chamber of Commerce event as her escort. They'd slipped into an easy relationship, which had gradually escalated to include sex. She'd wondered if sleeping together would ruin the companionship that she valued, but Frederick had continued in his easygoing way, never hinting that he wanted anything more, and she'd relaxed again. They'd been friends with benefits for a couple years now.

"So, why was it a week?" he said, emphasizing the last two words. "Troubles with the gallery renovations?"

"Nothing out of the ordinary." She recounted Cecil's insurrection and had Frederick laughing. "My biggest worry right now is I still haven't heard from Titus Wilcox. I'm giving him the weekend, but if I don't hear from him by Monday, I'm moving on to my next choice." She *really* didn't want to do that. As much as she loved the work of the local artist she had put second on her list, her name didn't have the pull—yet—that Titus had.

"It sounds like he might be playing you," Frederick said, "trying to put pressure on you for some reason."

She leaned her head back, feeling the warmth of his bicep under her neck. "I don't think so. He must know he has the upper hand. He has a reputation for being reclusive, and does hardly any public appearances. You either get Titus or you don't. I was shocked when he showed up at the door of the gallery. Nothing I've read gave any hint he took such a personal approach to his business."

"Well, I'm sure you'll handle it, whatever his decision."

His calm certainty usually soothed her, but for some reason tonight it made her restless. Indignation over the position Titus had put her in wouldn't be amiss. Couldn't Frederick show some emotion over the potential wreckage of her plans?

He slid his arm out from underneath her head and leaned forward to help himself from the charcuterie platter she'd placed on the low table in front of them before his arrival. She'd picked up the premade tray on her way home and transferred it to one of her own dishes to make it look less slapdash.

"We're still on for the Elizabeth Fry Society fundraiser next week, right?" he said, his fingers hovering over the plate as he studied the selection.

"Of course." The annual gala in support of programs to assist women and children in crisis was near and dear to Claudia's heart. In the past, she'd been on the organizing committee, but with launching Fauna she'd taken a step back. She planned to take a role next year and was also looking forward to doing more volunteer shifts at the shelter where she'd met Mae when things settled down again. "I'm supplying three prints from the frame shop for the silent auction. I've also bought a couple more tickets. Patsy needs to start attending these events, since she's taking over as manager."

He nodded and leaned back, munching on a cracker stacked with prosciutto and thinly shaved Parmigiano Reggiano. Silence settled once more. A less comfortable silence.

Maybe deciding to stay in had been a mistake. They

never seemed to have trouble making conversation when they were out and about.

Her phone rang. She sprang off the couch to retrieve it from the kitchen counter, and then stood staring at the screen.

"Aren't you going to answer it?" Frederick asked as the tone shrilled out again.

She looked up at him, heart pounding. "It's Titus Wilcox."

He nodded. "Go on, then."

She connected the call and put the phone to her ear. "Hello, Titus."

"Bring out the contract tomorrow. If my agent agrees, I'll sign it."

He sounded angry and her spine stiffened. She might want—*really* want—him for her exhibition, but she wasn't going to allow him to treat her with anything less than respect, artistic temperament be damned.

"I'm fine, how are you?" she said sweetly.

The pause on the other end of the line was heavy and taut and she held her breath. "I'm cranky," he finally replied, his voice a shade less irritated, and she relaxed. "I just had an argument with my agent and have no patience for contracts and legalese at the best of times. If I give you my word, that should be enough. But I told her I'd call you myself, so I am. Deal with it."

She almost laughed. She would put up with a lot more than surliness to have Titus as part of her grand opening. He didn't need to know that, though. "Tomorrow sounds fine. What time is best for you?"

"I paint every morning, so how about one o'clock?"

She could make that work but acquiescing to Titus' demands too easily might be a bad tactical error given his irascibility.

"I already have an appointment then. How about four?"

"Fine. I'll email you directions. Oh, and one more thing. Bring that painting the young woman gave you."

Claudia frowned. "Why?"

"I want to get another look at it."

"It has nothing to do with you."

"Bring the painting, or don't bother bringing the contract, Claudia."

The hair on the back of her neck stood up when he said her name. "I don't—"

"I've been thinking about it, and I want to see it again. We can discuss it more tomorrow." He hung up.

She placed the phone on the counter and turned to Frederick. "That was weird."

"Did he agree to the show?"

"I think so. But he has a condition."

"Is it one you can live with?"

Claudia noticed he didn't ask for specifics. Frederick was very careful never to overstep his bounds or offer advice unless she asked for it. She had a feeling Titus wouldn't be concerned with displaying the same civility.

"Yes. I just don't see how it relates to the show."

Frederick shrugged. "Then I don't see a problem."

Claudia didn't either. Which was one reason she didn't trust Titus' request.

CHAPTER FOUR

"Come here." Frederick held out his hand and Claudia stepped forward to take it. He tugged her down to sit beside him and she leaned into his shoulder. "Enough work." He pressed a kiss to her mouth, and she did her best to shove Titus from her mind.

Frederick's lips trailed along her jaw and she lifted her chin, waiting for the curl of gentle warmth his caresses usually lit in her. Their lovemaking had never been ravenously lustful, which was fine with her. She distrusted excess emotion.

"I was thinking," he said as he flicked her earlobe with his tongue, "that I should stay the night."

Claudia's pulse, steady and calm during his kisses, kicked into a higher gear. "You know the rule," she said, keeping her voice light. "No overnighters."

He lifted his head. "I've stayed before," he coaxed.

Yes, and I was in a low-grade panic every minute of every night. I have no desire to repeat a failed experiment. "I'm sorry. I'm not comfortable with it."

"We've been together two years," he said with a touch of asperity, "and I've stayed over fewer times than the fingers on one hand. You've *never* stayed at my place. Don't you think it's time to bend the rules?"

She shifted out of his loose embrace. "No, I don't."

"Claudia—" he said cajolingly.

"I'm sorry. I explained this right from the start. You said you understood." She would not give in. *Could* not give in. This was Frederick, her friend. He wouldn't make her do something she didn't want to.

"People change. Relationships change. I was thinking it might be time for *us* to change."

She searched his face, relieved to see no anger, but aware of a flickering frustration deep in his eyes. "Are you unhappy with what we have?"

"Not *unhappy*, no," he admitted. He took her hand and she let him hold it, but her fingers felt stiff and cold. "Am I interested in exploring more? Maybe."

A familiar sense of airlessness caused Claudia's heart to race. She stood up, pulling her hand out of his grip, and retreating to the far wall. "That's not what this is, Frederick. What we have now is all I want, all I can give."

"I didn't mean to upset you." Frederick rose and she tensed, relaxing only when he didn't approach. "I just thought it might be nice to spend the night with you more often."

She almost apologized for a third time but caught herself. She had nothing to apologize *for,* damn it. "Maybe it's best if you go."

His eyes widened. "You're sending me home?"

"I don't think either one of us is in the right frame of mind to spend time together," she said. "I'll see you next week for the gala. But right now, I think I need to be alone."

It was lucky Titus' directions were so detailed, otherwise Claudia might not have found his house. He'd told her to set her odometer to zero when she left the highway for the narrow, winding Blackwater Road, and then watch for the address marker on her left once it ticked over to thirteen kilometres. Black iron numbers attached to a rustic cedar plank marked the private drive, but the sign was set back from the road and easy to miss if you weren't looking for it.

The lane wound through thick forest, and an adventurous thrill, as if she were about to discover a fairy-tale castle or a dragon's lair, had Claudia's heart tripping lightly and her belly clenching.

The sensations had nothing to do with seeing Titus again. After all, she had no reason to be nervous anymore. He'd agreed verbally to do the exhibition. All was well.

It wasn't a castle, but the house did not disappoint when it finally came into view. Sleekly contemporary with a sharply slanted roofline, wood siding in matte black and deep cedar, and rugged stonework, it melded with its rustic setting yet made a bold statement. The landscaping was wild and relaxed—no manicured lawn or rigidly planted urns here. A detached two-car garage was set off to the side, and a large, dark green SUV was parked near the low flight of steps leading to the double-door entrance.

Claudia pulled her own SUV to a stop beside the one on the drive, lifted her purse from the passenger seat and stepped out. Opening the rear hatch, she retrieved Mae's painting from its safe storage and headed to the front door.

It opened before she reached it and Titus filled the frame. Unlike his disreputable look the day he'd come to the gallery, he was dressed in clean navy jeans and a white buttoned shirt. His dark beard looked newly trimmed, and she noticed for the first time threads of grey and silver. His scalp was smooth and gleaming.

"I'm not late," she stated, disconcerted that he appeared to have been watching for her arrival.

"No. I happened to be coming down the stairs and saw you pull up." He stepped back and gestured with one hand. "Come on in."

She came to an astonished halt a few feet into the entrance. "Oh, my god," she said breathlessly. "This is *gorgeous.*"

"My thoughts exactly. Go on, get a good look."

She didn't resist when he took the wrapped painting out of her grasp. Drifting forward, she tilted her head back and took in the enormous empty space above her, the huge wall of windows on the other side of the expanse of living room—and the view.

"It's like we're in the middle of nowhere," she said, drawn toward the French doors that led to the wide deck. "Wait. That's West Lake, right?"

"Yes. Although I find the Indigenous name more poetic—Nadsilnich."

"I didn't realize when I drove in that the lake was this close." She turned her back on the view. Titus stood in the centre of the conversation area. To his right a large gas fireplace was set in a white wall that soared to the ceiling far above. A huge canvas in an explosion of colours—nothing like Titus' own style—hung over it. The interior was even more modern than the exterior, yet he seemed right at home. Given the masculine yet sensual aura of his work, she'd always envisioned him somewhere rougher, more textured and primitive.

She blinked those thoughts away. "Now I know where this is. I call it the house on the bluff. Friends of mine have a boat, and most summers I spend an afternoon or two with them out here. I've seen this place from the water, but never dreamed I'd ever be inside."

"You're welcome to explore it more."

She was tempted, but that was something a person would do if the visit were for pleasure, not business. "Maybe another time," she said, and then realized *that* sounded like she was angling for a repeat invite. "I mean, I don't have time right now."

Slipping her purse off her shoulder, she grasped the folder with the contract and held it out. "I could have emailed it, you know."

"But then you would have missed seeing all this"—he swept his arms around in an all-encompassing motion—"and I would have missed a closer look at this." He sat on one of the low, chrome and white leather sofas that surrounded a square glass coffee table, lay Mae's painting on it, and used a blunt, heavily knuckled finger to peel off the tape sealing the package shut.

Claudia stood, arm outstretched awkwardly, still clutching the ignored contract. Taking a steadying breath, she approached and perched on the sofa next to him. "Why did you want to see it again?"

He didn't answer. Instead, he rose to his feet. She had to crane her neck to look up at him.

"How about a drink?" he said. "Wine? Whiskey? Soft drink?"

He had her so off balance she didn't dare have alcohol. Besides, she would be driving home soon.

"Do you have Club Soda? Any sort of sparkling water?

He nodded. "Lime? Lemon?"

"Lime, please."

He nodded again and disappeared behind her. She could hear him moving about in the kitchen—an open expanse of stainless steel, stark white stone countertops and glossy black cabinetry that she'd only glanced at on her way to the magnetic view.

She relaxed her shoulders. This was obviously not going to be a quick get-in-and-get-out visit. It was lucky she didn't have anything pressing to do later this evening, since she wasn't leaving until he'd signed the contract.

From the kitchen, Titus watched the set of Claudia's shoulders soften. She seemed anxious to get business out of the way, but he was in no hurry to have her leave. She was an intriguing blend of contradictions—sharp yet conciliatory, whimsical yet precise.

She was a lot like what he tried to portray in his art. He filed that thought away for future study.

He returned to the sofa with two glasses of sparkling water garnished with lime wedges.

Accepting hers, she smiled politely. Her professional smile, he decided. The one she used to placate clients and charm artists. He was fine with that for now, but he found himself increasingly curious about what was behind that facade.

"So, are you going to tell me?" she said. "Why did you want to see the painting again?"

While she appeared to have accepted he wasn't going to talk about the contract until they got the painting out of the way, he didn't think she'd be patient for long.

"Who was the young woman who brought it in?" he asked.

"Mae Smo—" She stopped and started again. "Mae Leung." At his raised brow she pinched her lips together, before adding. "She's recently left her husband and gone back to her maiden name."

That explained Claudia's odd look when she'd told him the painting had been a wedding gift. Placing his glass on the side table, he shifted to the edge of the sofa so he could get a better view of the artwork lying before him.

"Mae said it's been in the family for a few generations, right?"

"Her father told her that *his* grandfather was given it as a wedding present by *his* father. Her great-grandfather was married in the early 1930s. But she doesn't know how her—what are we up to now? Two greats?—grandfather acquired the painting. Whether it was already in the family or if he bought it specifically as a gift."

"It's an unusual subject to give to a young couple for their wedding. Three scruffy men camping out by a stream in the wilderness, panning for gold. Why this painting?"

Claudia leaned forward and he glanced at her profile as she studied the image with renewed interest. Her bright hair curled neatly around her ears and at the nape of her neck, and he was close enough to see the dusting of powder on her eyelids.

"Mae is of Chinese heritage," she said. "I wonder if the family has some connection to one of the gold rushes in British Columbia. I know for a fact Barkerville had a large Chinese population. I can ask her if you like."

"It's a place to start." He pulled his attention back to the image. "Even if we don't know where it came from or when it was painted, we know it's close to a hundred-years-old since it's been in the family that length of time." He leaned over further, examining the brush strokes, looking for craquelure, the tiny faults often seen in old oil paintings. "It really needs a cleaning." He rose, bringing the painting with him. "Come on."

He thought he heard a sigh, but without waiting for further protest, headed to the stairs beside the front door. Claudia followed and he led her to the second level, along the hallway that opened to the living area below, and into his studio.

A large rectangle of cabinets, much like an island in a kitchen and complete with two barstools tucked under an overhanging counter, took up a quarter of the floor space. He laid the painting on it and strode behind the island to the wall of shelves that contained his supplies.

"It is becoming more and more obvious why you chose this house," Claudia said, standing in the doorway and surveying the large room.

He grinned. "The view sold me, but this certainly didn't hurt. The wife of the couple I'm renting from is an artist, too. Not professionally, but seriously. They had the house custom built, and she designed this for herself." Like downstairs, one wall was almost completely glass, although these windows had heavy blinds for light control. The floor was a paint-speckled industrial tile which would be easy to clean if he ever decided to do it.

"Sometimes the planets align." She moved forward and the sunlight falling through the large skylights—which had blinds sandwiched between the panes that were controlled by an app—glinted off her hair.

"Do you believe in that stuff?" He chose a bottle of emulsion cleaner and grabbed a handful of cotton swabs. Returning to the counter, he said, "Astrological signs? Fate? Predestination?"

"Not really. But sometimes the coincidences are hard to ignore." She moved past his empty easel and toward the racks that held his canvases, both finished and unused. Her hand reached out but before she touched anything, she looked over her shoulder at him. "May I?"

"Go ahead."

He watched her lift a canvas out of its slot, study it, put it back, lift out another. She remained silent as she moved onto the third.

It didn't matter that he was a successful artist, one who made a good—very good, by many standards—living. It was always nerve-wracking to have someone new in his life look at his work. He could ignore the criticism of strangers. Nothing was more subjective than what a person wanted to hang on their wall, and he knew he couldn't please everyone. But some people—well, their opinions *did* matter.

He knew Claudia appreciated his work, or she wouldn't want him to do the exhibition at her new gallery.

But did she *like* it? Was it something she'd choose to live with herself, not just stock because she believed it would make her a profit?

He scowled.

CHAPTER FIVE

Claudia had been familiar with Titus' work for several years. She'd had prints available at Four Winds Framing, and when she'd decided she needed a strong hook for her first exhibition at Fauna, she'd researched him in detail.

Seeing his vision in its original oil paint, holding the actual canvases in her hands while standing in his studio...the effect was staggering. But the painting she held now went beyond anything she'd ever expected.

Without asking further permission, she lifted it clear of its rack and placed it on the empty easel in the centre of the room.

"This is..." She couldn't find the right word, couldn't lift her gaze from the image.

Titus came to stand behind her shoulder. "I'm trying something new. Opinions are welcome." The last words were said lightly, but a hint of tension teased Claudia's attention away from the painting. He, too, was studying the canvas, a muscle in his jaw flexing. Was he worried what she thought? She turned back to the easel.

The canvas was about thirty-six inches tall by twenty-four inches wide, an imposing size. A dramatic amount of white space surrounded a craggy, jagged-edged mountain peak. Framed within it, part of the mountain and yet separate, was a woman's face in three-quarter profile, her grey-streaked hair storm clouds streaming out of the rocks and blending into the stark white to vanish from sight. The wrinkles of her forehead and neck were the fissures and cracks of the mountainside, her shoulders and chest the slopes of the mountain, all fusing with the shrubs and grasses painted along the lower edge.

"I've never seen anything like it." The longer she looked, the more hidden details were revealed. It was like opening a treasure box. "How long have you been working on this style?"

"A few months now."

"Your other work is amazing. Landscapes that capture the sense of being there, portraits that show the soul of the person. But this—I think you've been working toward *this* your entire career. Now you're showing the soul of the land, the spirit inside nature."

She turned to him. He stood, arms crossed, staring at her as if testing her words for sincerity. His stone-grey eyes had dark rims around the irises.

Reaching out, she gripped his forearm. "It's *wonderful*, Titus. It's *beyond* wonderful."

The muscles under her palm flexed and he let his arms drop. For a moment, her hand hung suspended in space, and then she lowered it to her side. Still caught in the intensity of his gaze, she stood, barely breathing, her blood pumping heatedly in a way she hadn't felt for years. The memory of when she'd last felt such a visceral attraction—and the wreckage of her life it had caused—dashed her like a bucket of cold water and she took three steps back.

"I would be more than proud to be the first gallery to show this to the world," she said, clawing her way back to a professional footing. "Of course, you have to sign the contract first."

Titus rubbed a hand over his smooth skull, scratched

at his short, silver-shot beard, and remained unnervingly silent.

"I really need to get going soon," she said, backing up a few more steps. "Have you made a decision?"

After one more beat of silence, he said, "I want to do something first." He circled the easel and moved back to the counter where Mae's painting lay.

Irritation burned away the lingering traces of uneasiness when he once again ignored her direct question. "I still don't understand what one has to do with the other," she said, letting her annoyance bleed through into her tone.

"They don't," he said, dipping a cotton swab into a bottle of fluid and holding it over the bottom right corner of the painting. "I like puzzles. This is one."

Curiosity overcame her reluctance to stand near him and she drew close. He gently rolled the swab on the painting, his long back hunched, big hands delicate. In tiny degrees, he uncovered a one-inch square. The colours revealed glowed warm and luminous against the dinginess of the rest of the image.

"Leave it with me," he said, straightening up, a curl of satisfaction lifting the corner of his mouth. "You can't evaluate it properly until it's clean."

"Mae gave it to me to look after. I don't know if—"

"You can trust me, Claudia." She had the oddest sensation he wasn't only talking about the painting. "It needs to be cleaned, I want to do it, and you want to keep me happy."

"I do?" she said tartly.

"At least until I sign the contract." His eyes gleamed, letting her know he knew how much he was driving her crazy.

"I'm not leaving until you made a decision one way or the other. Either sign the contract or reject the offer, Titus."

"I'm not saying no, Claudia." He inflected her name just enough to alert her he'd heard the scold in her use of his—and was amused by her attempt at censure. "The exact opposite, in fact. I want to do your exhibition. I want your gallery to be the first one to present my newest work."

Her knees wobbled, relief making her weak. "I'll get the contract. I left it downstairs."

"You still have to leave without getting my signature, I'm afraid. My agent insists on reading everything first. I'll send her scanned copies tonight, and I'll bring the signed version by as soon as I get her go-ahead."

She couldn't make a fuss about what was simply common sense and good business practice. "I can understand that."

"Good. And I promise you, Yvette will have to prove there's something illegal in it to stop me from signing the contract. It's as good as done. Shake on it?" He held out his hand.

She took it, intending brief contact, a businesslike pledge. He didn't let her escape, though, instead turning her hand over and tracing the raised tendons on the back with one finger, his nail rimmed with green paint he hadn't managed to scrub away.

She swallowed and held still, refusing to give into the liquid heat his touch sparked. The reason her relationship with Frederick worked—or *had* worked, until last night, anyway—was because he was so undemanding. She couldn't imagine Titus would be as accommodating. Which meant, regardless of the attraction she could no longer deny, he was all wrong for her.

"You have beautiful hands," he said. "I noticed them when we met."

"I'm getting age spots," she blurted, and then winced.

He shook his head. "Hands reveal the person, almost as much as the face." His gaze unfocussed and she listened, fascinated, realizing she was seeing inspiration hit. "A tree. A big old cottonwood, the

45

fingers branching off the palm of the trunk." He blinked and came back from wherever he had gone. "Sorry. Thinking out loud."

She eased her hand out of his now lax grip. "It sounds like you might want to get to work. Let me know about the contract. Thanks for the drink." And she fairly flew down the stairs, snagging her purse on the way out, and fleeing to the safe sanity of her car.

"This is ready to put on the table, right, Mom?" Claudia asked. She slipped on flowered oven mitts and lifted the pan of lasagna from the counter where it was resting.

Julia Aronson finished tossing the green salad and tucked the utensils into the bowl. "Yes, thanks. I'll be right there."

It was just a few steps to the dining area, where the rest of the family attending Sunday dinner were already at the table. Her father, Harold, sat at the end, with Nicole, Claudia's youngest daughter, at his left, their heads close together as they had an intense but friendly discussion about the most recent movie in the *Star Wars* universe.

"I still say it was a silly ending," Nicole said, straightening up and putting a hand to her bulging belly.

"And I say you're not seeing the big picture," Harold insisted. "Are you feeling okay?"

Nicole winced. "She's kicking. At least she's awake now. Maybe she'll let me get some sleep tonight."

"Dinner is served." Claudia set the pan down and took a seat next to Nicole.

Five months ago, when her daughter had told her she was pregnant, her first response had been shock. It had nothing to do with the fact Nicole was unmarried and was going to raise the baby on her own. It was the incontrovertible realization that her children were now adults. Nicole was twenty-four, older than Claudia when she'd had her first daughter. Jill was soon to be twenty-seven and building a career as a microbiologist at an environmental consulting firm in Vancouver.

Her dismay only had a little to do with the fact she was not ready to be a *grandmother*. Only a tiny bit.

Her babies were grown. She'd protected them fiercely when they were younger and would continue to do so when needed. If they would let her.

That last little fact was causing tension between her and Nicole right now. Claudia knew from experience how tough it was to be a single mother, but when she had hesitantly asked about the baby's father Nicole had refused to tell her who he was. She'd also declared her intention not to tell him about the pregnancy. Claudia had definite reservations about that. Even if he and Nicole were no longer in a relationship, he could be expected to provide support, maybe even *want* to. But her attempts to convince her daughter had fallen on deaf ears, and she'd stopped pushing the issue. An abscess of distrust had formed between them because of it, and Claudia wasn't sure how to heal it.

"How's the gallery going?" Julia said as she took her place across from Nicole and everyone started serving themselves.

"It's coming together. I think I have Titus Wilcox signed on for the exhibition that will kick off the official opening."

"Excellent!" Harold offered the bottle of wine and Claudia gave him her glass. "You've been working on him for a while, haven't you?"

"It's not a done deal." She knocked her knuckles on the table superstitiously. "He's agreed verbally, but his agent needs to review the contract. It's pretty standard, except for one thing. I have asked him to provide a brand-new piece, one he must create specifically for the show itself. I want to auction it off, with fifty percent of the purchase price going to the Elizabeth Fry Society."

"He has to donate the painting?"

She shook her head. "I didn't think that was fair. That's why fifty percent. If we can bump up the bidding, which often happens when it's for a charitable cause, he should still recoup a reasonable amount. But it is a slightly unusual request, so we'll see."

"You'll need some heavy hitters at the auction, if you want to get more than retail value," Nicole said.

"I know. I'm sending personal invitations to my best clients from Four Winds, the ones I know have deep pockets, and especially the ones who have supported Elizabeth Fry in the past."

"Don't forget about my boss." Nicole worked in human resources for a local forestry company. Elwin Nyfield presided over a corporation that owned sawmills, pellet plants, and other forest industry related businesses. If Prince George had royalty, he would be a duke.

"Top of my list," Claudia said.

"I'd volunteer to help host," her daughter said with a rueful smile, "but it's a couple weeks before my due date. I'll be the size of a whale by then."

"You mean you're going to get bigger?" Harold said, pretending to be horrified. Claudia held her breath, and then relaxed when Nicole's reaction was a swat on the shoulder and a scowl, but no tears. Her father and daughter had a special relationship, and it made her wonder what kind of grandmother she'd make.

Grandmother. She was getting used to the idea, but it still didn't feel right. She was too young to be a grandmother, right? Sure, she was turning fifty in a few months, but still...

She tossed off the last of her wine. It was shaping up to be quite the year.

CHAPTER SIX

Titus spent several frustrating and unproductive hours in the studio on the weekend.

Yvette's news had rattled him even more than he'd revealed to her, and he hadn't been able to find his groove. She was his rock, his compass, his guiding star. In the heady first months of their relationship, he'd painted her obsessively. He knew now he hadn't ever loved her the way she deserved to be loved, and that she'd done the right thing in leaving him.

But damned if he could let her do it again.

He'd been desperate enough to call her on Sunday and attempt to bludgeon her into changing her mind. But she hadn't fallen for his pathos, his anger, or his wheedling. "I'll help you find a new agent," she'd said, "one that will put up with you."

"Put up with *me?*" He'd been honestly offended. "I'm the one that has to learn to work with someone new."

"I'll send you names," she'd said. "Do some internet stalking and let me know what you think."

She'd hung up during his blustering reply.

Now it was Monday morning, and the email she'd sent was still unread in his inbox. Needing to distract himself, he headed to his studio grumpy, surly, and ready to chew through a piece of canvas.

Yvette had no reason to roadblock his commitment to Claudia—especially since she was *dumping* him and no longer *cared* about him, he fumed. He was in no mood to pick up a paintbrush, but he could at least decide on a subject for the piece Claudia wanted to auction off.

First, he had to calm down. He sat quietly for a few minutes, his eyes closed, shoulders deliberately relaxed, not exactly meditating but smoothing his breath, soothing his mind. He was familiar with the Elizabeth Fry Society and approaching this project with anger and aggression would be grossly inappropriate.

His father had been a Royal Canadian Mounted Police officer for thirty years. He'd moved his wife and son numerous times throughout his career, so Titus had grown up in communities in the Yukon, northwestern British Columbia, and northern Saskatchewan. His father had never divulged details of the domestic incidents he attended, but in the smaller villages it had been impossible to avoid hearing about the horrendous things that went on behind closed doors.

He also suspected that Mae Leung might have required the services of the society. There had been something in the young woman's posture that day at the gallery, and the way Claudia was so protective of her, that hinted at abuse in her past. Given that she was also recently divorced, it seemed a logical conclusion. Domestic violence could happen anywhere, no matter the size of the community, the affluence of the family, or the age of the victim.

Once mentally prepared, he flipped through his sketchbooks, searching for something suitable. His art could be hard, masculine, even domineering. A piece done specifically for this cause would need to be sensitive without condescending. A landscape might be most appropriate.

As seemed par for the course these last few days,

none of the images he reviewed sparked any ideas.

Disgusted, he slid the last book back onto the shelf and pressed his fists on the counter. Waiting for inspiration to strike was a recipe for never getting any work done, but he also knew from experience that forcing himself to paint often ended in wasted supplies. What he needed was a distraction, something that would let his subconscious work away without him.

Cleaning Mae's painting would be perfect.

He gathered what he needed and set his playlist to Aerosmith. This wasn't work he'd done often, although one of his jobs while at university had been in a gallery, and he'd learned the basics there. If he believed the painting was valuable, he wouldn't touch it, but while the workmanship was above the usual ancestor's amateurish attempts, he doubted it was worth anything substantial.

The first step was removing the age-darkened frame. As befitted the rustic scene it surrounded, the wood was simply carved, with smoothly sanded swoops and swirls but no intricate designs. He flipped the painting over and hesitated. Brown kraft paper stretched across, hiding the reverse side of the canvas. Frowning at this unexpected sight, he took out his phone and snapped a couple of shots, both wide and close, instinct warning him it was a good idea to make a record of the original condition.

The paper had been stapled onto the frame. Very carefully, using needle-nose pliers he'd rummaged out of a drawer, he pulled out enough metal fasteners to allow him to peel the paper back.

Staring at what he'd revealed, he reached for his phone again.

To save money on the renovations, Claudia had told Cecil she was willing to do any jobs that might fit into her admittedly limited construction and renovation skill set. That morning she'd badgered him into giving her a task, and though he'd grumbled it was too soon, and complained he would have to store them until he was ready to install them, he'd set her to painting baseboards.

Now she stood in the main gallery, staring at the metres and metres of trim he had laid out on sawhorses while she'd made a quick visit to Four Winds. Cursing under her breath, she headed up to her apartment and changed into an old T-shirt and shorts, and then returned to the main floor and took up the paintbrush and gallon of paint Cecil had left out. She'd barely started when the phone she'd tucked into her back pocket began to ring.

Fishing it out, she balanced it on a section of unpainted trim and set it to speaker. "Hello, Titus," she said.

"Are you at the gallery?" he asked without preamble. She was beginning to think unintentional rudeness was his default setting. Well, two could play at that game.

"Yes. Do you have the contract signed?"

"Yes. And something else you need to see."

"What?"

"It has to do with Mae's painting."

Distracted for a moment, she said. "By the way, Mae called me yesterday. She talked with her dad, and he says the family *did* live in Barkerville. In fact, his grandfather, the one given the painting, was born there in the early nineteen-hundreds."

"I'll be there in half an hour."

Irritation at his abruptness overwhelmed her curiosity. "I know I was anxious to get the contract in my hands, but Mae's painting can definitely wait." She surveyed the cluttered room and any remaining interest in whatever he'd found waned. "I'm in the middle of something." *Literally.*

"I'm leaving now."

Her screen showed he'd disconnected. She was *not*

going back upstairs to change into more professional attire. If he was going to barge in with no regard to her own plans, he'd have to take her as she was.

Titus parked in front of the gallery entrance. Carrying a manila envelope with his discoveries tucked inside and the folder containing the contract, he tugged on the handle of the front door, expecting resistance. Instead, it gave way, and he strode into the building.

His progress was immediately impeded by a sea of long, narrow pieces of wood floating about four feet off the ground. Claudia stood in the middle of the chaos, paintbrush in hand. Sparing him a side-eyed glance, she completed swiping shiny white paint onto the dull white board in front of her, and then circled around the end and started on the next.

"Honestly," she said, concentrating on her work, "I could have waited a day longer for the contract. As you can see, I'm kind of busy right now."

Her prim, dismissive tone was in complete contrast to her dishevelled appearance. A bandanna was wrapped around her head, holding her short, golden curls off her face. Her makeup was discreet and casual, although a smear of white on her cheek and the tip of her nose ruined the effect. A tank top in a searing pink revealed toned arms and a deep cleavage, while denim shorts with a ragged hem hugged her hips and did nothing to detract from the long, curvy length of legs below them.

He swallowed.

"So, what's the panic?" she said dryly, looking up at him. "What was so urgent you couldn't wait a few hours until I was done this?"

"Right. Yes." He looked around, and then made his way to the table in the corner. He held up the folder. "Contract. Signed," he said, and laid it down. Then he held up the manila envelope. "And you'll want to see this for yourself."

She sighed and spread her arms out, wordlessly encompassing the vast amount of what he'd realized were baseboards and trim.

"Trust me," he said. "You're going to find this very, very interesting."

Laying the paintbrush across the top of the can at her feet, she threaded her way through the maze, stepping carefully on the thin plastic sheeting protecting the floor and wiping her hands on a rag as she did so.

"Okay, show me," she said. "What am I going to find so interesting it couldn't wait another minute?"

He lifted the flap of the envelope and pulled out several sheets of thick, glossy paper. "I left the originals where I found them," he said, "but these are high quality prints of the photos I took. For now, I thought that was best." He handed the first page to Claudia and watched her attention sharpen.

"What on earth..." she said.

"I thought I'd start cleaning Mae's painting and needed to take it out of the frame. When I peeled away the paper that had been stapled to the back, this is what I saw."

Claudia lifted the print closer to her face, peering at it. "There's a photograph of three men," she said, "and what looks like a letter written in Chinese characters."

"They are stuck to the back of the canvas. I didn't want to destroy anything by trying to remove them." He handed her another page, this one a full frame shot of the black and white photograph.

Three men stood on a raised wooden boardwalk in front of a two-storey building. The image was blurry, whether faded from age or simply the best technology at the time could do, she couldn't tell. Each wore dark trousers held up by suspenders, light-coloured long-sleeved shirts, and wide-brimmed hats tipped back on their heads. Each held a jar in his hands.

"What's in the jars?" she said. "I can't tell."

"How about gold?" Titus said.

She goggled. "You think so? That would be a fortune right there." She scanned the men's faces. "One of them appears to be Chinese." She looked up at Titus, eyes shining. "Do you think this might be a relative of Mae's?"

"That possibility certainly occurred to me." He handed her a third page, this one showing only the letter. "I suppose we shouldn't jump to conclusions about the writing system used here, as many Asian languages use similar characters, at least to Western eyes. But a starting point would definitely be Chinese."

"It definitely would." She stared at the page, fascination clear to read in her expression. "This is amazing! I wonder if Mae knows about these."

"I assume she would have mentioned them if she did. Again, I'm no expert, but my guess is that false back hasn't been touched since it was put in place. The staples felt like they had been embedded for years."

He pulled the print showing the full back of the canvas out of the sheaf she held loosely in her hand. "There's nothing written on the back of the canvas," he pointed out. "And since the letter and photograph are glued onto it, I don't imagine there's anything on the reverse side, either."

"This is so cool." She flipped slowly through the prints, her expression intent. "I'll call Mae right away. It doesn't seem right to keep it from her any longer than necessary."

Titus hesitated, and then said, "I'd really like to meet with her, talk to her about this, see what she knows. It's possible these two artifacts could increase the value of the painting. Like I said, I like puzzles. And this one just got a lot more interesting."

Claudia tapped the papers to her bottom lip, appraising him. "You're a very large man, aren't you?"

His eyes went blank, but she was pretty sure he'd noticed more than he had admitted the day Mae had come to the gallery. His oblique answer confirmed that. "Mae seems a little shy around men," he said.

"That's one way of putting it." Claudia let her gaze flick from his face to his feet and back again. He hadn't bothered to put on what her mother would have called "company clothes" and was wearing his paint-spattered jeans and a navy-blue T-shirt with a faded, cracked decal on the chest. His ratty appearance didn't stop a hum of attraction buzzing in her bones.

"Do you really think this painting might be worth something?" she said, blinking back to focus on the matter at hand.

"Probably not," he said bluntly. "But if we can track down the men in the photo—don't ask me how, but if we can—and translate the letter—and it turns out to be more than a grocery list—a museum might be interested enough to buy it. Sometimes it's not the art itself, but the story surrounding it that creates the value."

"That's true." Another thought struck her. "Maybe the letter tells where they buried the gold they're holding in the photo." She laughed at her whimsy, but to her surprise, Titus didn't.

"You never know," he said, perfectly serious. "Gold fever does odd things to people. When I was a teenager living in Dawson, I knew a woman who spent every spare moment looking for a cache of gold that legend said was buried on one of the hills surrounding the town." He paused, thinking. "For all I know, she's looking still. She was younger than my parents, so I'm guessing she'd be in her late sixties or early seventies now."

"You lived in the Yukon?" Claudia asked.

"Dad was an RCMP officer. He and Mom are real outdoors people, never wanted to live in big cities, so we spent a lot of years in small communities in the North.

He's retired now and they're settled in Whitehorse."

That explained quite a bit about Titus. It was part of his mystique that he didn't have a permanent base, that he moved from town to village to city as the mood struck him. And his art had a natural wildness to it that didn't come from an urban upbringing.

"About Mae..." he prompted.

Claudia came to a decision. "I can't give you details," she said, "but as you've noticed, Mae is leery around strangers, especially men. I trust you to treat her gently, but it's not me you have to worry about. I'll call her, explain what we—what *you*—want to do. We'll see what she says."

Mae answered right away. Since she and Titus hadn't officially met that first day, Claudia explained who he was, and how he'd ended up with Mae's painting. Then she told her about his discovery.

"I had no idea," the young woman said. "My dad didn't say anything when he gave it to us—to me."

"We've got copies of the letter and the photograph to give you. And Titus has some questions," Claudia said. "Are you comfortable meeting with us both?" She punched the last word a fraction.

There was a slight pause, and then Mae answered, her tone firm. "Of course. Is it okay if it's not until later? It's my afternoon for housekeeping duties."

"How does four o'clock sound? Tell you what—I'll buy coffee. We can meet you at Café Voltaire." The bookstore-slash-coffee shop was a short walk from the shelter, which would keep things simple for Mae, who didn't own a car.

"That's perfect." Mae's voice vibrated with excitement. "This is so neat. I can't wait to see what you found. It's like something out of a movie."

Claudia disconnected the call and looked at Titus, who had waited patiently, one hip resting on her table, throughout her conversation. "She couldn't meet until later."

"I gathered that. No problem." He straightened to his feet. "It's already after one. It doesn't seem worthwhile to drive the thirty minutes home only to come back less than two hours later. Is there another paintbrush around?"

She blinked at him. "Paintbrush?"

"You know." He made exaggerated swooping motions with his arm.

"What are you going to paint?"

He raised his eyebrows and tilted his head toward the ocean of trim. "It's my fault you won't have as much time as you'd planned to work on this. Seems polite to do what I can to help."

"You can't be serious."

"Why not?" he said, appearing genuinely confused.

"It's not exactly..." She trailed off, realizing how silly she was going to sound. Just because he painted art for a living didn't mean he'd consider painting baseboards slumming. "Are you sure? Wouldn't you rather go home and get changed before meeting Mae?"

He looked down at himself. "What's wrong with these clothes? How fancy is this café?"

She sighed, admitting defeat. "Never mind," she said. "Let me ask Cecil for another brush."

CHAPTER SEVEN

"I can't believe it," Mae said for the third time, staring down at the prints scattered on the table in front of her.

Titus and Claudia had arrived at Café Voltaire before Mae, and he had chosen a corner booth, sliding in so he was against the wall. His legs were uncomfortably cramped under the table and every time he took a drink his elbow bumped Claudia's. But this arrangement allowed Mae to take a chair opposite and sit as far away from him as possible, with a clear route to the exit. It was a small gesture, but the only one he could think of that might help the young woman feel more secure.

She was alone today, explaining she'd left Jasmine in the care of another mother at the shelter. Given his private conclusions and Claudia's hints, Titus wasn't completely surprised to learn where Mae and her daughter were living, though it might indicate her situation was more serious than he'd imagined.

At first, she'd done nothing more than send him quick, shy glances, but her anxious aura had slowly faded after Claudia handed over the photos.

"I made a number of copies," Titus said, "so you can take these with you. Is there someone you can ask about them? Your father, maybe?"

A shadow crossed the young woman's face. "I haven't told him I'm thinking of selling the painting. I don't want to explain how you found these."

If Mae's father was still in her life, Titus wondered, why was she living at a shelter and not with him? That was *definitely* none of his business, so he remained silent.

"I can understand he might be upset at first," Claudia said. "It's been in your family a long time. But thinking about selling doesn't mean you are committed to doing so. In fact, it is smart to have a professional look at it, for insurance purposes if nothing else."

She leaned in, focussing intensely on Mae, her shoulder brushing his in the tight quarters of the booth. When they'd finished the baseboards—he never wanted to paint trim again, as long as he lived—she'd changed out of her tank and shorts and into a silky summer dress that left her arms bare and flirted with her thighs. It had been a surprise to learn she lived above the gallery. He was used to living and working in the same space, but not everyone was comfortable with that arrangement.

"I suppose." Mae bit her lip, addressing herself to Claudia. "Not that I could afford insurance if I did want to keep it. You know I'm saving everything I can to start my daycare."

That solved at least one mystery—why Mae was even thinking about selling what seemed to be a prized heirloom. If she needed money for a business venture and didn't want to—or couldn't—get it from anywhere else, that would explain that.

"Not that I want to encourage dishonesty," he said, smiling, "but could you tell him you found them yourself, at least to start with? If it turns out they mean nothing, it won't matter. And if they are important, he might not care what started the search."

"I suppose so," Mae said, speaking directly to Titus for the first time, though she couldn't quite meet his eyes. "He knows I still have the painting, as he helped me pack up my stuff after...after I left my husband." Her chin jutted out.

"It's probably expecting a miracle to have him recognize the men in the photo, but the question needs to be asked," Titus said. "What about the writing? Could he read it?"

She shook her head. "No, he doesn't read Chinese. But I know someone who can. Our families were friends, and we grew up together. She went to the University of British Columbia and did a Master's in Asian Studies. She's in China right now, working at a Canadian government office there. If she can't translate it, I'm sure she would be able to find someone who can."

"That sounds great," Claudia said.

"Are you okay if Claudia and I try to find out more about the photograph?" Titus said, "Or do you want to talk to your dad, first?"

"It's fine, you go ahead. I don't know when I'll talk to him next. I wouldn't want to make you wait."

The more Titus got to know Mae, the more he wondered at the challenges she had to deal with. His interest in the painting and its secrets changed gears from sheer curiosity to defined purpose. This young woman needed some good news for a change. Maybe he could help.

Mae left soon after, taking the prints with her. Claudia and Titus finished their coffees and then stepped outside into the hot June sunshine. She raised her face briefly, enjoying the warmth on her skin, imagining her freckles popping out.

They started to where they'd parked their cars. "Thanks," she said.

"For what?" He walked easily, hands tucked into the pockets of his jeans, shoulders relaxed.

"Handling Mae gently, but without making a big deal

about it. There's nothing more annoying than being treated like a fragile flower when you're using all your strength to pull your life back together."

"That sounds like someone speaking from personal experience."

Her stride hitched and she had to take two long steps to catch up with him. She hadn't expected him to make the connection quite that quickly.

Thankfully, he didn't press the issue. He might look like an MMA fighter, and his personality could be demanding and arrogant, but he had patience, too.

"Mae mentioned her daughter was being looked after by another mother at the shelter," he said, emphasizing the last word. They stopped next to Claudia's SUV. "Would I be right in guessing that she is at least part of the reason the proceeds of the auction at my exhibition will go to the Elizabeth Fry Society?"

It would be ridiculous to deny. "Yes," she said, and then took a deep breath and looked him in the eye. "It is *part* of the reason." If he read the rest of the truth in her expression, so be it. She wasn't ashamed of her past, but it wasn't something she normally shared with a casual acquaintance. Whatever her relationship with Titus was, however, it wasn't casual. It had even moved beyond professional, after the afternoon they'd spent working together. She wouldn't have expected Frederick to step in and do such a mindless chore, let alone an artist she needed to keep pampered and appeased.

He nodded thoughtfully. "We have to start deciding details of the show soon," he said.

"What I really need to do is get the invites out," she said, relieved to be back on firm ground. "I sent a save-the-date type message to my client list already, because it is the official opening event, too, but couldn't go much further without the contract. Now I'd like to send out something more formal. What do you think of including the mountain spirit image I saw at your studio?"

His eyelids twitched. In a less confident man she would have taken the flinch as a sign of uncertainty. Remembering his initial reaction when she'd pulled the canvas out, she wondered again if he was really that worried about how his new work would be received.

"It's fabulous, Titus," she said. "You have to realize that."

He shook his head. "I'm too close to it," he said. "But if that's the one you want, I'll get some good shots tonight and email them to you. Also, most of my work is stored in rental space at a gallery in Vancouver. You'll need to decide which originals you want, which prints, so we can get them packaged and sent."

"Yvette sent me your catalogue when I first approached you. I've already got a list going."

"Good." He paused, spinning his keys in his hand absently. "I was wondering. Would you like to go out for dinner some time?"

Her eyes widened. "To talk about the show? Do you think that's necessary?"

He shrugged. "Why not? How about Friday?"

Was he asking her out on a date? If so, he'd be the first man to do so since she and Frederick had made their arrangement.

Frederick. "I can't Friday. I'm attending a fundraising gala." It was going to be awkward, there was no getting around that, but it was too late to break it off. She could only hope he'd revert to his usual, agreeable self by then.

"That's fine. Another time." He sketched her a salute. "Thanks for buying the coffee. See you later." And he was gone.

Shaking her head in confusion, she climbed into her vehicle. If he'd asked her out on any other night, she would have been tempted to say yes. And not for business reasons.

She had to get this attraction for Titus under control. He was off limits, for more than one reason. Besides, while she and Frederick had never discussed exclusivity, she owed him loyalty if nothing else.

It was a rather depressing thought.

During the next few days, Claudia communicated with Titus through brief emails and terse text messages. Even in her own head, her written words sounded formal and stiff, but she'd woken up Tuesday morning with the need to step back from whatever it was that had happened after their coffee with Mae.

And it wasn't just her conversation with him that had her worried. She had also been concerned about Mae's reaction to Titus' discovery. She didn't think he had noticed, but Claudia knew the younger woman well enough to have caught the gleam of hope in her eye. It was one thing for Claudia to playfully mention the possibility of buried treasure, but another entirely for Mae to put her trust in miracles—and if the painting's secrets were more than curiosities it truly would be a miracle.

She spent extra care on her appearance on Friday. She had her nails done in a shade to match the deep, jewel-tone blue of the shiny satin sheath she'd chosen to wear and visited the salon to have her highlights renewed and hair styled. Her height and size made it impossible to hide, no matter what she wore, and the days when she would have given anything to fade into the background were long gone. Now she embraced herself, enhancing her rounded, curvy form with colours and styles that accented her full figure.

Frederick arrived right on time, and she teetered carefully down the rear steps to the parking area behind the gallery. Her crystal sequined stilettos glinted in the early evening light and she grinned. Nothing like an awesome pair of shoes to make a woman feel sexy and confident.

"You look wonderful," Frederick said as he held open

the passenger door of his sedan.

She searched his face for any hint of his anger and frustration from a week ago but saw none. Relaxing, she replied honestly, "And you look very handsome." He wore a striking black suit with a crisp white shirt. A bow tie patterned in bright blues and shimmering golds lightened the sober look, and his brown hair was recently and fashionably cut. The pride he took in still having a head of full, dark hair had always amused her.

He kept the conversation to uncontroversial topics as they drove to the Prince George Civic Centre. He dropped her at the main doors, and she waited for him in the entry hall while he parked. She knew most of the people arriving by sight, if not by name, and was soon in conversation with two couples. She nodded at Frederick when he rejoined her, and a few minutes later when he touched her elbow and suggested they find their seats inside she made her excuses and followed agreeably.

Subdued lighting softened the high-ceilinged space, with round tables tucked cozily near each other. The chairs were draped in white fabric, big bows securing the coverings, while centerpieces glittering with silver and ebony flowers enhanced the formal look.

"About twenty-five tables," Frederick said. "That's a decent turn out."

"Yes." Claudia nodded at various acquaintances as they wended their way to their seats. "I'm glad. As long as the auctions go well, they should meet their goals." She'd have to keep track of the bidding on the three framed prints she'd donated, make sure she chivvied some of her clients into putting their names in.

Patsy and her partner, Chris, were already seated at the assigned table when Claudia and Frederick reached it. Frederick congratulated her on her promotion, and the four were discussing some of Patsy's plans for Four Winds when a voice spoke from behind Claudia.

"Good evening, everyone."

Claudia looked over her shoulder and up. Up and up and up. Titus stood with his hands resting on the back of the empty seat to her left. His scalp was newly shaved, if its gleam was anything to go by, and his black and silver beard freshly trimmed. He, too, wore a black suit with white shirt. No tie, though, bow or otherwise. Instead, the top buttons were undone revealing the strong, thick column of his neck.

She swallowed.

He looked down at her, eyes glinting with mischief. "Hello, Claudia. Aren't you going to introduce me?"

She did so, her thoughts whirling frantically. When the flurry of handshakes and greetings was over, Patsy drew Frederick's attention with a question about the frame shop accounts. Claudia, keeping her back straight, inclined her head to Titus and said quietly, "Why did you invite me out for dinner tonight if you had a ticket for this event?"

"Because I didn't have a ticket," he said reasonably. "I didn't even know about it until you mentioned it."

"Then how did you get one? It's been sold out for weeks. And who did you bump to get a seat at this table?" Elwin Nyfield was supposed to be joining them. She knew that, because she'd planned it with the gala organizers. Surely they hadn't moved the richest philanthropist attending to another table, not when Claudia needed to court him—for more than one reason.

Titus grinned and she couldn't stop her heart from giving a hard thump. "It didn't take much Googling to figure out this had to be the fundraiser you were attending. I then had a very lovely conversation with a young woman at the Elizabeth Fry office. She was quite accommodating, especially after I mentioned I was your artistic partner in another fundraiser for the society. As for who I bumped, if anyone"—he shrugged—"I have no idea."

She needed this evening to encourage Elwin

Nyfield's presence at Fauna's official opening. It was important, not just for the gallery but also for the success of her planned auction. Having two large fundraisers for the same organization a month apart was a risky move, and having Nyfield at the gallery, to help bid up the price if nothing else, was vital.

CHAPTER EIGHT

Titus realized the tight, cold sensation in his chest was jealousy.

He'd never felt that emotion before. Well, possibly about another artist's creation, but certainly not about a woman. Yet every time Frederick drew Claudia's attention to himself, Titus had to unclench his jaw. And his fists.

His parents had given up on him ever settling down with one person. He knew that, because his mother had stopped asking a few years ago, when he'd hit forty-five. And he used the non-gendered term deliberately, because in one amusingly awkward conversation when he was still in his thirties, his parents had explained that he could bring home *anyone* he wanted. They would love *whoever* he loved, his mother had assured him with pointed emphasis. He'd thanked them sincerely, knowing they meant it and just wanted him to be happy. But it wasn't fear of his parents' disapproval that stopped him from introducing them to any of his partners. It was a simple matter of logistics. He didn't stay in one place long enough to form solid friendships, let alone a committed relationship, and he'd yet to feel strongly enough about any woman to attempt a long-distance liaison.

At his shoulder, Claudia laughed, and he shifted in his seat, easing the growing tension in his groin.

Amongst the glitter and glamour filling the room, she was a brilliant beacon. In her vibrant blue dress, she shone among the more subdued colours most of the other diners had chosen. And it wasn't just her clothing. Her face beamed with charm and fervour.

After his arrival, she'd seemed tense and ill at ease. She'd relaxed when an older man and woman had joined them shortly before servers had brought out the first course. He'd already forgotten the couple's names, but reading between the lines, he gathered there was some big money sitting across the table. He also gathered Claudia had plans for them at her—at *his*—exhibition, from the determined way she manipulated the conversation.

More servers cleared the salad plates and began bringing in the main entrees. In the lull between courses, Frederick addressed Titus across Claudia. "I understand you're relatively new to town. How long do you intend to stay?"

He met the other man's gaze coolly. The question appeared simple on the surface, but he heard the challenge behind it.

"I'm not sure yet," he said, leaning out of the way so the server could place his roast beef and Yorkshire pudding in front of him. "My lease runs out in August, but I've enjoyed my time here, the people I've met." He cut his gaze suggestively toward Claudia, who narrowed her eyes. "I may decide to stick around a while longer."

"Claudia's told me you don't normally spend too much time in any one place but prefer to move on frequently," Frederick said, not backing down.

Titus wasn't sure if he was aware of his attraction to Claudia, but he knew that, if he were in Frederick's place, he'd be keeping a close eye on any potential rival. "Well, Freddy, that's true," he said, using the nickname deliberately, pleased to see his mouth tighten. He added, to be even more irritating, "But I'm not as young as I used to be, so maybe it's time for a change. Like I said, there's a lot to appreciate here."

Claudia's eyes were now thin slits. She was practically vibrating with the urge to tell him off. He still wasn't sure if *Frederick* had picked up all the innuendo, but Claudia certainly had.

Feeling more cheerful, he dug into his meal.

Claudia made it through the dessert course by resolutely ignoring Titus. Where did he come off, taunting Frederick like that? Not that she was happy with Frederick, either. He'd behaved extremely possessive ever since Titus had joined them, and after last week's discussion it made her very uneasy. She admitted he had a certain right to expect no one else flirt with his date—although she wasn't sure Titus *was* flirting—but that was as far as it went. Their relationship had been built on convenience and practicality, not desire and drama.

Miffed at both the men, she excused herself and headed for the silent auction tables while the others finished their coffees. She added her bid to a few items and noticed with satisfaction that her prints were already well above fifty percent of value.

"Anything I should put my name on?"

Stifling a resigned sigh, she acknowledged Titus with a raised shoulder. "Well, since you're planning on setting up house, there's a patio set and a barbeque that could use a bump in price."

"I said that to bug your boyfriend." He drifted along beside her as she scanned the bid sheets.

"Really?" she said dryly. "I had no idea. And Frederick isn't my boyfriend. Not exactly." Why had she added that disclaimer? Her arrangement with Frederick was none of Titus' business.

"You might want to ask him if he agrees with your *not exactly*." Without allowing her a chance to reply to this astonishing comment—astonishing because he'd noticed the undercurrents, not because it wasn't true—he went on. "What kind of name is Frederick, anyway? And why insist on using it in full?"

"Ever heard the saying about stones and glass houses, *Titus*?" she said mockingly.

"At least my name sounds manly, like a Roman gladiator. Not some prissy European royalty seventeenth from the throne." He stopped to put a bid down on a crate of local wines.

She choked back a laugh and turned toward him. In her stilettos she was almost the same height, and both of them were tall enough to see over the crowd. Which meant the crowd could easily see them, too. Aware that Frederick's gaze might, at this very moment, be directed their way, she resisted the urge to lay her hand on Titus' crossed arms.

"It suits you," she said. "Not everyone grows into their name, but you have."

He raised an eyebrow and opened his mouth, but before he could respond the Master of Ceremonies called everyone back to their tables for the live auction part of the evening. As they settled into their seats, Claudia was surprised to see Titus pull a bid card out of his inner pocket.

"You registered?" she said.

"It's a fundraiser, isn't it? Of course I did."

The society had hired a professional charity auctioneer. Along with her comical sidekick spotting bids from the floor, she deftly whipped up the excitement, and the pace was brisk through the first few items. Titus and Claudia each made bids but dropped out in the early stages. Frederick, who could normally be counted on to spend a sizable amount at events like these, won a unique garden bench made from driftwood. Elwin Nyfield watched the antics with a grin but made no movements that could be interpreted as interest, although his wife took part without success in a couple of small wars.

"We come now to the grand finale," the auctioneer said, her teeth flashing in a bright smile, silver bangles glinting as she waved her arm at the screen showing the featured item. "A trip for two to Mardi Gras in New Orleans! Airfare from Prince George, five nights accommodation included, as well as guided tours, meal vouchers, and more."

New Orleans, Claudia thought longingly. On the rare occasions she'd considered going on a holiday without her daughters it had been at the top of her list. And not only because of the food, the music, the history. When her loneliness had overwhelmed her, she'd contemplated the solace of a holiday fling. New Orleans was a less frequented destination for Northern British Columbian residents than Hawaii and Mexico and Las Vegas, which meant a lower chance of accidentally running into someone she knew.

Which knowing her luck, *would* have happened, despite the long odds.

"I've always wanted to go to New Orleans," Claudia said to the table at large. "But this is going to be too rich for my blood."

The auctioneer strode back and forth on her raised dais, energy pumping from her. "What an amazing opportunity. A fabulous trip, *and* you're helping women and children in your community. It's valued at seven thousand dollars. Who'll give me seven? We're going to get there eventually so why not jump right in?" She winked and nodded, making eye contact with a few in the crowd. "Playing hard to get, are you? Who'll give me six? Five? Four? All right, let's start at one. Who'll give me one thousand dollars for this stupendous trip?" Finally getting an opening bid, she began wrangling the total upward.

Paddles waved from all corners of the room, and

Claudia had no idea how anyone kept track. Not that it mattered much until the end.

The pace slowed as the price reached five thousand dollars. During a pause, as the auctioneer encouraged a bidder to go one more time, Claudia felt a whisper of movement at her shoulder. Titus spoke softly in her ear. "If I buy it, will you go with me?"

She turned her head to stare at him. He was so close she had to blink to put him in focus. His grey eyes gleamed. "Why on earth would I?"

"Because you want to go. And I would like to take you." Without looking away, he raised his bid card.

"We've got a new bidder!" called the auctioneer, and the spotter on the floor hurried over to stand behind Titus. "Fifty-five hundred to Paddle 187 at table nine. Six thousand to you, ma'am, here at the front."

For a moment, the vision of walking New Orleans' famed French Quarter hand in hand with Titus clouded Claudia's thoughts. Then she shook her head. "Bid all you want," she said, "but don't do it for me."

Turning her attention back to the stage, she noticed Frederick watching Titus with a suspicious expression. The auctioneer was still pleading with the woman bidder for six thousand dollars. Squaring his shoulders, Frederick lifted his paddle over his head.

The spotter behind Titus waved frantically, and the auctioneer cheered. "Another latecomer," she said, "and at the same table! This should be fun, folks. Hold on for the ride."

Claudia was still steaming with embarrassment as Frederick pulled into the parking stall at the base of the stairs leading to her apartment.

"I don't understand why you're angry," he repeated. "You wanted the fundraiser to be a success, and it was."

"Because you and Titus were in a...a *pissing* match." She refused to say it out loud, but she knew it had been over her. If only she'd kept her mouth shut about wanting to go to New Orleans.

Between the two idiots, they'd pushed the price of the trip to ten thousand, four hundred dollars. She had no idea—and neither did she care—if Titus could afford such an extravagance, but from the way Frederick's knuckles whitened on the paddle handle with each successive bid she knew he was in over his head.

"Thank goodness Elwyn stepped in and put an end to it all. Otherwise, we'd still be sitting there!" Elwyn had appeared to enjoy the antler-clashing going on at their table, and she could have kissed him when he made a final huge leap to eleven thousand dollars and allowed both Titus and Frederick to concede without losing face. But he'd spent way more than he should have because of the two numskulls, which very well could have put the success of her own auction at Fauna in jeopardy.

"I don't like that artist of yours," Frederick said. "He needed taking down a peg."

"What would you have done if you'd won? What if he'd dropped out? You'd be on the hook for a very expensive trip, one I don't think you could afford."

"I can afford it," he said stubbornly. "If he hadn't kept pushing it up..."

"Never mind." Claudia rubbed her forehead. "I'm glad *neither* of you won. I never would have heard the end of it, I'm sure. Goodnight, Frederick." She reached for the door handle.

"Claudia. Wait."

She hesitated.

"I'm sorry," he said quietly.

Determined not to let him off the hook too easily, she kept her gaze averted. "And you should be."

"It's just..." He trailed off, and something in his voice made her release the handle and sink back into her seat.

"Just *what*, Frederick?"

"Isn't it obvious? Especially given what we talked

about last week?"

She turned to face him. His lips were pressed together in a determined line and he stared at her intently. "Say it out loud, Frederick," she said, shaking off a disturbing sense of déjà vu. She'd spent much of her marriage trying to intuit what her husband wanted, and usually failing. No way was she putting up with that from Frederick. "You have to tell me."

"I was jealous!" he said. She flinched at his vehement outburst, but he didn't seem to notice. "That artist shows up, uninvited, and spends the evening whispering in your ear right in front of me. Who does he think he is?" He looked away from her, through the windshield to the grey brick wall in front of the car's bumper, and a muscle flexed in his jaw.

"You have nothing to be jealous about," she said, not sure who she was angrier with, Frederick for this new possessiveness or Titus for taunting him. Or herself for the white lie she had just told. She *was* attracted to Titus in a way that threw her comfortable relationship with Frederick into the shade. "Our relationship has always been one of convenience. Even if Titus was flirting with me, you have no *right* to be jealous."

Beams from the security light slanted steeply through the windshield, leaving his face in shadow. "I don't, do I," he said with a tang of bitterness. "But I want to change that, remember?"

Her stomach swooped queasily. "I thought we settled this last Friday."

"Well, you thought wrong." He tapped his index fingers rapidly on the lower arc of the steering wheel, and then faced her again. "I know when this started between us, I wasn't in a place to consider a long-term commitment. But that was years ago. I've changed." With a deep breath, he took her hand in his, pressing firmly. "We're good together, Claudia. In fact, I think we have something great, but it could be so much more. What do you say?"

She shook her head, helpless to give him the answer he wanted. "I'm sorry, Frederick. But I've told you more than once, I'm not looking for anything more. I can't *give* anything more."

"Why not? We enjoy each other's company, share the same interests." He winked, and for some reason the intimacy of the gesture caused her to shudder with something akin to revulsion. "The sex is good, too."

She pulled her hand out of his clasp with a jerk. "I'm not interested in anything deeper. I don't know how else to say it. I have no intention of ever getting married again." Long-term commitments were not healthy for her, as she'd learned the hard way.

"Who said anything about getting married?" he said in a soothing tone. "I'm not asking for drastic changes, not right now. I just want to...I don't know...make it more official. We never said we were exclusive, but I haven't been with another woman since you. And I don't think you've been with another man, either."

She hadn't, but that wasn't because of any special commitment to Frederick. It was more a result of her distrust of men in general. At this inopportune moment, her subconscious unhelpfully projected an image of Titus onto her mind's eye and she felt her blood warm, her belly coil heatedly.

Damn it. She had no intention of acting on the urges Titus kindled in her, but now that Frederick had revealed himself, change was being forced upon her regardless.

"I'm sorry," she repeated. She couldn't go forward, and they couldn't go back. It was time to end it. "I don't want anything more than what we have right now. I care for you, I do. But I don't think we should see each other anymore."

The silence was loaded with unspoken emotions. Her breath sounded loud in the stillness. Then—

"So that's it? We're done, just like that? You won't even give us a try?"

Frederick might not have the right to be jealous, but he did have the right to be angry and hurt. Yet his sharp tone made her uneasy and she inched back in her seat. "I know how I feel. There's no point in prolonging this. It wouldn't be fair to you."

"Well, this has been a goddamn night." He twisted away from her and pounded his fists on the steering wheel. The hairs on her neck prickled. "I can't believe it. Are you so hot for your artist that you couldn't wait until morning to get rid of me?"

His bitter words hit close to home, but she kept her voice calm. "This has to do with what is between us, Frederick, no one else." Despite her agitation, she forced herself to reach out a comforting hand. Frederick wasn't her ex-husband. There was nothing to fear from his anger.

Before she could touch him, he jerked his arm up, fingers clenched in a fist.

Her mind went blank. She squeezed her eyes shut and huddled against the door frame, freezing in place. *If I don't move, he won't hit me.* The words came from the dark place in her soul. The plea hadn't worked in the past, why would it work now? She waited for the blow.

"Claudia?"

The anger was gone from Frederick's tone, and she cautiously opened her eyes. He was staring at her, stricken, his arm relaxed in his lap. Not a weapon. A reflex.

"I didn't want you to touch me," he said. "What did you think I was going to do?"

"Nothing," she said through dry lips. "I just..." She swallowed down the fear. *Twenty-five years,* she thought. *Twenty-five years and I still haven't gotten past it.*

"Claudia..."

"Goodnight, Frederick," she said, fumbling for the door handle. "I'm tired, and we're both emotional. We'll talk more about this later."

She fled up the stairs, unlocked the door with a shaking hand, and bolted it behind her.

Only then did she sink to the floor and let the memories flood in.

CHAPTER NINE

Claudia allowed herself to wallow for a few minutes. Crying hadn't helped then, and it didn't help now, but she'd learned over the years that holding in her emotions when her trauma flashed back led to greater distress down the road.

She rubbed the tears out of her eyes with the heels of her hands, black marks on the insides of her wrists warning of the wreckage of her makeup. She unbuckled her sparkly shoes then rose from the floor and headed to her bedroom.

It was after midnight when she climbed between the sheets, face clean and moisturized, comforted by the soft, cool touch of the silky pajamas she favoured. She was exhausted, but sleep would be elusive while her mind was caught in nightmares from the past.

The next moment she was aware of the sound of running water.

She stared at the ceiling, disoriented, trying to figure out if she was dreaming or awake. The rushing sound came from behind the head of her bed, and she sat up, the last dregs of sleep fleeing. Kneeling on the mattress, she placed her ear against the wall over her headboard.

It sure sounded like pouring water. What the hell

was going on?

Tapping her phone to light the screen, she saw it was just gone four o'clock. She must have fallen asleep easier and quicker than she'd thought possible.

She walked barefooted out of the bedroom and the noise faded as she passed the bathroom, only to grow louder again when she entered the living area.

Nothing looked out of the ordinary there.

Her second-floor apartment ran from the front to the back of the building, half the width of the gallery below, which created the additional height on the main level. It was laid out rather like a single-wide trailer, with her bedroom at the front above the main entrance, the bathroom next to it. The doors for both led to a hallway that ran down the long edge of the apartment and opened into the living room and kitchen area. At the back, to the right of the exterior door, another door hid a flight of stairs that emerged beside her office on the floor below.

If there was water running somewhere, and it wasn't in her apartment...

With a gasp she threw open the interior door and tore down the stairs. As she entered the hall and flew to the main area, she stopped with a moan.

Her feet were wet.

Without heed for slipping, she raced to the gallery.

The glow from the streetlights outside shimmered on a thin layer of water spreading on the hardwood floor. In the far front corner, a cataract of water burst out of a fist-sized hole in the Gyproc, cannoning six feet into the room before raining down onto the table she used as a desk.

Claudia spun around and shot back to the stairs, this time heading down, taking them two at a time as she sprinted for the basement. The floor here was rough concrete but she paid no attention to the sharp grit cutting her soles. The main water shutoff valve was on a pipe jutting out of the floor and snugged up against the outer wall. The handle refused to turn, and with a sob Claudia gripped it with both hands, exerting all her strength. It finally gave way and she twisted until it refused to turn any more.

Dashing back up the stairs, Claudia saw with vast relief that the water was no longer cascading out of the wall, though it continued its merciless spread across the lovely, original hardwood floors.

Towels, she thought. *Sheets. Drop cloths.* Anything to stop the spread, to start mopping up the damaging moisture. Drywall could be easily replaced, but not these floors. She hurried to her apartment.

Titus figured he'd give Claudia the morning to cool down before apologizing for his behaviour at the auction. Well, not *apologize.* Explain. And say he might be a bit sorry she'd seemed upset about his bidding war with Frederick.

It was Freddy's *fault, really,* he thought as he prepped a canvas for his next piece. The man had obviously taken Titus' bid on the New Orleans trip as a declaration of intent regarding Claudia.

Which it had been, but still, what claim did *Freddy* have? Claudia had introduced him as her accountant, not as a friend or partner or anything more intimate.

Since he figured she was mad enough to refuse to answer his calls, shortly after twelve he stepped into his SUV and drove into town. He parked in front of the gallery and pulled open the door to a hive of activity.

The buzz and whir of a half-dozen large fans competed with the sucking growls of wet-dry vacuums. One machine was operated by a young woman with the large, tight belly of late pregnancy, the other by Cecil. An older couple was using two wide-headed contractor's brooms to push around a swathe of fabric, wielding the daisy-patterned cloth like a mop. Much of the floor was covered in an odd assortment of materials—bath towels in purple and yellow checks, sheets in blue and grey plaid, and even a duvet in a gingham print.

To his left, Claudia stood facing the wall. He had no trouble reading the fury in her fierce, jerky movements as she tore large chunks of ruined drywall off water-stained studs, revealing the concrete that formed the divider between her gallery and the business next door.

And two lengths of plastic pipe that had apparently come loose at the join and caused the destruction he was witnessing.

Claudia turned to toss a handful of debris into the garbage can beside her and saw him. Her lips tightened and for an instant he saw devastation in her expression, but it was swiftly replaced by the intensity of a warrior.

His fingers curled instinctively, as if holding a paintbrush. He needed to capture that look. And he would. Soon.

"What are you doing here?" she said, raising her voice over the cacophony. The couple working the brooms looked up but returned to their chore when they realized she was talking to Titus. They were both tall and strongly built, and there was something in the set of the woman's shoulders and the sharp glance the man had given him that was familiar.

"Your parents?" he asked.

"Yes. Cecil you've met. And before you ask, the pregnant one is my youngest daughter."

Wasn't that a smack between the eyes. Claudia was going to be a grandmother. A sexy, vibrant granny, but still...

Cautious about stirring her up even further, he said, "Should she be here right now? In her condition?"

"A pregnant woman is not an invalid," she replied through tight lips. "I didn't ask her or my parents to come, but when my mother called this morning, I mentioned what was going on. The three of them showed up at the door half an hour later, ready to help.

It's what family does, you know."

He held up his hands placatingly. "I wasn't criticizing, just asking."

Her stern glare didn't relent. "As you can see, I'm busy. Why are you here?" she repeated.

"It can wait. What can I do?"

For a moment, her shoulders remained strong and sturdy. Then they sagged. Blue shadows bruised the skin beneath her eyes, her curls were unruly, and her jeans damp from the knees down.

"Go home," she said wearily. "It's under control."

He shook his head. "Don't be stubborn. If you don't want this to push your opening back any further than necessary, take all the help you can get. Did you get any sleep last night?"

"A few hours. I didn't notice the leak until about four."

"Do you have more sheets? These damp ones need to be replaced."

She wiped a wrist across her forehead, leaving specks of drywall material behind like freckles. "You really don't have to do this."

"I know. Consider it my way of paying you back for the fun I had last night."

That had sparks shooting from her tired eyes. "I *knew* you were doing it just to bug Frederick. I am furious at both of you." She surveyed the mess in front of her. "You know what, you *do* owe me. Let me introduce you to my parents. The bigger sheets and blankets are really heavy once they're wet, and I don't want them lifting the weight. There's a laundromat a couple of blocks over. We already have machines spinning out the first sheets I laid down. You are now on laundry detail."

By late that afternoon, the worst of the water had been removed from the floor. The wood was still damp to the touch, but Claudia and Titus arranged the fans so they were blowing cool air onto the worst spots.

"I'll leave them like this all night," she said, watching the caged heads oscillate back and forth slowly, like so many demented sunflowers. "Maybe move them around tomorrow morning."

"It'll probably take a few days to really dry the boards out," Titus said. "Don't turn the fans off too soon. You'll want to get someone in to a do a moisture reading, too. But I think the floors can be saved."

"I hope so." It had been unusual to find a building of this size with hardwood floors, and she'd really wanted to preserve them. "I suppose one blessing is that we hadn't yet stripped and re-stained them. And the bazillion baseboards and trim you and I painted are stored in the back, along with the portable walls Cecil built, and the water didn't get to them."

"Thank god." Titus' heartfelt reply had one corner of her mouth lifting.

"Cecil thinks we can get away with replacing the one sheet of drywall. The water shot out with such force little of it ended up in the walls, though he's going to double check before he closes it up."

An accommodating grunt sounded from the man beside her.

Only the two of them remained at the gallery. Nicole had left shortly after Titus arrived, finally shooed home by Claudia, who had been feeling guilty about accepting her daughter's help even before Titus had expressed his concern. Her parents had stuck around until he had brought the last load of sheets back from the laundromat, spun dry but still damp. Then they had taken all the makeshift mops home for further cleaning and drying.

"Cecil says he'll get the pipes refitted tomorrow, even though it's Sunday. But until then, no water." Claudia moved her shoulders restlessly. "And, boy, could I use a shower."

"Why did you refuse your mom and dad's offer to stay the night?" Titus asked, his grey eyes calmly curious.

"They don't really have a spare room. They say they do, but it's a convertible sofa in my mom's very crowded sewing room. I've tried to sleep on that so-called bed before." She shuddered melodramatically. "Never again."

Titus grinned, as she'd meant him to. "Well," he said. "I have a *real* spare room, and while I can't vouch for the mattress personally, given the one I am sleeping on, I think you'd be perfectly comfortable."

"Thanks, but I'll be fine in a hotel for one night."

"What about dinner?" he said.

"I'll order in after I get a room."

"You're exhausted," he said, "and no one gets a good night's sleep in a hotel."

She'd been treating his offer casually because she was certain he didn't mean it. If not a confirmed recluse, he was someone who preferred to be on his own. "You don't really want me to stay. You're just being polite. I appreciate it, but—"

"Come for dinner, Claudia. Stay the night. No strings attached. Just a home-cooked meal and a comfortable bed after a terrible day."

God, she was tempted. She just wasn't sure she was *able* to accept his invitation.

A therapist might have an official term for whatever it was that prevented her from staying overnight with a man. Once she'd finally started dating, many years after her divorce, she simply hadn't felt safe doing so, no matter how well she knew her partner. She had hoped her relationship with Frederick would help her over this hurdle and had tried—really tried—to make it work. But she'd been wrong. The rare time her anxiety didn't flare was in the neutral territory of a hotel room.

Titus' home was definitely not a hotel room.

"Just dinner and a bed, right?" she said. "Nothing

more."

"I think I can control my animal urges for one night." He waited patiently, arms crossed.

Surprisingly, his flippant reply calmed her nerves. She really didn't want to be alone. It would give her time to obsess about how much the flood was going to cost her, in time, money, and energy. What if other joints were about to give way? Would she come back tomorrow to an even bigger disaster? She squeezed her eyes shut. *That way madness lies...*

"All right," she said slowly. "Thank you. I'll pack a bag and be right down."

"We'll go in my car," Titus said. "Tomorrow, I'll bring you back whenever you like. I don't want you falling asleep at the wheel."

"I'm not in that bad of shape," she protested.

"You're not seeing what I'm seeing," he said. "You might be a warrior, but right now you're a warrior on her feet only by grace of her last ounce of strength. Go get your stuff." He nudged her gently toward the hall. "Don't forget to lock up."

CHAPTER TEN

A few minutes later, Claudia buckled herself into the passenger seat of Titus' SUV as he tossed her overnight bag into the back.

"I need to make a quick stop at the grocery store," he said. "Do you mind?"

"Since I'm more than likely the reason you need to, I don't have the right to complain, do I?" Ignoring her slightly self-pitying reply, he simply put the SUV in gear and reversed out of the stall.

Conscious of her bedraggled appearance, she waited in the vehicle while Titus went inside the store. She probably should insist he take her to a hotel, but she was too tired to argue anymore. If he wanted to play knight, who was she to say no? *I'll pretend I'm at a bed and breakfast,* she thought through a jaw-cracking yawn.

She leaned back and closed her eyes. It was possible she dozed off as she jolted when Titus opened the door behind the driver's seat to place four bags on the floor.

Although the day had felt unbearably long already, it wasn't yet seven o'clock when he parked outside his house. In mid-June in Northern British Columbia, the sun didn't set until well after nine-thirty, so bright sunshine still gilded the impressive structure.

Without fanfare, he showed her directly to the guest room, pointed out the en suite, and then excused himself.

"Take your time," he said. "I'll get dinner prepped, but I won't put the fish on until you're ready."

Claudia looked longingly at the bed but couldn't bear the thought of collapsing onto its pristine surface in her current state. Stripping off her clothes, she walked into the bathroom and stopped in awe.

As befitted the rest of the house, it was a sophisticated, elegant space of gleaming tile, polished glass, and shining fixtures. A freestanding oval tub was placed in front of a large window, the bottom sill so low that anyone soaking could look out into the deep green depths of the forest. The colours of the trees were repeated in the cabinetry, a sleek blend of indoor and outdoor.

It was tempting to lose herself in the luxury the tub offered, but she didn't want to keep Titus waiting any longer than necessary. Besides, the lavish shower with its rain head and body jets was just as appealing.

Feeling almost human after ten minutes under the invigorating spray, with her hair towel-dried and curling naturally as she'd forgotten to bring her hair dryer, she added a swipe of gloss to her lips and mascara to her lashes. Then, wearing a maxi dress patterned in burgundy paisley, she padded bare footed down the open tread staircase and went to find Titus.

She didn't have far to look. Since the lower floor was open concept to take full advantage of the view, she spotted him in the kitchen immediately. He stood on the other side of the enormous flat-topped island and didn't look up from his work. His arm moved in smooth, practiced motions as he chopped at something green and leafy. He'd changed as well, and now wore a pale grey dress shirt, with a white dish towel tossed over his shoulder.

Music drifted through the air, soft and soothing, harmonized voices in a flowing, lilting chant. Her spine relaxed further listening to it.

As she approached the kitchen, Titus looked up and smiled. "Feel better?"

"Oh, my god," she said, "yes. I almost didn't come down. That bathroom is to die for. And I didn't even sit on the bed. It looks so cozy I was afraid I'd never get up again."

"Drink?" He nodded at a half-empty glass on the counter in front of him. "I'm having a mojito."

"I'd love one."

Putting aside his knife, he moved to the end of the counter, which was doing service as a bar as evidenced by the variety of bottles clustered on it. She watched him deftly muddle mint and lime as he assembled her drink.

"Something smells great," she said politely. She couldn't remember the last time a man had made her dinner—if ever. The intimacy of the scene was beginning to make her feel nervous. She breathed deeply and reassured herself that, if necessary, she could make up some excuse and have Titus drive her back into town. She knew he wouldn't refuse.

And knowing that, calm settled on her once more.

"I'm roasting butternut squash," he said, handing her the drink and taking a sip of his own before returning to his work. "There's a fresh salad ready in the fridge and I'll keep the rice dish warm while I barbeque the salmon fillet. It will only take a few minutes to cook, so there's no hurry to finish your drink. Unless you're hungry. I can get it started now if you like."

She was starving, and probably shouldn't be drinking on an empty stomach, but a feeling of recklessness floated through her. "I can wait," she said. "I'd love to sit on the deck before we eat, if that's okay."

"Go ahead. I'm about done in here. I'll join you in a minute."

Titus tossed butternut squash cubes with the wild rice he had waiting on the stove. Then he added cranberries, pecans, and the fresh parsley he'd finished chopping. It was a dish he'd made so many times he could put himself on autopilot and watch Claudia through the glass as she explored the deck.

She drifted along the railing, her dress blowing in the breeze sweeping up the cliff. The thin fabric outlined her full thighs and lush breasts.

Offering her sanctuary for the night had been an impulse. Other than when his parents came to visit, he couldn't remember the last time he'd hosted a guest in the place he was temporarily calling home. Probably because he had so few friends. His nomadic childhood had made it hard to create close ties, and the friends he'd cultivated during his university days were scattered far and wide. As for his relationships with women—he wouldn't classify any of them as *friends*, exactly. Other than Yvette, of course, but she was a special case.

He was beginning to wonder if Claudia might fall into the same category as Yvette. He couldn't deny he was sexually attracted to her. He wanted to paint her. And he wanted to get to know her.

To be honest, it was quite disconcerting.

Freshening his drink, he joined her on the deck. The sun was dipping behind the tips of the trees and golden streaks slanted across the shadowy, peaty depths of the water far below.

"I don't know how you get any work done," she said, her hands resting lightly on the top rail. "I think I'd spend all day looking at the view."

"Don't tell my agent, but I pretty much did exactly that the first week I was here. I'm learning to use it as inspiration, not distraction."

She turned to him, her face lit by the glowing amber

rays streaming from behind him. Lines fanned out from the corners of her eyes and mouth, and the skin of her throat had lost some of the tautness of youth. The stories hiding behind her frank blue eyes intrigued him more than he cared to admit.

"How is it going?" she asked, sipping her drink. "Your work?"

A fleck of lime flesh caught on her upper lip. She was so tall he would barely have to dip his head to kiss it off, but before he could her tongue flicked out and licked it away.

"Fine," he said gruffly, his throat suddenly scratchy and dry. "It's going fine." The problem was, *fine* wasn't good enough. He was still struggling to find the vision for the Elizabeth Fry piece. He wasn't worried. Yet. Once he latched onto something, it would only take him a few days to complete. He still had time.

She raised an eyebrow, and he had the unsettled feeling she'd read more into his curt reply than he'd intended. But she didn't press. "How about Mae's painting? She told me a couple of days ago that she's reached out to her friend for the translation and will let me know when she hears anything. What with one thing and another, I haven't had a chance to think much about how we might find the men in the photo."

"I finished cleaning it," he said. "I can show you later. It's actually a particularly good piece of art." So good as to add yet another mystery, but he didn't mention that to Claudia. He needed to find an expert who could provide a more informed evaluation, and until then he didn't want to say more. "I still can't see a signature, which is a little odd, but not totally unusual."

"We could search the web for paintings whose subject is Barkerville. Given the family's connection to the town, that seems logical." She moved away from him and sank onto a large, cozily cushioned, metal-framed sofa, one of a set of three that surrounded a low, square table with a gas fire pit in its centre. Tucking her feet under her bottom, she went on. "As for the photo, I think the Barkerville Historic Society has an online collection. If we are really lucky, it's a copy, and the other is neatly labelled and searchable in their database."

"Somehow that seems a bit much to ask. Why hide it so carefully and yet let a copy wander around loose?" Straightening from his stance against the rail, he gestured toward the barbeque—a gleaming monster he'd conquered his first week in the house. "Should I put the salmon on? Or how about another drink?"

Claudia smiled. "Yes to the salmon, but no to the drink. I didn't have lunch today and this one went straight to my head."

The thought of Claudia languorous and limp and pleasantly buzzed on alcohol was uncomfortably arousing. While he preferred his women active participants, the idea of Claudia letting go of the control he knew she so rigidly exerted was overwhelmingly erotic.

He went inside to fetch the salmon before he embarrassed himself.

Claudia crossed her knife and fork on her plate and leaned back with a contented sigh. "Were you a chef in a prior life?" she asked. "That's the best meal I've ever had. Don't tell my mom."

They'd served themselves in the kitchen but had eaten outside at a table in the top corner of the large deck. Fresh air and a gorgeous view had enhanced the delicious meal. The company hadn't hurt either, Claudia admitted. Conversation with Titus ranged far and wide and she had to be sharp to keep up.

He grinned. "Both my parents worked twelve-hour shifts, my dad as an RCMP officer and my mom as a civilian member. I was six feet tall by the time I was thirteen and could empty a refrigerator in less than forty-eight hours if you believe the stories they tell. Once I was old enough, it became my job to get dinner on the table. Macaroni and wieners gets old pretty fast, so I taught myself. Specialized ingredients were sometimes hard to come by in the smaller places we lived, which meant I had to be creative. It involved a lot of trial and error, and the occasional last-minute call for delivery when the experiment was truly inedible."

The thought of a gangly, loose-limbed Titus finding his way around the kitchen caused a warm ball of tenderness to light in her chest. She had allowed him to talk her into a small glass of wine with the meal, and she blamed her sentimentality on that. "I hate cooking," she said. "I did it, of course, as a mom with two children to raise. But it was only to keep body and soul together. Once the girls were out of the house, doing anything requiring more than two pots seemed a waste of time." She waved at her empty plate. "If I could cook like *this*, maybe I'd do it more often."

"I find it relaxing," Titus said. "I don't even mind cleaning up."

Before her brain could catch up with her mouth, she said teasingly, "How has no woman snapped you up? You'd make an excellent husband," then flushed, glaring at her wineglass as if it had made the inappropriately flirtatious comment.

If Titus noticed her discomfort, he chose to ignore it, saying lightly, "You haven't seen me in the throes of an artistic tantrum, have you?"

For some reason, the thought of Titus in a temper was titillating and gave her no cause for alarm. She felt confident his anger would be turned inward, not directed at an innocent bystander. She tilted her head to one side, considering. "Do you get all broody and sulky? Or throw things?"

The tips of his ears flushed red and his mouth lifted in a sheepish smile. "Both, on occasion."

She wanted to laugh, but a thrum of sexuality

vibrated deep in her belly. What lures would a woman have to use to coax Titus out of sullenness? How would he respond to having something thrown back at him by someone who refused to be intimidated by his fury? Each had their own appeal, she realized with a shock.

Scrambling for a distraction from her provocative thoughts, she blurted, "You look like you take out your frustrations on a punching bag, not a dish or vase."

"I do that, too. My dad is a firm believer that teenage boys must expend pent up energy, and if they don't do it in safe ways, they'll find *un*safe ways. Most places we lived, he taught sports like boxing, martial arts. Nothing formal, just for fun. He dragged me along more often than not, and the habit stuck."

Well, that hadn't helped. Now she was envisioning Titus wearing nothing but loose shorts, sweat glistening on the muscles of his arms and chest.

Claudia deliberately brought images of the flood to mind, reminding herself of what was important—getting her gallery back on track. But thinking about the gallery reminded her of the hard work Titus had done this afternoon. Work he hadn't been required or even requested to do. Which in turn reminded her—

"Why did you come to the gallery today?" she said. "You never did say."

CHAPTER ELEVEN

Titus spun his nearly empty wine glass slowly by the stem, rich red clinging to the sides. "No, I didn't." He sighed and tossed back the last of the liquid. "I came to apologize."

That reason hadn't even been on her radar. "You what?"

"I didn't mean to upset you last night."

Claudia blinked. The reason for her rage after the auction seemed pale and insignificant now. "Oh. Well, that's all right then. Thank you."

"If I'd known you and Frederick were serious, I wouldn't have tweaked him quite so hard. But I thought you were just business acquaintances, and that he wouldn't take offense to friendly competition for your attention."

Something in his tone alerted her to the fact he was fishing for details. He didn't actually believe she and Frederick were a couple. He wanted her to confirm or deny.

She toyed with the idea of keeping him wondering. It would be a buffer, one she could use as a shield if her attraction grew too intense. But that would be a lie, and while she and Frederick still needed to clear the air between them, it was obvious their relationship was over. It would be dishonest to let Titus go on thinking she was committed to another man, when she wasn't.

She'd have to examine *why* she couldn't lie to him later. It would be so much safer if she could.

"Frederick and I have…I mean, we had…an understanding," she said, choosing her words carefully, "for a few years now. But I've recently decided things will be…changing…between us."

Something flashed in the depths of Titus' grey eyes. "He was your sex buddy," he said, a grin lighting up his face.

She wouldn't dignify that with an answer. "We were two single people who needed escorts to various functions and enjoyed each other's company."

"So why are you breaking it off? Does it have anything to do with me?"

Gritting her teeth and wondering how on earth she'd ever thought she was attracted to such an arrogant man, she said, "My reasons are none of your business. And stop looking so smug."

He kept grinning. Irritated that even now she could feel a tug of amused sensuality, she rose to her feet and reached for his plate. "You cooked," she said, smiling with teeth still clenched, "so I'll clean."

She gathered the plates, cutlery and glasses, her cool poise fracturing a crack at the French doors when she had to juggle her load in order to twist the handle, but she managed before he could come to her aid.

It was time to put some distance between them, to get back to a professional relationship. "I assume you have a laptop," she said over her shoulder as she made her way to the kitchen.

"I do." His voice was right behind her and she suppressed a shiver at his nearness.

"Why don't you do some online sleuthing while I wash up?"

"Just toss them in the dishwasher."

"There's not too many. Really, I don't mind." She risked a glance at him. He was no longer looking at her like she was on the dessert menu, and the fierce mix of exasperation, attraction, and tenderness that had sent her scurrying from the table loosened its hold. "Go on. It won't take me long and then I'll join you. I'd really like to have some news for Mae when she calls next."

She half-filled the large farmhouse sink inset into the island with sudsy water as Titus retrieved a large, thin laptop from somewhere upstairs. Taking a stool on the opposite side of the island, he flipped open the lid.

"Where do you want to start?" he asked, tapping keys.

"How about the photo? Do a search for Barkerville Historic Society," she said.

"Top return is Barkerville dot C-A, the site promoting the park. Let's see what's there."

"Have you ever been?" Claudia asked as Titus typed and clicked.

"No. This is the first time I've lived in the area. It's on my list, though."

"You should go." She rinsed a saucepan and placed it on the drying tray. "It's kitschy and touristy but well worth the visit. And the drive is beautiful."

"Found the photo archives," he said. "You can filter so that when you search only entries that have online visuals show up. Should we start there?"

"Why not?"

Once Claudia had tidied his kitchen, she pulled up a stool next to him and began offering suggestions on what to look for in the archives. Titus found her a distinct distraction and kept up the search for more than an hour only because she seemed so keen. What he really wanted to do was pull her into his arms and kiss her.

Finally, she leaned away from the screen with a sigh.

"I knew it was too much to hope that we'd strike gold on our first try."

"Haha," he said drily.

She looked blank for a moment, and then realized what she'd said and smiled. "Pun not intended. We've tried everything I can think of for now. We should get permission from Mae to send a copy of the photo to the museum and ask for help."

"That sounds like a good next step." He shut the lid of the laptop before she could come up with any other ideas. "Did you want to see her painting? It's in my studio."

"Of course." She stretched her arms above her head, her breasts lifting delightfully, her bountiful cleavage deepening. "And then I should head to bed. I've been up since four."

He eased off his stool, discreetly rearranging himself in his jeans before following Claudia up the stairs. Her hips swayed with every step and he swallowed a groan. He really hadn't thought this through when he'd invited her to stay the night. He hoped she'd get some sleep, but he was pretty sure the thought of her nestled in bed a few steps down the hall was going to cause him insomnia.

In his studio, he left the overheads off and flicked on the small clamp light attached to the easel where he'd placed Mae's now clean painting.

"Oh," Claudia breathed, moving so close she looked like she was sniffing the canvas. "It is lovely, isn't it? The colours are so vibrant. And the faces of the men..." She trailed off, two lines forming between her brows. "Is the man panning for gold Chinese?"

"I think so. The fine details weren't visible, not until I cleaned it."

She glanced at Titus, her eyes sparkling, all trace of the tiredness he'd noted downstairs gone. "So, we have a photo of two white men and one Chinese man hidden on the back of a painting with the same subjects."

"I compared both images. I'm not sure we'll ever be able to state without a doubt that they are the same men, but there is no evidence to negate the possibility. It has to be more than a coincidence."

"This is awesome." Claudia straightened, her attention still absorbed by the painting, her face softly lit by the single bulb clipped to the easel, her profile outlined against the wall of windows.

"Come here." He took her arm and urged her toward the middle of the room, snagging one of the barstools as he went.

"What are you doing?" she asked but went willingly enough. He set down the stool, placed his hands on her shoulders and pressed her onto it.

"I'm going to draw you."

"Don't be silly." She shifted as if to stand, and he held her down. Even in his furor to get a pencil and paper, he kept his touch gentle.

"I have to. I've been thinking about it for days. And now, with the moonlight streaming in..." He gestured to the nearly full moon glowing outside the window and she lifted her chin to look where he pointed. "Don't move!" he said urgently. He wanted that exact tilt of her jaw, the angle of her head over her shoulder.

She ignored him and turned to look at him again. "I am not going to model for you, Titus."

Desperation to create welled up inside of him, fierce and strong in a way he rarely experienced. He didn't have time to argue.

So, he kissed her.

His palms on her cheeks, he pressed his mouth softly to hers, doing his best to wordlessly convey his need. She gripped his wrists but as he deepened the kiss her touch grew slack. Her mouth opened, welcoming him in, and her hands slid up his arms to his chest, and then wrapped around his neck.

He'd wanted to distract her, bewilder her so she'd sit for him without complaint. Instead, the heat of her passion was like a backdraft, the fire he'd set roaring out to consume him.

He dragged his mouth away reluctantly. Her eyelids fluttered open, and raw satisfaction filled his chest. Her gaze was dreamy and dazed. She didn't resist when he took her chin in his fingertips and placed her exactly where he wanted her.

"Look at the moon," he said. "And think about me."

He went to get his sketchpad.

Claudia woke Sunday morning with Titus' kiss still burning on her lips.

She'd sat on that stool, exactly as he had placed her, and stared at the moon until her eyes watered. He'd told her to think of him, and she'd desperately wanted to ignore that demand, but the confident gentleness with which he'd claimed her lips had been dizzying. How could she *not* think of him?

When she couldn't take it anymore, when her spine and shoulders and neck were throbbing from the immobility, she had told him she was done, stating she was going to bed no matter what he said.

He'd flapped a hand dismissively and grunted, never lifting his focus from the sketchbook.

More than mildly miffed, she had stomped back to the guest room and gone through her nighttime routine, muttering under her breath about ungrateful, self-absorbed artists. She'd lain stiff and tense between the smooth, cool sheets, grumbling about his arrogance, his refusal to consider other people's sentiments, his sheer *cheek,* until she'd fallen asleep.

Now, as she dressed and packed her bag, she determined to treat him with cool politeness. There was no need to mention the kiss, to make a fuss about it. She'd just be more careful in future to avoid any similar situation.

When she came down from the second floor, he

greeted her with fresh coffee, a bagel ready to toast, and a chipper smile.

"Morning," he said brightly. "Sleep well?"

"Yes, thank you." *I won't bring it up,* she thought self-righteously. *But if he does, I'll laugh it off, tell him not to worry, it meant nothing to me.*

He didn't bring it up.

She bit off a chunk of bagel with ferocious force, as if it were made of steel. Had the kiss meant so little to him that he'd forgotten about it already? Of course, it had meant *nothing* to her.

But still.

Titus didn't appear to notice her irritation. In fact, he didn't appear to notice *her*. He drank his coffee, lost in his thoughts, and she refused to prod him into sharing.

Breakfast, therefore, was a silent meal, with no other conversation than "More coffee?" and "Can you pass the butter?" As soon as it was done, he drove her back to the gallery and waved goodbye without even getting out of his SUV.

She watched him leave in a welter of confused emotions, none of which she wanted to examine closely. With a frustrated shake of her head, she went inside.

Cecil was already at work, along with the plumber he'd sub-contracted to do all the repairs and check the rest of the piping. She headed upstairs to unpack her overnight bag, nodding at Cecil's reminder there was still no water to her apartment.

And that's when Frederick phoned.

Heaving in a deep breath, she connected the call.

"I'm sorry I didn't get in touch yesterday," she said before he had a chance to speak. "It's a long story that I will explain. Are you free this afternoon? We need to finish our talk."

CHAPTER TWELVE

From the safety of Monday morning, Claudia could categorically state that she'd had one of the most chaotic, distressing, and troubled weekends of her life. She'd had *worse* days—*weeks* of her marriage had been unbearable—but since her divorce, she'd lived relatively drama free.

She wanted those days back.

Sitting behind her desk—now Patsy's desk, she reminded herself—at Four Winds, she tried to focus on the inventory sheets spread out in front of her. This was one part of the job Patsy had little experience with, so Claudia was training her as they went along. The other woman had been called away to deal with a customer at the front, which meant Claudia was forced to wait for her return, giving unwelcome thoughts the chance to creep in.

It was no use reliving her conversation with Frederick on Sunday afternoon. It had merely been a repetition of what they'd both said on Friday night. She'd listened patiently as he'd first requested then pleaded that she reconsider her decision to break off the relationship, surprised and dismayed at his obvious distress. But she knew they couldn't go on the way they had been, and it would be cruel to give him any hope she might change her mind. The discussion went around in circles before Frederick reluctantly acknowledged defeat, and by the time he left her apartment she was emotionally exhausted.

At least the water had been reconnected by then, so she had been able to have a long, hot bath to soak away her tension.

Her cell phone rang, and she flinched. Checking the screen with trepidation, her shoulders relaxed when she saw Mae's name.

"Hello, there!" she said, in her relief answering with what was probably over the top cheerfulness.

In comparison to her own strident tones, Mae's voice was soft. "Hi. How was your weekend?"

"Do *not* ask. Did you hear from your friend? Has she done the translation yet?" The mystery of Mae's painting brought Titus to mind, but for now, she'd take whatever distraction from Frederick she could get.

"I did." If anything, Mae's voice was even more hesitant. "I don't think it will be very helpful, though."

"What does it say?"

"Honestly, it makes no sense. I'll read it to you. *Knowledge is weightless, a treasure easily carried.*"

Claudia waited, but there was only silence on the other end. "That's it?"

"I told you it's useless." Mae sounded dejected.

She couldn't deny her own disappointment. "It's very poetic."

"I suppose it is rather pretty. But it doesn't tell us anything about the painting, or the photo."

"Why would someone go to the bother of hiding a piece of poetry on the back of a painting?" Claudia mused aloud.

"I have no idea."

"Well, don't get discouraged," Claudia said. "It's still a step forward."

"I guess I shouldn't have let myself hope," Mae said.

"You'll think I'm stupid, but I wondered...never mind."

Claudia had a sinking feeling she knew where this was going. "I would never think you stupid, Mae. What did you wonder?"

She paused, and then answered in a rush, as if saying the words quickly gave them less importance. "I'm having trouble getting loans to start my daycare. When I saw the photo, I thought—well, it made me think of buried treasure. I thought maybe the men had hidden the jars filled with gold and the writing was directions for how to find them."

Titus sat back with a sigh and rubbed his gritty eyes. With a faint sense of surprise, he noted the sunlight falling through the glass above his head created narrow shadows on the studio floor. He was pretty sure it was Monday and given the sun's angle it was probably midday-ish. However, with his phone nowhere to be seen, he couldn't confirm either belief.

He'd barely slept since Saturday night, snatching a couple of hours before breakfast with Claudia the day before, and a few more very early this morning.

He had the niggling feeling he owed Claudia an apology for his distraction. What had they talked about during breakfast Sunday, or when he'd driven her home—or had they talked at all? When his brain was bursting with ideas, he found it difficult to interact normally. He should probably explain himself, say he was sorry if he'd seemed cold and brusque.

He'd done more apologizing since meeting Claudia than the rest of his life put together.

But he wasn't going to apologize for the kiss. Not that, not ever.

Clenching and releasing his fist, he worked out a cramp in his fingers. His sketchbook was filled with drawings inspired by the glowing moon, the mystery of night—and Claudia. He slowly turned the pages, reviewing the work he'd done in a fever of inspiration, and her face radiated up at him from each.

He'd found his muse for the Elizabeth Fry piece. And for any number of others, too, he realized. The thought was more than a little disconcerting. He'd never needed one particular subject, one specific model, to feel inspired before. He wasn't sure he wanted it that way now.

It was time to take a break, let the ideas percolate after the first frenzy of creation.

Ninety minutes later, after a long workout in the small personal gym in the basement—including a round with the punching bag Claudia had imagined—and a hot shower, he headed to the kitchen. He remembered having a bagel with her on Sunday, so at least he hadn't been so far gone that he'd forgotten to feed his guest. Given the gnawing ache in his stomach, he wasn't sure if he'd eaten since. Splitting a small loaf of focaccia bread through the middle, he layered it with sprouts, tomatoes, red onion, and the salmon leftover from Saturday night. Carrying it and a large glass of milk outside, he sprawled on the outdoor sofa and propped his feet on the fire pit table.

His phone—which he'd found in the refrigerator, cool but unharmed—dinged, signalling an incoming email. One hand holding his sandwich while busily chewing on a large mouthful, he pulled it out of the pocket of his hoodie and thumbed to the message.

It was from Yvette. He ignored it for now, along with the five or so other unread messages he noted as he scrolled through his inbox. The only one he was interested in reading was from Claudia. She'd sent it just before noon with a subject line of *Translation*.

The tone of her email was crisp and business-like. She provided the text Mae's friend has supplied and stated that neither she nor Mae had any idea what it meant. If he had suggestions, she wrote, he was welcome to offer them, but she held little hope of anything useful coming from it.

She signed off with a polite thank you for hosting her on Saturday. No mention of what had passed between them.

It might have been written by a random acquaintance, and one who didn't particularly like him. Not the warm, luscious woman he had kissed into a daze. And intended to kiss again.

He dashed off a short reply, acknowledging receipt of the email and graciously accepting her thanks. Two could play at the politeness game, though it was one he rarely bothered with. Finishing off his meal, he went back inside and found his laptop. Claudia might have given up on the translation, but he had a few ideas about the painting he wanted to explore.

Claudia was already in her pajamas when the knock sounded at her apartment door. It was only eight o'clock in the evening, but when she'd gotten home after a day of crunching numbers with Patsy, she'd wanted the comfort of elastic waisted pants, a loose, flowing top, and no bra. Wearing what you wanted when you wanted was one of the advantages to living alone.

The knock sounded again, brisk and peremptory. It was such a rare sound she considered ignoring it. If her parents or her daughter wanted to visit, they would have called first. She doubted Frederick would want to speak to her any time soon, if ever. And she lived in a non-residential area which made a visit from band students selling chocolates or young athletes collecting bottles extremely unlikely.

Thinking of that isolation, she decided she should at least make sure it wasn't someone scouting the place for a way to break in. With no intention of opening the door, she peered through the peephole.

Titus.

She glanced down at her silky pajamas. They were

perfectly presentable for company, but she was suddenly fiercely aware of the way the material brushed against her naked buttocks, how her breasts swung heavily under the thin fabric.

Another knock.

Peering through the tiny lens again, she reached for the lock, and then hesitated once more. He had taken a step back and was turning to the stairs leading down to the parking area, as if preparing to leave. She could let him go...

Taking a deep breath, she opened the door.

He stopped, one tread below the top step. She was met by the tang of dampness, and she realized it was drizzling. Light from the security bulb in the upper corner of the building sparked off the water droplets clinging to his shaved skull and cast his eyes in shadow under their heavy brows.

"Sorry for taking so long," she said. "I wasn't expecting company."

His gaze swept her from head to toe, and despite the fact there wasn't an inch of flesh showing from the soles of her feet to her neck, it was as if she was naked before him. Her nipples pebbled and she crossed her arms over her chest, hoping he wouldn't notice.

"I suppose I should have called first," he said. "I didn't think of it."

"It's raining," she said, stating the obvious. "You might as well come in." She pulled the door open wider as she stepped back.

After a pause, he strode past, bringing the scent of rain and pine with him. She noticed for the first time he carried a small black case.

"Let me take your coat." He shrugged out of his thin leather jacket and wiped his forearm over his skull, using the long sleeve of his pale blue Henley to mop up the moisture beading it.

She locked the door, hung his coat on the knob, and followed him past the kitchen area into the living room, trying not to watch his ass, clad in dark denim unsplattered by paint. He turned to face her and she hurriedly lifted her eyes.

He made a small gesture toward her. "I gather you weren't expecting visitors."

For a moment she considered asking him to wait while she changed, but that seemed like drawing more attention to her attire. "So, why are you?" she said. "Interrupting my evening, I mean."

He straightened his shoulders. "First—about Sunday. I was in the throes of, for want of a better phrase, a creative epiphany." Without waiting for her reply, he lifted the hand carrying the case. "Second—I have something to show you. About Mae's painting."

She couldn't help the bubble of amusement at his non-apology apology. Oddly enough, it was enough to evaporate the last lingering traces of her resentment. Remembering her manners, she said, "Have a seat. Would you like a drink? I was about to make myself some tea."

"That would be great." He sat on the edge of a cushion and unzipped the case, pulling out his laptop.

For the next few minutes, neither of them spoke. Titus focused on his computer screen and Claudia busied herself with setting the water to boil and assembling the tea things. The silence wasn't as awkward as she had expected. When she brought over his mug, he smiled up at her and patted the cushion beside him. "Sit here. You'll want a good view of the screen."

She lowered herself, careful to keep enough space so her hip didn't brush his. Resting her forearms on her knees, she cupped her mug in her palms. "Does this have anything to do with the translation?"

He shook his head as he sipped his tea, and then placed the mug on the coffee table next to his laptop. "No. I'm as confused by that as you and Mae. But I had a couple ideas about the painting itself."

Tapping a tab at the top of his internet search screen, he brought up a page full of text results with the words Barkerville and oil paintings.

"You mentioned we could try searching for paintings about Barkerville. I figured we could narrow that search even further. Mae said the painting was given to her great-grandfather when he was married, right?"

Claudia nodded. "In 1931. And did I tell you that the family *did* live in Barkerville at the time? Her grandfather was born there, and possibly his father, too."

"Barkerville was at its biggest, with a population of around six thousand, in the 1860s." On another tab, he brought up a timeline of the Cariboo Gold Rush. "1862 to 1868 was its heyday, although there was still considerable mining until the end of the nineteenth century. By then, most of it was being done on a large scale, not by the romantic miner panning all alone in a mountain stream."

"So, not like the miners in the painting."

"Exactly." Titus' eyes gleamed with the fervour of the hunt, and Claudia felt her spirits rising to meet his. "What if the painting was done by someone who had actually been to Barkerville in the 1860s?"

"We're still just guessing this whole thing is connected to Barkerville," Claudia said. "The photograph has nothing to identify it, and neither does the painting. It's only mountains and trees and a creek."

"We've got to start somewhere. If this leads to a dead end, we'll try again. But why not take the easy route first?"

"I suppose. So where did the easy route take you?"

"Here." Another tap, and the screen filled with a new image. Claudia leaned forward.

The colours were subdued, the brushwork soft. As for setting, it was as if the painter had been on a high peak, looking across a wide valley toward a mountain capped in white far in the distance. In the foreground, scrubby bushes and white flecked rocks filled the frame. In the middle of the scene, a man followed the faint trail that meandered from the lowest edge of the painting and over the edge of the foreground peak.

"He's carrying a shovel," Claudia said, peering closer, "and is that a gold pan strapped to his pack?"

"Here's a photo of Mae's painting." Titus tapped an icon on the bottom of the screen and that image replaced the first. "What do you see?" He flicked back and forth between the two paintings, giving Claudia plenty of time to compare them as he did so.

"I see two paintings that share certain similarities," Claudia said, tamping down a blossoming excitement. "The colour palettes are similar—muted, earthy tones. The trees and mountains are rendered in comparable styles." She put her half-drunk tea down and clasped her hands together. "Who did the first painting you showed me, Titus? How on earth did you discover it? And what do you think this means?"

CHAPTER THIRTEEN

Claudia stared at him, eyes wide with anticipation. Titus wished he could tell her a story of days hunched over a keyboard, of hands cramping from using a mouse, of frantic calls to museums and galleries.

With a self-deprecating laugh, he told her the truth.

"I Googled for images using the keywords *Barkerville, oil painting,* and *1860s.* This was on the second line of results. It's called *Scene in British Columbia* and it's by William George Richardson Hind. It is believed to have been done in 1863."

"I'm not an expert. I was in university the last time I had to compare and contrast two images, and that was an exercise for a class. But at first glance, wouldn't you say..." She trailed off, as if afraid to speak her hope aloud. Titus had no such hesitation.

"Yes. At first glance, I would say these are done by the same person."

Claudia rose to her feet and started pacing. He kept his eyes firmly on her face, but that didn't stop his body from reacting to the sway of her breasts as she moved.

"What was his name again?" she said.

"William George Richardson Hind." He pulled his gaze reluctantly back to his laptop and switched to another screen. Summarizing what he read there, he said, "He was born in England in 1833 and came to Canada in 1851 to join his older brother. Even at eighteen his artistic talent must have been evident, as he was given a job as Drawing Master at a prestigious school in Toronto. His work was also included in a provincial exhibition the next year."

Claudia continued to stalk back and forth in front of him, her expression fierce and concentrated. "I did a Canadian Art History course when I took my degree at the University of Toronto," she said. "I don't recognize the name, but I could have forgotten it."

"By all accounts, he stopped painting in 1870. Or at least painted nothing that was considered worth preserving, either in his own opinion or whoever handled his estate."

"How did he end up in Barkerville?" She came to a stop directly in front of him and put her hands on her hips. He planted his elbows on his knees and leaned forward, hoping to hide his growing erection. "If the painting was done in 1863, he must have been there during the biggest years of the rush, right?"

"Have you heard of the Overlanders?" he said.

She frowned. "It sounds familiar."

"Most miners who joined the Cariboo Gold Rush arrived in what would become the Province of British Columbia by boat, usually landing at Victoria. But one group decided to follow the old fur trader's trail across the Prairies and through the Rocky Mountains. Hind was part of that expedition. Supposedly he was so annoying they kicked him out and he had to drag along after them for days until they let him join again."

"Artists," Claudia snorted, shooting him a glance. "Can't live with them, pass the beer nuts."

Titus grinned. He enjoyed sparring with Claudia more than he should.

"The group arrived in the Cariboo in the fall of 1862, but according to the article I found on biographi.ca,

Hind was living in Victoria by early 1863 and making a name for himself as a sign painter. In those days, business signs could be works of art, with depictions of local landmarks and landscapes. He did continue to paint for personal reasons during the seven years he lived there, and it's believed he made another trip into the Cariboo in 1864. He left Victoria in 1869 or so, stopping for a few months in Winnipeg, which resulted in a few paintings of varying quality—again, according to the writeup I found. He died, unmarried, in New Brunswick in 1889."

"Mae's painting is unsigned, right?"

"Yes. From the images I've seen, I can't tell if Hind regularly signed his work or not."

Her gazed sharpened. "You found more online?"

"Quite a few, actually. A good dozen or so are of miners or life in mining camps. I'll send you a link so you can take a look. I found the best images on a website that sells on-demand print copies of old works. Most of the originals seem to be in the McCord Museum in Montreal."

"Can we contact them? Do you think they'd look at Mae's painting for us?"

"I don't see why not, but—" He was strangely loath to allow strangers, however expert, into the search. If others joined them, it would lose the intimacy he and Claudia now shared. "Let's not rush into anything. I can do more exploring online. And it would be great if we could identify the men in the photo first."

"It would." Claudia settled next to him again, her excited energy dissipating. She lay back and put her bare feet up on the low table. He saw with lustful delight her toenails were painted a stunning red, matching the rich, Oriental pattern of her pajamas. "You're not the only one that's done some sleuthing, by the way," she said.

"Oh? What have you been up to?"

"I spent more time on the Barkerville site last night.

Not that I found anything useful. I've pretty much exhausted the images that are available online. I have Mae's permission to share the photo, so tomorrow I'll reach out to the curator and see if it's okay to send it. It's possible what we're looking for is in an offline collection." She sunk lower and studied the ceiling with unseeing eyes. "Also, Mae said something about the translation that got me thinking."

He lay his arm along the back of the couch, close enough that her hair tickled his inner wrist. "What was that?"

"She wondered if it pointed to buried treasure." She rolled her head toward him. "You know, if it's a code to show where the gold—if it is gold in the jars the men are holding in the photo—is hidden."

"I seem to remember someone else mentioning that possibility when *she* first saw the photo," he said cheerfully. "Common sense dictates it is unlikely."

"That's what I told her. It's too bad, because she could really use the money. Still, I can't get it out of my mind. It would be like something out of a book or movie."

Titus was getting used to the low buzz of sexual tension he felt when in Claudia's presence. But as they sat there in the thoughtful quiet following her words, he was shocked by how content he felt, simply sitting next to her warmth, watching her breathe.

Perplexed at this discovery, he lifted his arm over her head, snapped the lid of his laptop shut, and stood as he slid it back into its case. "I should get going," he said.

She stayed where she was and looked up at him from lazily hooded eyes. "I'm glad you came," she said. Reaching out, she took his free hand as it hung lax at his side and used it to pull herself to her feet. The motion brought her so close the silk of her clothing brushed his chest. It did little to conceal the heat and weight of her breasts.

"Claudia..." He wasn't sure if he spoke her name in

warning or in want.

The merest lift of her chin allowed her lips to whisper against his. "Kiss me again," she said. Her breath, flowery and sweet like the tea she'd drank, flowed against his cheek.

He had enough brain power left to make sure he dropped his laptop onto the softness of the sofa cushion before he wrapped his arms around her waist and pulled her tight.

For years, Claudia had been wary of her instincts when it came to the opposite sex. The brutality of her marriage had stripped her confidence in her ability to read men—their wants, their needs, their desires. She'd taken refuge with those who were quiet, undemanding, and often physically smaller. It had allowed her to feel in control, to believe she could overpower them if necessary.

Teasing Titus was a different kind of power. One she hadn't exercised in a long time.

A frisson bolted down her spine as his mouth crushed hers, his arms banded around her. Not fear. Lust and longing and a sudden unexpected need to let herself be, without worrying about what might become.

Dragging her lips from his, she brushed her nose in the soft scruff of his beard and dropped kisses on his strong, thick neck. "You told me to think about you," she said between nibbles. "On Saturday, in your studio. I haven't stopped." She'd tried. Damn, she'd tried, but hadn't been able to.

His hands moved restlessly on her back, the satiny fabric erotic and sensuous against her skin. "I didn't come here for this."

Her hands slipped under his shirt and her palms spread against his abdomen. "I know." He hissed as she scraped her nails above the waist of his jeans. "And I had no intention of doing this when I let you in." Lifting the hem, she dropped kisses on his chest, pausing to lap dreamily at one nipple.

She felt drunk, dizzy and floating. Then his touch swept from her back to her hips to her breasts and the sparks humming in her veins turned to rockets of flame. She leaned back, closing her eyes and thrusting her chest forward into those big, strong hands.

"I knew it," he murmured. "No bra."

"Who wears a bra under pajamas?" She gasped when his thumbs brushed her nipples. Her breasts tingled, grew heavy and tender. He held them carefully, lifting them as he bent forward and pressed his face between their swells. Her knees weakened. "Oh, god."

"I've been wanting to do that for a long time," he said, licking the hollow of her throat before nuzzling between her breasts again. "I don't want to let you go. You'll have to undo your buttons."

With hands that trembled, she flicked open the fastenings, streaks of lightning flashing along her nerves as he continued to play with her nipples. He watched her fingers, an intense red flush painting his hard cheekbones. Once the two sides of the material separated, he tortured her further by using his thumbs to work the fabric to the side, never losing contact with her breasts, until he revealed their hard, pulsing tips.

He nudged her with his hip. "Sit."

She dropped to the sofa so quickly his hands slipped from her body, but she barely had time to give a disappointed moan when his mouth replaced his fingers. Vaguely aware he had somehow jammed his huge body in the narrow space between the coffee table and the couch, she gave herself up to sensation.

"Oh, oh, oh!" She panted, her hips jerking, as he feasted on one breast then the other. Gripping his head, his smooth skull slick and cool under her palms, she wordlessly demanded his attention. A throaty hum buzzed on her oversensitive skin, which she took as approval. His hands gripped her hips—big hands more than capable of holding her generous body—and slid her so her buttocks were on the edge of the cushion, her feet planted on the table on either side of him.

He slipped a hand between their bodies, and his hum grew to a low growl. "You're wet," he said.

She pressed against his hand, seeking, searching, pleading.

Instead of responding with stronger pressure, deeper caresses, he withdrew. "No," she protested, opening her heavy-lidded eyes. "Touch me."

"Trust me, Claudia, there is nothing I would like to do more. But if I stay in this position much longer, I'm going to be crippled for life." With a groan that was less passion and more pain he levered himself from the floor and sat carefully on the table between her feet. "I'm not a teenager anymore," he said, "although you make me feel as randy as one."

She lay sprawled on the sofa, panting softly, coming down from the heights he'd shot her into. Her knees had dropped open and her unbuttoned pajama shirt hung off her elbows, doing nothing to cover her torso. Suddenly self-conscious, she made a hurried movement to shift into a less wanton position, but Titus' hand on her knee stopped her.

"Don't," he said. "Don't cover yourself. God, you're gorgeous."

The flush of desire that had started to fade flared up again. "Let's go to the bedroom."

His eyes glittered with a dangerous light. It should frighten her, seeing that deep-seated desire. It should worry her.

It made her even damper.

"I can't believe I'm going to say this, but not tonight," he said.

That got her attention.

"Why on earth not?" Shaking off his light touch, she struggled to a more dignified position and buttoned her shirt.

"To be honest, I'm not entirely sure." Titus appeared sincerely confused. "I think—I don't think—" He shook his head, sucked in a breath, and started over. "I don't want it to be spur of the moment. Not with you. I'm usually all for spontaneity, but...well, I want you to be sure. After all, you just broke up with Frederick."

Claudia blinked. "What I had with Frederick was more of a mutual agreement than a relationship. I am not suffering from a broken heart." That sounded harsh but was nothing more than the truth. And Frederick had *never* ignited the burning need Titus lit within her. Which, now she could think again, was a huge, red warning sign blinking urgently at the top of a cliff.

Titus scowled. "Well, we *are* going to have a relationship. And if it doesn't end well, you *will* have a broken heart. Which means this is not something I am going to rush into." He rose and circled round the table to put space between them.

She scrambled to her feet. "I knew you were arrogant," she said, her fingers clutched into fists, "but that's over the top. *I* decide if I'll have a relationship with you. And as for a broken heart"—she flapped one hand dismissively—"you'll be the one snivelling in your sleeve."

"I'm almost fifty years old," Titus said bluntly. "I've had one long-term relationship in my entire life, because I never found another woman I thought worth the effort."

She glared. "Of all the chauvinistic—"

"Not chauvinistic. Honest." He pointed a finger. "Then I met you. Yes, I'm arrogant. Yes, I'm used to having things my way. And, no, I don't know if I can handle a committed relationship. But I've finally found someone I want to try with. For some reason, that also means I can't have sex with you. Not tonight."

"What if I don't *want* a relationship?" she said, clutching her anger around her like a cloak. No matter how much turmoil Titus had thrown her into, she could cling to that. She didn't do relationships, not like he was describing. "What if all I want is hot and dirty sex?"

For one terrifying moment, she thought he might take her up on her taunt. *Hot* and *dirty* did not describe her recent sex life, and she had never wanted it to.

He shrugged. "Then I guess we'll both be disappointed."

How dare he be so autocratic? Her temper soared higher, its searing blaze incinerating the panic tickling at the edges of her soul.

He moved toward the door. "When you are willing to explore something deeper, something more than the *mutual arrangement* you had with Frederick, you know where to find me."

Titus sat in the driver's seat of his SUV, gripped the steering wheel, and stared blankly at the grey brick wall outside the windshield. He didn't remember leaving Claudia's apartment or climbing down the stairs. It was probably a good idea to wait until his nerves steadied before turning on the ignition.

"Where the *hell* did that come from?" he said. He'd heard the words that had spouted from his mouth, but from a distance, as if he'd been standing in another corner of the room, watching someone who looked very much like himself make a declaration to Claudia.

He could still feel her heat in his arms, taste her flavour in his mouth. He could also still feel the ache in his knees and lower back from his awkward stance between the couch and the table. *Middle-age sucks,* he thought grimly. If he hadn't had to adjust his position, his mind wouldn't have cleared long enough to have second thoughts, and he'd still have a luscious bundle of woman pressed against him.

As an artist, he was used to his subconscious springing surprises on him. Few paintings ended up being exactly as he envisioned them when he brushed on the first strokes. But to have his soul rear up and slap him upside the head like this was unexpected and unprecedented.

Claudia as his muse was one thing.

Claudia as the woman he intended to pursue a commitment with was something else entirely.

Yet he felt oddly calm about that revelation. He hadn't been looking for a long-term relationship, had never worried about being alone. He'd accepted female companionship when convenient for both, but never looked back when he left. Yvette had been the exception that proved the rule, but so long ago he thought he was past all that neediness.

The thing was, the longer he stayed in Prince George, the more he wondered if he'd finally found a home base, a place he could grow roots, one that didn't give him the itch to leave as everywhere else had. Was his reaction to Claudia mixed up in that new, as yet unexplored feeling?

Whatever the reason for his outburst, he hoped his honesty hadn't put paid to discovering what he and Claudia might have together before it even started.

CHAPTER FOURTEEN

After she'd calmed down, Claudia realized—rather against her will—that she was a teensy-tiny bit flattered by Titus' announcement.

He had basically said he was thinking of her in a way he had thought of no other woman before. What woman wouldn't be complimented by that?

She was still ticked off at him for leaving her in a fever pitch of lust and fury, but she was beginning to understand that any sort of life with Titus—be it friendship, business connection, or something as yet undefined—was going to be rife with drama and upheaval. His decidedly masculine appearance hid a temperament that would do the most flamboyant Hollywood star proud.

And despite the fact she'd avoided any hint of conflict or theatrics for years, she found herself energized by their quarrel, not fearful. Anticipation of their next meeting spiced her coffee like a shot of Bailey's as she practically skipped down the stairs to meet Cecil in the gallery the following morning.

"How's it looking?" she said.

The handyman was crouched near the base of the wall that had suffered the most damage during the flood, a black, square, plastic rectangle about the size of a cell phone pressed to the floor. Grunting, he pushed to his feet. "Not bad, not bad at all." He held out the gizmo, showing her a screen with meaningless numbers displayed. "Moisture reading is good. We can start refinishing the floors today. Probably begin on the far side, where the water didn't reach as much, give this longer to dry just in case."

"That's great. We won't get pushed too far behind, then."

Cecil nodded. "Lucky you noticed when you did. If you didn't live here, that water could have gushed for days. Would have been a lot worse."

"How long will the floor take to finish?"

Cecil scratched his grizzled chin. "It's a big job. Got to sand it all a couple times before staining. Then got to let that dry before varnishing. The crew I hired are experts, do this all the time, but it'll still be five, six days. And you might not want to be here while they're varnishing. The fumes can be pretty strong."

"Thanks for the warning." She did some quick plotting. "If all goes as scheduled, you figure they'll reach that stage by the weekend?"

"Yeah. You'd want to be out early Saturday for sure, maybe come back no sooner than late Sunday afternoon. Monday she should be ready."

Claudia intended to send the photo found behind Mae's painting to the Barkerville museum as soon as she got settled at her laptop. She supposed she could leave it at that, but the idea of visiting the historic town with Titus had taken hold. Fitting in the trip would be near impossible in the weeks remaining before the gallery's opening, but if she couldn't work or live there this weekend anyway...

"Keep me in the loop," she told Cecil as she headed to the rear and the steps leading up to her apartment. "I'll be working upstairs most of the day, give your guys a clear run of the gallery." And avoid what she assumed was going to be a lot of loud noises.

Titus didn't set foot in the studio on Tuesday. After returning from Claudia's, he'd dropped into bed and hadn't awoken until almost noon. He often indulged in a day off after a long stretch of concentrated work, but it wasn't only the need for refreshing his well of creativity that kept him away from his easel. He was also worried that it had been the solid hours immersed in sketching Claudia that had inspired his outburst at her apartment. He figured it would be a good idea to test himself by refusing to think of her for twenty-four hours. And since his idea book was now filled with various views of her face, the studio wasn't the best place to be.

But Wednesday he woke early and had a paintbrush in hand minutes later. The image burned into the back of his eyelids before they'd opened to the dawn formed smoothly and easily on the canvas. It was one of those sessions when his hand moved without thought, when the colours went on perfectly, when that ephemeral *something* blessed his work.

Leaning away from the easel, he stretched his spine, flexed his shoulders. Judging by his stiffness, it was time for a break. His stomach rumbled, and he realized he hadn't had breakfast. The overcast sky visible through the glass above him gave no clue if it was closer to lunch or dinner.

He tilted his head and studied what he'd completed so far. It wasn't finished, but he'd accomplished a lot for one day.

On a stark white background, a huge, aged cottonwood tree in its autumnal glory sprang straight and tall from the shore of the small, blue-grey creek that formed the bottom edge. He'd gone for a more subtle double-image than the woman in the mountain that Claudia had singled out. The forearm with its timeworn skin and the back of the hand with its ridged veins that formed the trunk blended into the rough bark he'd wrought so they were almost indistinguishable. The eye was drawn instead to the heavy branches—long, slender fingers tipped by painted nails like over-sized leaves in autumn orange and gold.

Satisfied with his progress, and growing more aware of his hunger every moment, he tidied up and prepared his work area for the next day. As he walked by his bedroom on his way to the kitchen, a chirruping noise led him to his phone.

A voicemail from Claudia.

Putting it on speaker, he listened as he continued downstairs and raided the fridge.

"If you think dropping a bombshell the way you did and then not calling me is going to piss me off, you're wrong." Her voice was light and cheerful, and he shook his head. She never seemed to do what he expected. Not that he *wanted* her to be angry. But he had wondered what she'd think of his silence since Monday evening.

"I don't scare that easily," she continued, "and as much as it pains me, you've got my attention. Happy now? When you deign to speak to me again, I've got an update on the photo. Also, if you don't have any plans for this weekend, I have an invitation for you. *You* know where to find *me*." From the inflection, he understood she was tossing his last words to her on purpose.

The avocado he was pitting had made his hands messy, but he managed to use the tip of his pinkie to hit the buttons necessary to call her back, grinning all the while.

Claudia and Patsy were in the basement of Four Winds, a large, well-lit storage area neatly cluttered with framed and unframed prints, long lengths of uncut trim, and stacks of fresh matte boards.

"We have to decide what is staying here and what will

be moving to the gallery." Claudia flipped through a rack of sunset photographs printed on shiny aluminum. "I won't strip the shop of everything high quality, that's not the goal. I want each location to have its own ambiance, its own personality. So modern and contemporary looks, like these, will stay here. Anything with a more traditional, rustic feel goes to the gallery." She moved to the next holding rack, which featured unframed prints of a well-known local wildlife artist.

Patsy followed her, peering over her shoulder. "You're not sticking exclusively with originals at the gallery?"

Claudia shook her head, moved one print from the middle of the rack to the front. "Only if it's a special exhibition, like the one we're doing with Titus. I'm planning two of those each year. But prints will be featured as well." She pushed away the thought Fauna might not make it past the first year. She'd put a lot of time and effort into the business plan. It *would* be a success. Thinking anything else was pointless.

She chose four more of the wildlife prints. "Let's get these done up. Double mattes with reveal for each."

They had worked their way halfway down one wall when Claudia's phone rang. She couldn't help the clutch in her belly at seeing Titus' name on the screen. The lures she'd cast in her voicemail had obviously worked.

"Hello, Titus. Give me a minute," she said coolly without giving him a chance to speak. Holding the phone against her shoulder, she said to Patsy, "I should take this."

"No worries. I'll head upstairs, start choosing frames and mattes. You can decide which you like best later." Patsy gripped a slippery pile of prints, each protected in a clear cellophane sleeve, and disappeared.

Claudia lifted the phone to her ear. "Sorry about that."

"I'm not sure I like this side of you," Titus said, although she thought she heard a smile, not censure, in his voice.

"What side would that be?"

"You're turning into quite the tease." His voice rumbled through the speaker, stroking her skin like velvet. "So, what's with this invite you mentioned?"

All in good time, she thought. *See how* you *like delayed gratification.* She leaned against the stout wooden rack behind her. "I sent the photo to the Barkerville Museum yesterday and heard back this morning. The curator is quite intrigued with our little mystery. She says she'll look into it."

"That is good news. But what does that have to do with this weekend?"

"Can you take a high-quality photo of the painting and send it to me? I want to make a print so I can study it more."

"Fine. The weekend?" he added, single-mindedly.

"The contractors are working on the floors in the gallery. They'll be varnishing on Saturday, and I've been told I shouldn't be in my apartment until that's done and dry. If you don't have any plans, I thought maybe we could make a trip to Barkerville. Leave Saturday morning, explore the town, meet with the curator, spend the night and come home Sunday."

There was a short pause. "Spend the night?" Titus said.

Even though he had no inkling of the hang up that caused her to shy away from sharing a bed with a man in the intimacy of his or her home, he obviously knew her offer indicated a potential shift in their...whatever it was they had.

"There are accommodations in the historic town itself," she said, "but they book up weeks in advance. I put in a call to the Bowron Lake Lodge, which is nearby. They have a cottage available."

"I see."

"I also figured the two-hour drive gives us plenty of time to talk things out," she said. "You said no sex until

I decide where I stand. Maybe by the time we get there, I'll know."

"And if you don't?"

"There are two beds in the cottage," she said cheerfully.

Thursday evening, Claudia set her laptop on a stack of books on the coffee table in front of her sofa and arranged the screen so she and Nicole were both visible.

"Oh, god, I look like a whale," her daughter moaned. "My stomach's even bigger from that angle."

"You look wonderful," Claudia said as the video call signalled and she connected with Jill. "Hi, there!" she said, waving. "So good to see you! It's been a while."

"Hi, Mom. Hi, Nicole." Jill waved back. "I'm sorry I've been so busy. I miss talking to you guys."

Claudia settled back with her mug of tea. "It's not just you. The gallery is keeping me hopping, too."

"I live in town and I hardly see her," Nicole said.

Claudia refused to feel guilty. It was a fine line, staying connected with grown children. She didn't want to hover by constantly calling. But that meant they had to take responsibility for staying in touch with *her*. Phones worked both ways, after all.

"How are things going? Ready for the opening?" Jill asked.

"Almost. No thanks to the flood."

"Flood? What flood?"

Claudia and Nicole filled Jill in. "But that's all fixed now," Claudia concluded. "I don't even think it will affect the soft open, which is two weeks today. And it definitely won't affect Titus' exhibition two weeks after that, thank goodness."

"Speaking of Titus," Nicole said, looking at Claudia with an adult gleam, "is there something going on between you two?"

"What?" Jill asked. "Mom and the artist?"

Off step at the quick switch, Claudia stalled for time. "What makes you think so?"

"Gramma and Grampa told me he stuck around all afternoon, helping clean up. That's not exactly in his contract."

There had been a few men in Claudia's life between Saul—her ex and the girls' father—and Frederick, and she'd never hidden them from her daughters. She wouldn't hide Titus, either. The problem was, *she* wasn't sure what was going on, so how could she explain it to them? "I won't deny there is definitely an attraction," she said slowly. "But I don't know if it will lead anywhere. He's leaving town shortly after his exhibition."

"Then you better not waste any time." Jill pointed a finger at her through the screen and winked. "Get to know him now, decide what to do with him later."

It was pointless to tell her daughters Titus was pressing for something other than an affair. For more than twenty years, she'd stuck to her vow never to be in another man's control. She wasn't going to break it now. He was attractive to her in part *because* he was leaving soon, not despite it.

"We're going to Barkerville this weekend. Staying overnight at Bowron Lake Lodge."

She briefly explained about the quest she, Titus, and Mae were on, hoping it would distract them from her love life.

No such luck. As soon as she was done, Jill said, "That sounds so romantic. Don't forget to bring condoms."

"Jill!"

"Hey, you're the one that taught us to be careful, so take your own advice and be responsible."

Nicole shifted, and Jill's expression froze. "Sorry, Nic. I didn't mean you weren't. Accidents happen."

"I might not have planned this pregnancy, but my baby is *not* an accident," Nicole said fiercely. "And anyone that makes her feel that way is not welcome in her life."

"I'm sorry, I'm sorry! That's not what I meant."

"It's what you think, though. What you both think." As if a dam had broken, she turned to Claudia, colour high in her cheeks, breath rapid. "I know you believe I'm making a mistake, not telling L—the father. But you don't know him. So how do you know that's the right thing to do?"

Slightly stunned at the turn of the conversation, a chill slid down Claudia's spine. "He didn't hurt you, did he? Nicole, tell me he didn't hurt you." Abuse was a cycle, but the last thing she'd thought was one of her daughters would fall into the same trap she had, not when they'd been so young when she'd escaped.

"Of course not! But you didn't need a man to help raise us, so why should I?"

The ache in her lungs eased at Nicole's vehement denial. "If you think raising you girls on my own was easy, then I'm a better actress than I thought. Even with Gramma and Grampa to help, it was *hard*, so hard. And even if the father wants to have nothing to do with you or the baby, he has an obligation to support you financially at the very least."

"Haven't you told Mom?" Jill said. A look passed between the sisters, and not for the first time Claudia wondered if Nicole had confided more in Jill than she had with her.

"You don't have to," she said hastily. "I'd never insist you tell me anything you don't want to share. But you know you can, right? I love you. No matter what, I love you."

Nicole's face dissolved into tears and she leaned against Claudia's shoulder. "He doesn't love me," she sobbed. "I told him I loved him and he broke it off with me the next night. I didn't know I was pregnant yet."

It was a shock to hear her daughter was in love with a man Claudia had never met. "How long did you know him?"

Nicole sat upright. "It doesn't matter! I knew the second I saw him I loved him. But he didn't feel the same way, and I *refuse* to tell him about the baby. I don't want him if the only reason he wants me is because of the baby."

Claudia wrapped her arms around her daughter's stiff shoulders and rocked her. Nothing she could say would mend a broken heart. Her embrace was the sole comfort she could offer.

CHAPTER FIFTEEN

Claudia locked the apartment door behind her. Heavy fumes of varnish were already creeping up from the main floor, making even the scent of stale garbage sweeping through the alley preferable. Carrying her small overnight bag, she headed down the stairs to the parking area to wait for Titus.

Her stomach curled in delightful twists of anticipation. During the last few days, ever since making their plans to go to Barkerville, she and he had been engaged in a virtual flirtation. In the guise of planning for the exhibition, they'd exchanged texts and emails. Each had started business-like enough, but along the way, the conversations had slipped into moments of personal sharing.

It was quite delicious and whetted her appetite for more.

Hidden beneath her excitement, however, was a jittery layer of anxiety. If Titus was as serious about her as he professed to be, she owed him honesty about her past, and not just hints and innuendo. She never enjoyed talking about her marriage, and not only because reliving it was vastly unpleasant more than two decades later. But because she'd seen how the knowledge changed people's perceptions. The thought that Titus might think differently about her caused her more than a touch of uneasiness.

His SUV turned the corner into the narrow lane and pulled to a stop. Shaking off her apprehension, she hopped in, tossing her bag into the back.

"Good morning," she said, smiling as she fastened her seatbelt.

"Morning." He smiled back. "There's one thing I have to do before we get going."

Before she could assure him running an errand wasn't a problem, his fingers cupped her chin, holding her in place as he pressed his mouth to hers. Caught by surprise, her eyes stayed open.

He pulled away. "There. Something for you to think about while we drive," he said, grey eyes intense.

She blinked, enjoying the buzzing warmth, momentarily speechless.

Ten minutes later they were out of the city on the highway heading south. To Claudia, the silence between them, at first comfortable and natural, had grown edgy and tense. *It's just me,* she assured herself. Titus seemed perfectly relaxed, his hands loose on the steering wheel, shoulders slouched.

Time to get it over with.

"All right," she said, taking a deep breath and keeping her gaze focussed out the windshield. "Since I'm the one who declared this would be a good time to talk things out, I'll start."

She could feel Titus slant her a glance, but his only vocal answer was a soft grunt.

"We can agree we're attracted to each other, right?"

A definitive humming assent from the driver's seat.

"And that we're too old to waste time on a relationship that doesn't work for both of us?"

This time, a huffing chuckle was his answer.

She twisted in her seat and glared at his profile. "You know, this will probably work better if you actually speak."

His mouth quirked. "I thought I'd let you get everything out of your system first."

"I don't have to get anything out of my system," she said testily. "This is supposed to be a discussion, not a monologue."

"I was pretty clear on where I stand, that night at your apartment."

She tossed her hands in the air. "You expect me to believe that after less than a month's acquaintance you've decided I might be *the one*"—she placed derisive air quotes around the last two words—"the first woman you've ever considered good enough to spend the rest of your life with."

He took his eyes off the road long enough to meet hers levelly. "Yes."

"You don't even know me!" she said.

"That's easily fixed," he said, his attention once more back on the highway unspooling before them. "Start talking."

Still, she hesitated. Her fingers tangled together in her lap and she shifted to face forward again.

"Would it help if I told you I'm pretty sure I know what you're going to say?"

It was her turn to answer with a wordless noise. It was certainly possible he had deduced the truth, but there was a yawning chasm between guessing and knowing.

In a soft voice, Titus said, "He abused you, didn't he? Your ex-husband?"

In the close confines of the SUV's interior, Titus felt Claudia stiffen. Her fingers, which had been fidgeting restlessly in her lap, froze.

Keeping his eyes on the road, he said, "I might be off base with the *ex-husband* part, since I'm not certain you've ever been married." But that was just semantics.

The breeze from her whirring thoughts was nearly tangible. Waves of tension rolled off her, abating slowly when he remained silent. They reached the base of a long hill and he pulled into the passing lane to slip by a slow-moving transport truck.

"Yes, we were married," she said finally. "When did you figure it out?"

"A few things made me wonder. The first day we met, you seemed uncomfortable around me. Not scared so much as wary. You're very protective of Mae, and after we met with her at the coffee shop you said a few things that showed you related to her situation. Also, I get the feeling your involvement with the Elizabeth Fry Society is deeply personal. Then there's Frederick."

"What about Frederick?"

As he shoulder-checked to move back into the right-hand lane he snuck a glance at her. She was studying him suspiciously. "You had a relationship with him for years. Casual, easy. He was someone you felt you could control. I also think that, once you met me, you realized he bored you silly."

She hissed in a breath. "I'll have you know I broke it off with him because he wanted to get serious, and I don't do serious. It was *not* because of you."

That gave him pause. This wasn't the first time she'd implied she wanted nothing more than an affair. If she was willing to end a lengthy relationship because Frederick had wanted *more,* he might have to change his tactics.

"Fine," he said. "We can table that for later. Tell me about your ex. Does he live in Prince George?"

After a short pause, during which he could feel her eyes boring into his temple, she turned to the front and answered, "No." She crossed her arms under her breasts, making them lift. It didn't seem to matter if he was painting or cooking or driving—he was completely aware of Claudia at every second. "We met in Toronto. When we split, he stayed there, and I brought the girls home."

"He ever visit?"

"Not once. I was granted full custody, and when I applied to take the girls out of province he didn't even bother to argue."

"Sounds a real peach." He was pleased when she let out a soft chuckle. "How old were you?"

"I was still in university." She shifted lower in the seat, laying her head against the rest. "I left Prince George at eighteen. I'd always known I wanted to do Art History, and U of T was where I wanted to go. I met Saul in my fourth year. He was in construction, was working on renovations to one of the buildings on campus. He whistled at me one day when I went by." She laughed self-deprecatingly. "I suppose that should have been my first clue. But in more than three years of school I'd been on fewer than ten dates, and having someone express any sort of interest, no matter how chauvinistic, was flattering."

She turned her head toward him and he tipped his toward her to let her know he was listening. "Saul was a big guy, maybe even bigger than you. His work kept him fit, but he liked to lift weights, too. I was a lot heavier then, and he made me feel small, delicate. I liked that."

He wanted to tell her he liked her size, how she was solid and soft and strong and sexy, but didn't want to break her rhythm now that she'd started.

"One of the first things I did when I began putting my life back together was join a gym. I'm never going to be slim, but I'm much healthier than I used to be." There was a hint of defiance in her voice when she added, "It took awhile, but I learned to accept myself. I like my body the way it is."

He couldn't let that remark go by. "So do I," he agreed, letting some of the heat he felt seep into his tone.

Out of the corner of his eye he caught a glimpse of pink flushing her cheek.

"Anyway," she said, "to make a long story short, he romanced me for a few months and we married as soon as I graduated. Looking back, I can see the signs were there almost from the start. But hindsight truly is twenty-twenty, and I've had enough therapy to know better than to dwell on it. I've also forgiven myself for staying with him for as long as I did, even after the abuse changed from verbal to physical. The first time he hit me was a month after our daughter, Jill, was born. She was colicky and had been crying non-stop for days. He blamed his bad temper on lack of sleep, even though I was the one that spent the nights rocking her. I'd wanted my mother to come stay with us after the baby was born, but he said he wanted us to be a family ourselves before strangers burst in." This time her laugh was sad. "He'd been walling me off from my support system right from the beginning, but it was so gradual I didn't notice. I was upset my parents weren't welcome, but by then he'd pretty much convinced me we only needed each other. And it turned out that what I needed, according to him, was a punch upside the head occasionally. Among other things."

Titus realized he was breathing raggedly through his nose, as if he'd run a long distance. His knuckles ached from clenching the wheel.

"He'd said he wanted kids, but really he wanted a son. When Nicole was born a year and a half after Jill, he was furious. He didn't wait a month to hurt me. That was the last time, though. We'd been together about three years by then, and I was done making excuses, for him and for myself. He went to work the next morning, and I packed a couple bags, put the girls in the double stroller, and walked away. There was a church two blocks over. I rang the doorbell and said, 'My husband beats me and I need a safe place to stay. Can you help?' They were the hardest words I've ever had to say."

A blue and white sign advertised a rest stop a couple hundred metres ahead. Titus signalled and pulled off the highway. It was a simple paved area surrounded by pine forest, with a couple concrete outhouses and a few scattered picnic tables. No other vehicles were there. He parked and turned off the ignition, noting vaguely that his hand was trembling.

"Titus?" Claudia reached over and touch his arm.

"Wait right there," he said, and unbuckling his belt, he stepped out of the SUV. Rounding the hood, he opened the passenger door. Claudia stared, her blue eyes wide. He ducked in, unfastened her belt, straightened up, and held out his hand.

She raised her eyebrows, and then placed her hand in his. Gently tugging, he urged her from the seat, and when she was standing, wrapped his arms around her fiercely, breathing her in.

After a moment, her arms came around his waist and she hugged him back. "Titus—"

"Shhh," he said, eyes closed, nose buried in the crook of her neck. "I just need to hold you for a minute."

And he did, while traffic whooshed and chickadees chirped.

Titus' beard bristled softly against her collarbone. He hugged her like her daughters used to when they needed comforting—nestling against her as if the mere contact could fix his troubles. His back hunched as he laid his head on her shoulder, and she lifted her chin to rest it against his smooth scalp.

"His name was Saul?" Titus' voice was muffled against her skin, and she shivered at the sensation of his breath skimming her neck. "Aronson?"

"No. Aronson's my maiden name. I didn't want anything from him. Except our daughters. If he had cared enough to oppose me bringing them back to Prince George, I would have fought like a tiger."

He lifted his head and she immediately missed the weight of it on her shoulder. "Was he charged?"

She toyed with a button on his shirt. "Yes. He was given a suspended sentence."

"A slap on the wrist." Titus winced. "Sorry, poor choice of words."

She surprised herself by laughing. "At the time, I thought the same thing. But in the end, all I wanted was to be safe, for my daughters to be safe. I was happy with anything that kept him away from us, and his probation did that. Once we moved home, back to my parents, it was even easier to forget about him. Now, months go by without me thinking of it." Remembering her reaction to Frederick's innocent movement after the auction, she felt obliged to explain further. "I should warn you, on the odd occasion something will trigger me. In case you're around when it happens."

"How do you deal with it? The flashbacks or whatever you want to call them?"

"Usually, I have an ugly cry and then move on."

He unwound his arms from her waist and brushed the pad of his thumb over her cheekbone. "I don't know what I'd do if I saw you cry."

"Run the other direction?" she teased. She felt light, buoyant. Titus had been affected by her story, but the warm compassion she saw in his expression was not the disturbing pity she had feared.

He opened his mouth, and then closed it, and let a wry smile lift one corner. "Probably," he said with the same lighthearted tone, and dropped a quick kiss on the tip of her nose. "Thank you for telling me. Even though I did have to worm it out of you. Now, let's get back on the road."

CHAPTER SIXTEEN

Shortly after they resumed their journey, Titus turned off the main highway and headed east on the smaller, winding road that led into the mountains.

If anyone had asked Claudia how she'd feel after telling Titus of her past, *playful* was not the word that would have come to mind. But she seemed to have experienced a catharsis, and with Titus' sympathetic but matter-of-fact acceptance, she felt carefree and open, like a child escaping school at the end of June.

They still needed to talk about *them*—about Titus and Claudia—but as he'd said, that could wait for a little while. They were both clear about what each other wanted, but she wasn't going to toss away what they could have right now on a nebulous some day.

"Have you heard of ArtsWells?" she asked as the scattered residences outside her window grew fewer and farther between, to be replaced by forests of pine and poplar interspersed with shrubby, marshy areas.

"Maybe?"

"No one lives in Barkerville itself, but there's a village a few kilometres this side of the Historic Town and Park called Wells. It has a reputation as an artists' haven. Every summer it hosts ArtsWells, a festival of all things art. Music, dance, visual—you name it. Usually the last weekend in July."

"Yvette will know all about it. That might be why it sounds familiar—she's probably wanted me to go. More than likely too late for this year, but I'll tell her to consider it for next."

Claudia suppressed a surge of unease. No matter what his supposed feelings for her, she was depending on his vagabond lifestyle to put a natural end to whatever might grow between them. She reminded herself that planning to attend a nearby festival didn't mean he'd still be living in Prince George at the time. He'd simply travel from wherever he ended up.

Giving in to curiosity, she asked a question that had been on her mind since her first discussions with Yvette. "Has she been your agent long? She sounded very protective when I talked to her."

"And you find that surprising?" Titus slid her a sideways glance.

She swept him with her eyes, taking in his heavy, athletic build, the determined set of his jaw, the confident way he held his shoulders. "Yes, actually," she said drily. "I don't know what it was, but she sounded more like a friend than a businessperson."

"Remember I told you I've had one long-term relationship in my life?"

Claudia's eyebrows shot to her hairline. "You had a personal relationship with your *agent*?"

"She wasn't my agent at the time. We met in university, lived together for two years. She is an excellent artist in her own right. Not that I ever told her that. If I had, maybe things would have been different."

Claudia tried to fit the pieces of the story into a shape that made sense and gave up. "How did she go from living with you and being an artist to being your agent?"

"As you know, I can be occasionally self-involved." Ignoring her snort, he continued calmly. "I was worse in my twenties, believe it or not. Selfish, narcissistic, proud. Yvette was smart enough to know I wasn't a good bet for the long haul and left me."

"That must have been upsetting." Especially given he hadn't had another even remotely serious relationship since.

"Probably less than it should have, but yes. I had loved her, as much as I was capable at the time. Looking back, I know leaving was the best thing for her. Probably both of us. We kept in touch, very loosely, so I knew she'd become an agent. When my career started to take off, she was the first person I called."

"And she took you on as a client? Just like that?"

"Oh, no, it wasn't that easy. I had to do some grovelling. But your instincts are right. She is more than a business partner." His tone, easy and reminiscent through the conversation, turned bitter. "Not that she will be for much longer."

"She won't? Why not?"

"She's dumping me. Again. For a job running a gallery in Toronto."

If Titus had been a toddler, she would have said he was pouting. On a man with such heavy features, the downturn of his mouth only made him look ferocious. "You need a new agent?"

"I don't want a new agent. But it doesn't look like I have a choice." He pressed his lips together.

The road dipped around a curve, and a wide-open space with neatly maintained square-cut log buildings came into view. A sign declared it Cottonwood House Historic Site. Titus remained silent, apparently done talking about Yvette. Searching for a new topic, she said, "I find it fascinating that the road we're on is basically the same route thousands of people used to get to the gold fields."

A short pause followed. Even though she kept her gaze averted, she was conscious of Titus' tightly wound emotions. The last thing she wanted was to spend the rest of the drive with a petulant driver. She held back a sigh of relief when he finally replied. "And most of them had already travelled thousands of kilometres to get this close."

She nodded in agreement, watching the log fence snaking by. "They must have wanted to get to Barkerville very, very badly."

Titus shifted, his posture relaxing further as he bent one knee up as far as he could under the dash. "So, who are we going to see at the museum?"

"Nadia Yu. I sent the original email to a generic inbox, but the reply came directly from her, complete with name and credentials in her signature. I did some research. According to her bio, Ms. Yu's area of study while getting her Master's was Chinese emigration to British Columbia in the 1800s."

"That sounds serendipitous."

She shot him a look. "Big word, big guy. But yes. Although it isn't unlikely that someone with her specialized knowledge would work there. Barkerville's Chinatown is famous as one of the oldest in North America."

They swept around yet another corner of this winding mountain byway and headed down into a narrow valley, a tumbling rocky stream racing along with them.

"Originally I communicated with Ms. Yu about the photo. But once I found out more about her, I figured I might as well bring the document, too, in both its original and translated form. It can't hurt for someone else to look at it. And I brought a colour print of the painting, too."

"Covering all your bases."

"You bet. There's something special about this painting, about these mementos. And we're going to get to the bottom of it."

The last few kilometres of the journey took Titus

and Claudia past the interestingly named Jack of Clubs Lake—he wondered what the story was there—and through the community of Wells she had mentioned. Titus approved of the old wooden buildings painted in bright, eye-catching colours housing cafés, galleries, and souvenir shops. These were interspersed with the drab, shuttered buildings found in many rural places. A tiny RCMP detachment suggested it wasn't always as quiet as it appeared now—though given the road he had just driven, he wouldn't doubt if most of the officers' time was taken up with vehicle incidents.

Past the village, the road twisted along the base of a series of low hills to the right, and a vast expanse to the left.

"That looks like a river delta," he said. "It's flat and wide and swampy."

"I'd forgotten what this approach is like," Claudia said, leaning toward him and peering past. "It's always so much more open than I remember. Of course, I haven't been here since Nicole's class came when she was in Grade Four or Five, so it's been a while."

The road straightened out, long sweeping curves replacing the tight corners to the west of Wells, and gradually the valley narrowed. Traffic was scarce, with no one ahead of him, only a motorhome in his rear-view mirror, and just the occasional vehicle going the other direction.

Claudia pointed out a road branching off to the left. "That's the way to Bowron Lake, where we're staying tonight," she said. "It's about twenty minutes in, I think."

He nodded, and a few minutes later pulled into a parking space outside the Barkerville Visitor Centre.

"So, what's first on the agenda?" he said as they left the SUV. Even though it was late June and the sun was shining brightly, the air was brisk and chilly. He imagined that at this altitude it rarely got too hot.

Claudia reached into the back and dug out a folder

from the bag she'd tossed there. "We're right on time. Our appointment with Ms. Yu is in ten minutes. We'll get our business done first and explore the town later."

Titus supposed it was a failing of his, but he'd rarely played tourist in his own country, preferring to do his leisure travel internationally. He was looking forward to meandering through the streets, poking his nose into the displays and shops, discovering the living museum with Claudia at his side.

Instead of heading into the Visitor Centre, she led the way across the parking lot to a different building. Steps led to a central structure with a peaked roof and long, single-storey wings stretching out to the right and left. They entered a tidy but shabby hall with an alcove that housed an old metal desk with a modern laptop and multi-line phone perched on it, a row of battered filing cabinets, and a cheerful young man.

"Hello, there!" he said. "How can I help you today?"

"Claudia Aronson and Titus Wilcox to see Nadia Yu. We have an appointment."

He beamed. "I'll let her know you're here," he said, reaching for the handset.

Moments after he delivered his message, steps could be heard coming from the hall that led to the right wing, and a woman appeared. Titus guessed she was in her early forties, just above average height, with a slim build that made him think of a marathon runner. Wire-framed glasses were perched on her head, glinting brightly on her short dark hair. A few silver strands threading through it matched the frames.

"Claudia?" she said, stretching out a hand. "Nadia Yu. And this must be Titus." She smiled at him. "When Claudia mentioned your name, I wondered why it sounded familiar. Then I realized I had seen your work in a gallery in Vancouver recently. I very much enjoyed it."

"Thank you," he said, uncomfortable at the praise yet revelling in it at the same time. He caught the sly glance

Claudia shot him and realized she understood what he was feeling. Did she really know him that well? He wasn't sure whether to be pleased or concerned.

"I have some things to tell you," Nadia said, motioning them to follow her. "I think you'll find them interesting."

Titus let the two women precede him into what appeared to be a windowless, soulless boardroom. A long oval table, big enough to seat ten people, took up most of the floor space. A few of the chairs had been pushed against the walls to allow easier access to the artifacts spread across the surface.

Claudia's heart beat faster as she surveyed the documents, maps, and photos. She put the folder she'd brought off to the side and faced Nadia.

"Have you identified them?" she asked. "The men in the photo?"

"Yes and no." Nadia picked up a sepia-toned page covered in faded writing from the littered table. "Given the circumstances in which you found the photograph, I started with a search for the family name. Barkerville's Chinese community was vibrant and well documented. It didn't take long to find a man named Leung Ah—proper Chinese usage puts the surname first—in a register of residents living in the Chee Kung Tong building." Smiling, she offered the paper to Claudia. "This is a scanned copy, showing entries from June 1864. Leung Ah is mentioned here." She pointed to a series of characters about halfway down the first column.

Titus moved closer and Claudia held the page so he could see it, too. Even though it was a copy, and in a language she couldn't read, it made her tingle to be this close to something so old, to think of the person whose pen had touched the page, to imagine the world surrounding him as he'd written these names.

"What exactly was the Chee—what was the name again?" Titus asked.

"The Chee Kung Tong are Chinese Freemasons. Their society hall here in Barkerville is a National Historic Site of Canada and is the oldest ethnic Chinese structure in the country. Since the town is also a National Historic Site, that makes it the only NHS with another NHS nested inside it. The society was a hub for Chinese men, and the building was used for ceremonial, residential and social purposes." She gave a sheepish grin. "I could go on, but I think that's all you need to know for now."

"This Leung Ah." Claudia moved her fingertip gently across the paper, invisibly underlining the name. "You think he is the man in the photo?"

"Based on circumstantial evidence alone, I'm afraid. The photo was found in the possession of the Leung family. Leung Ah was in Barkerville—the single Chinese man with that surname, which is helpful. And the photo was taken here."

Claudia looked up sharply. "You know that for a fact?"

Nadia nodded. "I do." She chose two photos from the small stack on the table. The first, a copy of Mae's photo presumably printed from the file Claudia had sent, she handed to Titus. The second she held so they could all see.

"Almost ninety percent of Barkerville burned to the ground in September 1868. More than one hundred buildings had to be immediately rebuilt before winter hit. See the building the men are standing in front of?" Nadia tapped the page Titus held. "You can see it here, in this photo"—she tapped the page she held—"showing the main street as it was reconstructed after the fire. And we know this photo was taken in 1870."

"So, our photograph had to have been taken later than September 1868," Claudia said thoughtfully.

"Actually, I can date it better than that." Nadia drew

a large sheet of paper closer, tugging it gently so the two empty coffee cups and stapler holding down three of the corners came along with it. "This is a copy of a map from 1875, showing all the registered claims around Barkerville." The paper was riddled with thin lines and greyed out blocks in irregular shapes. "I cross-referenced Leung Ah in the Gold Commissioner's records, and found his name assigned to this one." She pointed to a block in the bottom right-hand corner, somewhere to the southeast of the townsite. "Despite the fact that Ah arrived in Barkerville in 1864, it wasn't until five years later, August 1869, that he registered a gold claim. I haven't discovered what he was doing before that time. He might have been working for another miner or at one of the many Chinese businesses that serviced the town. The boom was mostly over by the fire in 1868, so there would have been plenty of claims for sale. Maybe he simply decided it was time to try his luck. He was the owner of record until 1889, when the title lapsed."

"No other names are associated with the claim?" Claudia asked.

Nadia shook her head. "Not at the relevant time. I'm collecting data on the surrounding claims, on the surmise that the other men in the photo are miners from the same area, but I haven't anything worth sharing yet. I'll keep looking."

"You said the title lapsed. Does anyone own the claim now?" Claudia asked.

"In these mountains, you can't set foot out of your car without stepping onto someone's claim," Nadia said. "And I'm only half-joking. But I can help you find the current owner, if there is one, should it become necessary."

"Is the claim accessible?" Titus asked.

"I would imagine so, if you're willing to do some bushwhacking. It's not that far away from the townsite as the crow flies—less than five kilometres. There might even be a reasonable trail part of the way, but you'd probably need to rely on GPS coordinates to make sure you hit the right spot."

"Why would you want to go?" Claudia asked, looking over her shoulder at Titus. Light glinted off the scattered silver hairs in his beard and she could smell his aftershave.

He shrugged. "I wondered if the painting was done near the claim."

"Oh! The painting." Claudia opened the folder she'd brought and handed a page to Nadia. "I thought you might be interested in seeing what the photograph is attached to."

"Of course I am." Nadia patted the top of her head absently, searching for her glasses, and placed them on her nose. For a few moments she studied the print in silence. "It really is quite lovely, isn't it. Wonderful colours, an unusual subject...can I keep this?"

"Of course. Show it around. Maybe someone will know something about it...maybe even recognize the area it depicts."

"No signature," Nadia said, tilting the print toward the light.

Claudia motioned to Titus to take up the conversation. "No," he said. "We haven't confirmed it yet—I'm not even sure we will be *able* to confirm it—but we think it might have been done by William George Richardson Hind."

Nadia's head jerked up. "Hind? Really?"

"You recognize the name?" Claudia asked.

"Of course. There were very few artists who painted Barkerville during its heyday. Hind is probably the most notable."

"From what we found online, it seems the McCord Museum in Montreal has the biggest collection of Hind originals," Titus said. "You wouldn't happen to know anyone there who might be willing to take a look at our painting, give us their opinion?"

"Let me make some calls." Nadia's attention was back on the image she held. "This could be quite valuable, if it is an unknown Hind."

Claudia wondered if it would be inappropriate to ask for an estimated value. Titus, obviously less inhibited, said bluntly, "How valuable?"

She tucked away the smile that threatened and waited for Nadia's reply.

CHAPTER SEVENTEEN

Nadia spread her hands and rolled her shoulders. "In dollars, I have no idea. The McCord Museum might be able to help you there, too. In significance, it would be of major interest." She placed the print on the table and held out her hand for the photo of the men Titus still held. He released it agreeably. "I'm going to keep studying your photo, probably share it with colleagues, see if we can find anything else that might help us date it more positively."

The room fell quiet. Claudia was overwhelmed by the information Nadia had gleaned, yet there was so much more to learn. Into the silence, Titus said, "What do you think of those jars they're holding? We can't really tell, but we're assuming they're filled with gold."

"Dreaming of treasure?" Nadia laughed, dark eyes gleaming. "As I said, the main boom was over by 1868, at least as far as most of the smaller placer miners were concerned. I would have thought a find substantial enough to fill those jars would have been well known, but I'm not aware of any. From the fact the photo was taken in town, I would assume they were on their way to deposit it in the bank."

"Then why go to the trouble of hiding the document

and the photo?" Claudia asked. As laughable as it was to believe the photo might lead to buried gold, she wasn't quite ready to let go of Mae's romantic notion.

"Document?" Nadia asked. "What document?"

"I brought these for you, too." Claudia handed her copies of the original and the translation. "It was attached to the back of the painting, next to the photo. We've had it translated, but it means nothing to us. Maybe you could give us your thoughts."

"*Knowledge is weightless, a treasure easily carried,*" Nadia read. "You really did uncover a mystery. I would be more than happy to study this. I can see my evenings are going to be full for the next while."

Conscience-stricken, Claudia said, "We don't mean to take up your personal time."

"It's no trouble at all. I'll get in touch with McCord right away. And if you find anything yourselves, be sure to let me know."

"Well, remember there is no real rush, other than sheer curiosity." Mae might disagree with Claudia's view. If the painting was valuable—or if, against all odds, it did lead to buried treasure—she could use it to support her daycare business. Claudia might find the search an intriguing puzzle, but to Mae it might be the difference between financial independence and smothering debt.

Claudia and Titus spent the rest of the morning wandering the streets of the reconstructed town, watching the street performers, and exploring the shops. When a hailstorm swept through with little warning, they sought shelter in Wake Up Jake's and fortified themselves with thick, hearty soup served in a sourdough bowl. In the afternoon they explored Chinatown.

"It gives me chills," Claudia said, staring up at the Chee Kung Tong building. "Mae's ancestor would have walked these same streets, climbed these same stairs, lived in this very building."

"Have you ever been to Europe?" Titus asked. He took her hand as they resumed their stroll. His was warm and large and Claudia felt heat kindle in her belly. She was doing her best to ignore the fact that every minute brought them closer to a night together. She knew how *she* wanted to spend it—wrapped in Titus' arms—but he'd been the one to say no last time.

"Claudia?" He quirked an eyebrow.

"Sorry," she said, flushing. "I was thinking of something else. No, I've never been to Europe."

"I spent a month in the south of France about ten years ago. It's full of ancient structures—Roman aqueducts, medieval castles, walled cities. And many still in daily use, not just tourist attractions. I went to a concert in the amphitheatre in Arles. The atmosphere was amazing."

"I'm jealous. I've never been out of North America. When the girls were young and we had the money for a holiday, we still couldn't afford to go far from home. Once the gallery is up and running and doing well"—she crossed her fingers superstitiously—"maybe I'll treat myself to an adventure." Though the idea of travelling alone, whether to her dream location of New Orleans or any other spot, no longer seemed appealing. Not after the comradeship of the last few hours, and the potential the night held.

Delving into the nooks and crannies of Chinatown whiled away the time before dinner, which they agreed was only appropriate to eat at the Lung Duck Tong Restaurant. Pleasantly sated on the excellent food, they ambled down the main street, passing St. Saviour's Anglican Church before reaching the exit gates.

"Ready to go?" Titus asked.

Claudia nodded, nerves sparking delightfully. "It's been a great day. I'm so glad we came."

"Me, too." Once again, he reached for her hand, this

time tucking it into his elbow in an old-fashioned gesture.

"Do you think Nadia will find anything else?"

"I hope so. She seemed pretty confident. We'll have to be patient, I guess."

The drive to Bowron Lake Lodge was quiet. They rolled smoothly along the well-maintained gravel road at a steady pace, and Claudia found herself hypnotically soothed by the rumble of the tires. Her eyelids drooped.

A soft exclamation from Titus woke her from a light doze. Forests had hemmed the road on both sides for most of the journey, but the vista now before her was breathtaking. A huge lake stretched into the distance, long and narrow, the mountains ranged along its shores navy blue with white shoulders.

"I need to paint this," he said, the vehicle slowing as he craned to look out the windshield. The road made a sharp corner to rim the end of the lake.

"Right now?"

"Right now." To their left, a low building painted red with white trim bore a round wooden sign declaring it the resort office. Titus pulled into the parking area and handed the keys to Claudia. "I'll be on the beach. Come find me when you know what cabin we're in."

Opening the back, he pulled out what looked like a large suitcase and hurried across the road to the gravel shore. It wasn't quite seven o'clock, so there was plenty of daylight left, though it would disappear fast in this mountainous terrain. Amused rather than upset at the rapidity of his desertion, Claudia climbed out and headed into the office.

It wasn't often that Titus had the luxury of painting outside of his studio. In the interests of efficiency, his usual process while on location was to sketch in pencil— or take photos if he was really in a hurry—then use those images to inspire later works. When Claudia had told him where they'd be staying, he'd looked it up online, and what he'd seen had convinced him to bring his travelling paint kit with him.

The photographs on the internet had done pale justice to what was now spread before him.

His kit had been cleverly designed to hold all he needed, including various sized canvases. Choosing the largest, he hurriedly set up his easel. Experience and instinct had him choosing colours for his palette without conscious thought.

Rich gold and cobalt violet...

Cool white and ivory black...

Venetian red and Prussian blue...

He added tints and tones to reflect the pinks and purples turning the slate-grey water opalescent, dying the snowy peaks unearthly hues. From one blink to the next, it seemed, the light was gone, snuffed out behind him. He stood back from his easel, laid his palette and brush down on the closed lid of his kit, and worked the kinks out of his hands.

"It's gorgeous."

Some part of his mind had been aware of Claudia's presence, as he felt no surprise at hearing her voice. He turned to find her perched on a picnic table—sitting on its top, her feet on the bench seat. She had a blanket wrapped tightly around her shoulders, her hands hidden in its folds.

He said nothing, still trapped in a daze of creation. In the growing dusk he couldn't make out her features, but an errant shaft of the setting sun teased gold glints from her hair, gone in a flash.

"I hope you don't mind that I watched." She huddled deeper into the blanket. He became aware of the chill nipping the end of his nose, a biting wind sweeping off the lake and down the back of his neck.

"No, I don't mind." Which wasn't usual for him. Normally having someone peering over his shoulder would have irritated him. Extremely.

She studied him, head tilted to one side. Stepping off the table, she approached, standing so close her crossed arms brushed his chest. "I had no idea that watching you paint would be so arousing."

He hissed in a breath, his body reacting instantly to her words.

"You had no idea I was here," she went on. "It was like watching someone sleep. Vulnerable, because you were so unaware of your surroundings. Yet powerful, because it energized you, took you to a different place."

She kissed the corner of his mouth, rubbed her nose in his whiskers. "I love your beard," she said. "I want to feel it on my skin. Everywhere." Her eyes, black in the now almost complete dark, met his in challenge.

He had to clear his throat before he could speak. "I'll clean up and meet you at the cabin. Which one is it?"

"Number nine," she said over her shoulder as she sashayed away.

Claudia entered the tiny cabin tingling with anticipation. Titus hadn't wanted their first time together to be spur of the moment. He couldn't use that excuse tonight. She'd made sure of it.

The floor space wasn't much larger than the average hotel room, with a minuscule kitchen in one corner, an equally tiny bathroom in another, and a table with four chairs tucked under the front window. It did have two beds, as she had promised—threatened?—Titus. What she hadn't told him was that it was a bunkbed anchored to the back wall. The lower mattress was a double, the upper a single. She hoped he was a snuggler, because she doubted the upper bunk would hold either one of them and the lower was a far cry from the king mattress she preferred.

Tossing aside the blanket she'd taken from the cabin earlier, she stripped off her clothes and left them strategically scattered between the door and the bed before climbing under the sheet. Propping herself on one hip, bent arm supporting her head, she draped the covers artistically to reveal her naked shoulders and the upper slopes of her breasts.

Titus was going to regret making her wait almost a week.

Her ears buzzed with the silence. No appliances hummed, no vehicles roared by. There were other campers—she'd seen the RVs set up at the far end of the beach and vehicles were parked outside a few of the other cabins—but nothing disturbed the heavy quiet.

She heard the click of the SUV's rear door opening, followed shortly by the chunk of it closing. Footsteps thudded on the short flight of stairs and across the narrow porch.

The door opened.

Though the cabin did have electricity, she'd opted for the thick candles she'd brought. In their flickering light, Titus' face appeared dark and dangerous, his bulk nearly filling the doorway.

Her toes curled in anticipation.

His gaze traced the trail of clothes, from the jeans at his feet to the T-shirt, the bra, and the panties leading to the bed, lifting to sweep over her shoulders to her face, as intense as a touch. The brisk breeze swept past him and swirled around the room and she shivered. He stepped in and closed the door.

The silence between them grew tighter, thicker. Claudia licked her lips but refused to speak. He was the one who wanted something deeper, something more than the *mutual arrangement* he'd openly scorned.

Let's see how long that vow lasted—when she was naked and waiting.

He pulled one of the chairs away from the table and spun it to face her. Lowering himself carefully, he lifted his right foot onto his left knee and untied the light hiking boot he wore. All without taking his eyes off her.

"I said I wasn't going to be casual with you." He

peeled off his sock, tucked it into the boot, and tossed it to the floor with a thump. He switched legs.

"I said I wanted a relationship." The second boot dropped. He planted both bare feet on the ancient linoleum covering the cabin floor.

"I said we needed to know each other better before we fell into bed." He shrugged out of the flannel shirt he'd worn unbuttoned over a white Henley T-shirt.

Claudia worked saliva into her mouth. He was still clothed yet she was wet with wanting. "I can't promise you more than I had with Frederick." She flung the covers to her hips. Her breasts were so full and heavy they mounded on the mattress like pillows. From the harsh glitter in his eyes and the way his breath grew ragged, Titus liked what he saw. "But I can promise you I'll give as much as I can."

"That's a start." He pulled his T-shirt over his head. "What about me, Claudia? What do you want from me?"

His chest was lightly furred with silvery hair, a dusting across his pectorals that arrowed down a firm belly to his jeans. His abdominals were not overly defined, but she thought they might have been in his younger years.

"Claudia?" he prompted. "What do you want from me?"

She'd promised herself she'd never again be trapped by a serious commitment. It wasn't healthy to be so wrapped up in one person you lost yourself. But she couldn't tell Titus that. It would bare too much of her soul, and she done enough of that today.

"I want you," she said. "I want your hands, your lips, your mouth."

He studied her for a moment, and then rose from the chair. His hands went to the button at the waist of his jeans, unfastened it. Heat flooded her body, softened her bones. "That's a start," he repeated, the words both a promise and a threat. He unzipped his fly.

She was dizzy with lust but forced herself to say,

"You're leaving in a month. It can't be anything more."

"We'll see about that." He shoved his underwear and jeans down in a smooth motion, stepped out of them, stood naked and ready before her. "Is there anything that might trigger you? Anything I shouldn't do, any way I shouldn't touch you?"

And despite her best intentions, the armour she'd built around her heart cracked.

"I trust you," she said around the lump in her throat. "I trust you enough to tell you if I don't like something, and know you'll understand. But don't hold back. I need you, Titus. I don't think I've ever needed anyone like this before in my life."

She held out her hand. "Come to bed," she said. "Make love to me."

CHAPTER EIGHTEEN

Titus approached the bed, took Claudia's hand in his. She stared up at him, blue eyes dark and dilated, a flush spreading across the top of her splendid breasts.

"You are magnificent," he said, and then knelt beside the bunk. It was so low to the floor he had to sit on his heels to avoid waving his cock in her face. *Too soon,* he thought with an inward grin. He released her hand, let his palm hover over her opalescent skin. "May I?"

She said, "If you ask my permission every time you want to do something, Titus, you're going to tick me off. I said I trust you. Trust *me* to tell you what I like, what I don't like. I'm sure we'll figure it out." She drew his hands to her breasts.

They were so large his palms couldn't encompass them. They flowed soft and silken, the nipples dusky brown and pebbled to points. With a moan he took to be encouragement, Claudia rolled to her back, and he lifted her breasts, held them together so he could bury his face in her cleavage. Her hands gripped his head, and he did what she had asked on the beach—caressed every inch he could reach with his beard.

She'd climaxed so quickly, the first time he'd feasted on her breasts. This time, he listened carefully to her sighs, paid close attention to the tension in her body. When she reached the edge, he pulled back, easing her down. Over and over again, until she writhed uncontrollably.

Kicking the covers off, Claudia groped for his hand, dragged it between her legs and held him there. "Yes," she demanded, her hips lifting, and warmth gushed against his palm.

"You are so sexy," he whispered against her nipple. "So incredibly arousing. I've barely touched you."

"I don't understand," she said huskily. "It's so easy with you."

A surge of pride and tenderness and delight surprised a chuckle out of him. He lifted his head and studied her face. Her eyes were closed, one arm crooked over her head, and he tickled the corner of her mouth with his tongue. "I'll take that as a compliment."

"Idiot," she said, her voice indulgent. Her lids lifted and his rampant desire spiked at the passion in her eyes. "Come here."

He slid onto the mattress. Her arms wrapped around his torso, sweeping from shoulder blades to waist, as she wriggled against him. "Lay down," she said.

In the cramped, narrow space, it took some manoeuvring to get into position. Claudia was flushed and giggling by the time she straddled his stomach, her head dipped forward to avoid the bottom of the bunk above. "We're too old for these sorts of gymnastics," she said, leaning down to nibble at his lips, her breasts soft and full against his chest, her hands planted on either side of his head.

"Speak for yourself." He gripped her hips, holding her securely against him, as his cock nudged between the softness of her buttocks. "I'd put up with much worse conditions to be with you."

Her mouth commanded his, open and seeking, and he lost himself in the tangling of tongues and sharing of breath.

Long, sensuous minutes later, Claudia whispered, "I want you inside me."

There was so much more he wanted to do with her, but they had the luxury of time. He'd been serious when he'd said he was ready to explore long-term with her, whether she believed it or not. "I want that, too."

"Lift your head." Puzzled but willing, he did as she asked, and took advantage of his position to lick and suck her breasts. Though distracted by this bounty, he could feel her rummaging under the pillow. "Got it." She sat up and he reluctantly released her. She held a foil wrapped package between her fingers.

"I haven't hit menopause yet," she said, "and while the odds are astronomically low, I'm taking my daughter's advice."

"You told her we were going to have sex?" He wasn't sure how he felt about being the subject of a mother/daughter discussion of that nature.

"Told *them*," she clarified. "Said it was a distinct possibility." She ripped the package open. "A condom is obligatory. Pregnancy aside, we've both been with other people recently."

He was finding this frank conversation oddly arousing. Claudia wriggled further down so she sat warm and wet across his thighs. Squeezing his eyes shut and gathering his galloping thoughts, he said, "My last time was more than six months ago. And I'm always safe."

"Then we'll keep being safe." With a dexterity that had him shuddering, she rolled the condom on. "It looks like I bought the right size," she said in a pleased tone. "Extra small."

His eyes popped open. "Extra *small*?" he growled, enjoying the devilry in her expression. "Let's see if you think it's still small when it's inside you."

Bending his knee, he prepared to flip her to her back. She pressed his shoulders down. "I said I'd tell you what I need," she said. "And I need to be on top."

Relaxing, he smiled up at her. "Absolutely no problem."

Rising on her knees, Claudia guided him to her entrance. She was hot and tight and ready, and he bit back a groan as she settled on to him, buried him deep. Her hands spread on his belly and her head dropped forward as she circled her hips.

He couldn't help it. He thrust upward, bending his knees and pressing into his feet to lift off the bed. "Yes," Claudia hissed. "Like that." He thrust again and her nails dug into his abdomen. "Oh, god, yes."

He stopped thinking, stopped worrying, certain now she would let him know what he needed to do to make it good, make it right. The wooden frame squeaked with his frantic pace, drowned out by Claudia's loud demands and uninhibited pleas. When her release flooded through her, set her body stiffening and clutching, lightning flashed down his spine and through his groin, fusing them together. She collapsed on top of him, a warm, pliant weight, as his hips jerked in the last spasms of his climax, and he held her against him, not certain if he would ever let her go.

Claudia woke the next morning to the unusual yet satisfying sensation of a man spooned behind her.

She lay there, eyes closed, and took stock of her feelings.

One she was surprised to discover *missing* from her self-appraisal was, well, *surprise*. Titus' warm breath on the back of her neck, even the soft, rolling snore he rhythmically emitted, felt comfortable, natural.

Physically, she was aware of a sensation of satiation, repletion. She and Titus were well matched, physically and sexually—as he'd demonstrated a second time sometime in the darkness before dawn. Even when she'd whacked her head on the top bunk during a particularly vigorous movement, their shared laughter had only enhanced the connection they were building.

Testing, she wiggled her butt and felt his cock twitch. She was toying with the idea of being less subtle when a hoarse voice growled in her ear, "Are you *trying* to kill me?"

"Of course not." She squirmed again. "You feel pretty lively to me."

The hand of the arm draped over her waist squeezed her breast gently. "How many condoms did you bring?"

She held back a chuckle. "The whole box."

The hand stilled. "You did have high hopes."

This time, her laughter rang through the room. She rolled onto her back and Titus obligingly made room for her. His bald head and trimmed beard appeared exactly as they did at any other time of day. It made her conscious that her own hair was probably standing up in spikes.

As if reading her mind, Titus said, "I like you like this. All rumpled after a night of sex. With me," he clarified, and she felt another laugh rise. At this rate, she'd do nothing but giggle the entire ride home.

With a sigh, she rubbed her nose against his. "I guess we should get up. There's no restaurant here so we'll have to drive into Wells to eat."

"I'm not sure I can fold myself into that shower," Titus said, "let alone share it with you."

"Was that part of your plan?" she asked, raising an eyebrow.

"A shower with you?" He nodded, his beard rustling against the pillowcase. "Getting you all slippery and soapy is definitely on my list. But it will have to wait until I can get you back to my place."

"I'll pencil that in," she said, and then slipped out of bed before she ignored her own intentions and tackled him again.

If Titus hadn't come into the gallery with her,

Claudia thought she might have lain down on the newly finished floor and caressed it like a lover.

"It's beautiful," she crooned, giving in to temptation so far as to crouch down and smooth her fingertips over the glossy surface.

"It's coming together, isn't it?" Titus said, hands on his hips as his gaze swept the room.

She gave the floor one last pat and stood up. They'd come in the rear entrance, and from their vantage point the sun streaming in the large windows on the far wall made the varnished hardwood glow like dandelion honey, the reflected light warming the soft white of the walls. The baseboards would be installed tomorrow, and then she could start arranging the artwork that would bring it all to life. Her stomach lurched.

"I'm getting more nervous, not less, the closer we get to opening," she said. "All this preparation and planning—that's the fun stuff. But once it's open, there are no more excuses."

"I won't try to comfort you with platitudes," Titus said. "Success can be elusive. But as long as you know you did your best, that's all that matters."

"And *that's* a cliché if I ever heard one," she replied with a laugh, but felt better all the same. "RSVPs are starting to come back for your exhibition, which kicks off the official opening. Even though it's not ticketed, I need a head count to make sure I'm fully prepared." In her mind, she started going over the lengthy to-do list— caterer, decor, gift bags...

A hand waved in front of her face, startling her out of her reverie. "You zoned out there for a minute," Titus said, smiling, "so I think I'll get going, leave you to it."

"Sorry. There's so much still to be done..."

"It's okay." He kissed her firmly. "Thank you for a great weekend." His next kiss banished the to-do list from her mind.

"I'm not *that* pushed for time. Want to come upstairs with me?" she said, wriggling her hips against his suggestively. "Maybe we can have that shower you mentioned."

He groaned, and this time his kiss was deliciously rough and demanding. "We'll save that for when I have your full attention," he said, and with a light tap on her ass, he was gone.

Grinning inanely, Claudia nodded in pleased satisfaction at the gleaming floor stretching in front of her then turned to the stairs. She picked up the bag she'd left at the landing and headed to the apartment, humming with happiness.

Since she'd been off the grid for much of the weekend—cell and data service were spotty at best in the mountains around Barkerville—her first order of business was to check emails. Scrolling through her phone as she waited for water to boil for a cup of tea, she almost ignored the message from a rival business. She'd signed up for their newsletter months ago, to make sure she stayed in the loop on what they were offering clients, but rarely did more than scan them.

This subject line had her heart dropping, and she tapped to open it with a sense of dread.

According to the professionally designed invitation now on her screen, River's Edge Framing and Art Gallery was pleased to announce a special exhibition by wildlife artist Robert Bateman. Limited edition prints as well as select originals would be available for sale and viewing at this invite-only event. The artist himself would be in attendance on Thursday, July 23.

Titus' exhibition at Fauna was scheduled for Friday, July 24.

A flush of icy heat swept up Claudia's neck and prickled her cheeks. She leaned heavily against the counter.

Robert Bateman. Arguably the world's best-known wildlife artist. Born in 1930, he was still a driving force in the art world, and an appearance by him was sure to draw a large, enthusiastic crowd.

As much as she loved Titus' work, the comparison between their two careers was like watching a tuna swim with a shark. And while their visions were diverse and individual, their shared exploration of nature and humanity's response to it would appeal to the same audience.

Her grand opening now had *disaster* written all over it.

CHAPTER NINETEEN

Claudia spent a restless night, seesawing from *It's not that big a deal* to *Might as well give up now*. But the resilience she had built, painfully and persistently, after she left Saul was so ingrained now that defeat was not in her vocabulary.

As she showered Monday morning, she planned her strategy. It wouldn't hurt to send out a reminder to those she'd invited to the grand opening, even though it was still four weeks away. Just a gentle nudge to encourage them to RSVP sooner rather than later and remind them of the charitable aspect of the evening. It was also time to start updating Fauna's social media pages in the lead up to the soft open. Now that the main chaos of construction was over, she could post photos that didn't show the place looking like a war zone.

Most of her time that day, however, was taken up with her new staff. Now that opening was less than two weeks away, it was time to kick training into gear.

They were an eclectic group but, watching them interact as they reviewed the on-boarding package she'd prepared for them, Claudia thought they might make a good team given the chance. Bernadette Jenkins, a retired art teacher, had a warm but no-

nonsense attitude that the two younger women, Karina Spencer and Tanya Prince, seemed to welcome. Tanya was of Indigenous heritage and had caught Claudia's attention by including her own excellent artwork in her resume. Karina had no art background at all, but a wealth of customer service experience and an appealing eagerness to learn.

"As you can see from your package," Claudia said, "there will be a reception desk at the front entrance, but all financial transactions will take place here, in this room, which will eventually be set up as a lounge as well as a secondary showroom." Right now, they were perched on folding metal chairs around the banquet table that used to be up front. "While selling artwork is our ultimate goal, I want the atmosphere to reflect that of a museum or public gallery, not a retail business. Also, the value of some of the work we'll have available may require payment plans or other financial arrangements. We'll want a private space for those discussions."

Her cell phone rattled against the table and Titus' name lit up the screen. Her fingers itched to answer it, just to hear his voice—*How pathetic is that?* she thought—but sent it to voicemail with a quick apology to her staff and muted her phone to avoid further interruptions.

"What happens if only one of us is on and we need to leave the front?" Karina asked. A slender redhead in her late twenties, she was living at the same shelter as Mae. Claudia was always looking for ways to support the women who took refuge there, though she wouldn't have hired Karina if she hadn't had applicable skills.

"To start with," Claudia replied, "I'll be here all hours we're open, so there will always be two of us available. If we feel we need to expand from the Tuesday through Saturday, 10am to 7pm hours currently scheduled, I'll review staffing to make sure we're covered."

The rhythmic barrage of a nail gun started up in the

front room. Raising her voice, Tanya said, "When is construction supposed to be done?"

"Not soon enough," Claudia said with a wry grin. "I shouldn't say that. It's gone reasonably well, knock on wood." She rapped the table to ward off bad luck. "The main gallery should be done today, and then the rear rooms by the end of the week. Tomorrow we start moving stock from Four Winds and taking deliveries of the new products. It might be a bit tricky, but we should be able to work around everything."

She spent another hour or so answering questions, going over timelines and explaining expectations. When they'd covered everything on Claudia's agenda, she asked once more if there were any concerns. Three heads shook in the negative, and Bernadette closed her binder briskly. "Tomorrow at nine?" she said.

"Yes. Casual clothes, please. We'll be doing some grunt work."

The three women were barely out the door when she reached for her cell phone. Titus had compared himself to a teenager the first night they'd kissed and now she knew what he meant. It had been difficult to concentrate on her training after he'd tried to reach her. Simply knowing the voicemail was there had been more distracting than it should.

The notifications on her lock screen showed that not only Titus had called—so had Nadia Yu. Cautioning herself against getting her hopes up, she connected to the recordings.

Titus' message was first. If she'd thought their relationship would now include sentimental expressions of longing, it would have shattered that assumption.

"I've got an idea for the Elizabeth Fry piece. The contract demands I run the concept by you. Call me."

She couldn't help but laugh. It was so Titus. Grinning, she pushed the buttons to hear Nadia's.

"You're not going to believe this, but I found the

other men in the photo. They did have a claim next to Leung Ah. I'm going to email you details, but I couldn't wait to tell you. Of course, maybe you've seen the email already, since this is going to voicemail, and you already know what I'm talking about. Sorry, I'm rambling. I'm still stunned. If you haven't yet, read the email. I can't wait to hear what you think."

To: Claudia Aronson (claudia@fourwinds.com)
From: Nadia Yu (Yu.Nadia@barkerville.ca)
Subject: Identification of Men in Photo

As I mentioned to you Saturday, I wanted to determine who owned the claims surrounding Ah's. They weren't difficult to discover once I had time to do some proper digging. Then, with those names in hand, I searched our archives to see if I could find any photos of those miners, in the hopes of being able to compare them with the one you provided.

Of the twenty or so names I had shortlisted—that is, those with claims nearest to Leung Ah—none resulted in a photo match. Undaunted, my next step was to search the names in the Cariboo Sentinel archive. This was the newspaper published in Barkerville from 1865 to 1875, and digitized pages are available through the University of British Columbia's open library.

There, I hit pay dirt (isn't it funny how many of our sayings relating to lucky finds use terminology tied to the search for precious metals?).

One claim that directly bordered Ah's was owned by Julius H. Franklyn and Lloyd Bilsland. If you remember, Leung Ah registered his claim in August 1869, on the site of an existing claim abandoned by a miner from Wales. Franklyn and Bilsland had registered their claim almost three years earlier, in June 1866.

I found a newspaper report stating Julius H. Franklyn died on June 15, 1870 as the result of a fall down a mineshaft at the claim he owned with Lloyd Bilsland. He was twenty-three years old. A photo printed with the article, showing both men, has allowed me to conclude they are the men with Leung Ah in your photo.

The names appear again, about a month later, in an article announcing the claim had been sold, and that Bilsland intended to return home to England. There is no mention of Leung Ah in either article, but I am certain they are the right men.

Your search has sucked me in, so I promise to keep on looking. But I was only able to spend time on it this weekend because plans I had fell through, so I'm not sure when I'll next be able to provide an update. Rest assured, I will not forget about it.

Sincerely,
Nadia Yu

Titus finished reading the email—for the third time—and then laid his phone on his thigh. On the outdoor sofa next to him, Claudia shifted, bending one knee so she could turn to face him.

"She found them, Titus," she said, her blue eyes glowing like the depths of a glacier-fed lake. She'd come to his house after work, and the sole topic through dinner, kitchen clean up and now coffee on his deck had been Nadia's email. "We know who all three men are."

"It's amazing, it really is. Now we have to figure out how this knowledge helps." He didn't want to quench her excitement, but someone had to keep a level head. He tapped the mug she appeared to have forgotten she was holding. "Drink your coffee before it gets cold. What did Mae say when you talked to her?"

Obediently she took a sip before replying. "She couldn't believe it either. She was thrilled enough when Nadia found her great-great-great-grandfather but putting names to the other faces in the photo always felt like we were asking too much."

"Does she still think the gold from the photo is buried somewhere?"

Claudia pursed her lips and shrugged. "She did mention that again. I'm not sure how deeply she believes in it, though. She's too realistic to depend on it." Something flared in her blue eyes, something Titus saw with a touch of misgiving. "If it does exist, what about Ah's claim? Could it have been buried there?"

"Sure. Also, anywhere else in the world." It was ridiculous to believe in hidden treasure, but he couldn't help wishing, just a tiny bit, that it was true.

Brows creased, Claudia placed her now empty mug on the low table in front of them and flopped back onto the seat in what he might describe as a huff. "I want to help Mae so much," she said. "She deserves a break."

"Finding buried treasure is more than a break—it's a fairy tale come true. And we all know that real life isn't a fairy tale." Seeking a distraction, he said, "We haven't talked about my painting for the auction."

"Oh, I'm sorry! I'm afraid I forgot all about your message after I listened to Nadia's."

He supposed he couldn't blame her, although he wasn't particularly thrilled to be relegated to second place. "I only agreed to this condition because of the charity you chose. No one tells me what I can and can't paint. However, I understand why you want to ensure I'll provide something appropriate. As a white male I appreciate I might never fully understand the nuances involved."

Claudia's eyebrows rose. "There's something in that admission that feels condescending, but I'm going to assume you didn't mean it that way. What's your concept?"

Despite his assertion no one could dictate his work, he once again felt the need for Claudia's approval. He'd had an art teacher in university that believed every artist created their work for an audience of one, that everything they did was conceived to elicit acclaim from that ideal viewer. Titus had scoffed at that thought then and had had no reason to change his mind since. Until Claudia.

He was beginning to believe she might be his audience of one. And his muse. And his love.

"It will be in my new double exposure style," he said. "A female face blended with a sunrise over a mountain lake, conveying resilience, strength and new life." He rarely put into words what he wanted one of his paintings to say, so working out how to explain it to Claudia had been an interesting exercise in frustration, and he had no intention of telling her that the female face would be inspired by her. "Concepts often morph during the actual execution, but I promise you it will be a positive, encouraging image."

She tilted her head to one side, eyes thoughtful. "It sounds just right."

Tension he hadn't realized he'd been holding flowed out of his shoulders. "Great. I'll start working on it tomorrow."

He did his best not to be insulted when Claudia returned to the subject that had monopolized the evening. The world didn't have to revolve around his art *all* the time. Though it would be nice. "Nadia didn't get in touch with you, did she?" Claudia asked. "Regarding the McCord Museum? In all the excitement of identifying Franklyn and Bilsland, I forgot to ask."

"Not yet. If I don't hear from her in a couple of days, I'll send a reminder."

"Okay." She rolled her neck as if resetting her thoughts, and then in one swift motion moved his phone from his thigh to the coffee table, hiked up her skirt, and straddled his lap. His hands went automatically to her hips. "I missed you today," she said, running her fingers through his whiskers and toying with his earlobes. Since her breasts were right *there,* he pillowed his head on them and her hands slipped over his skull to the back of his neck, pressing.

"I didn't even think of you once," he said.

He felt her low hum of amusement and her nails pinched his nape. "Not once?"

"Not more than once every fifteen minutes," he said, relenting, letting his lips brush against her skin as he spoke. She arched her back, offering him even easier access. "Maybe every ten."

"Let's see if we can get that to five," she murmured, and pulled the silky, flowing top she wore over her head and unclasped her bra.

CHAPTER TWENTY

The next morning, Titus had every intention of working on the Elizabeth Fry painting as he'd promised Claudia. But he found himself restless and unable to settle. It wasn't a completely unusual state when he was between pieces. What was unusual was the reason *why*.

Claudia hadn't stayed the night.

After an al fresco interlude that had left him as boneless as a sponge with Claudia draped over him in what had appeared an equally satiated state, he hadn't wanted her to leave. Which was new territory for him. He rarely enjoyed sharing his space with anyone, be they family, friends, or lovers.

Yet when Claudia had lifted off him and started to put herself back together, one word had popped out of his mouth. "Stay."

She'd given him a cheerful grin without meeting his eyes. "I can't. I didn't bring any of my stuff."

"What do you need? I have a spare toothbrush somewhere. And you had no problem sleeping naked at Bowron."

"I have to go home," she said, her voice muffled as she pulled her shirt back on.

He wouldn't beg, but he could plan. "Why don't you

bring some things with you the next time you come? Leave them here." He folded into a sitting position and stroked his hand up her back.

"Maybe." She stood up, away from his touch. "I'll call you." For a moment he thought she was going to lean down and kiss him, but instead she'd wiggled her fingers in a friendly but dismissive wave and vanished. Something in her departure had made him think of a prisoner escaping her jail cell. But she'd been perfectly happy sleeping in his arms in the cabin, so what had changed?

The only thing that managed to hold his attention this morning had been an email from his absentee landlords. They'd decided to extend their commitment to Doctors Without Borders and were asking if he wanted to renew his lease another twelve months. If he didn't, they were going to put the house on the market.

He'd replied immediately, asking for time to consider his options. The email had coalesced ideas floating around in the back of his brain for a few weeks now, but he had to ensure he was making his decision for the right reasons. *Not* reasons driven by his libido.

After that distraction, he'd returned to his studio and back to mooning over the Claudia conundrum. Like a romantic fool, he was now flipping through the pages of his sketchbook—the pages he'd filled with Claudia's face and figure the night of the full moon. He hadn't looked at them for almost a week, and as he studied them, he grew more and more thoughtful.

He turned back to the first sketch. It showed Claudia from head to toe, her chin lifted over her shoulder. The expression on her face was soft and yearning, and he remembered telling her to think of him, of the kiss he'd pressed upon her, as she posed.

It wasn't only her expression that intrigued him. It was what he saw in his own work. No longer caught up in the fever of creation, he couldn't avoid seeing his own feelings in the strokes and lines—tenderness, admiration, passion.

Love.

In all his dramatic declarations, he'd never used that word. It gave him pause even now. Was he truly in love with Claudia? Is that what had prompted him to challenge her insistence there could be nothing more between them that a short-term fling?

He glanced down at the sketch again. The answer was there, right in front of him.

Yes.

Given her reaction to his invitation to stay the night, he was thankful he hadn't known the depth of his own feelings sooner. He had no doubt that hearing that word would have sent her fleeing faster and farther.

But what to do about it? How could he get her to open her heart and mind, to give him a chance to be a part of her life?

The canvas he'd prepped for the Elizabeth Fry piece was waiting, blank and ready. Propping up his sketchbook so Claudia's portrait was in his eye line, he set to work.

For Claudia, the next several days flew by. Her new team lived up to her expectations and the gallery was taking shape. Signage went up as scheduled, the point of sale and inventory system was installed, and Cecil and his crew finished the work in the backrooms right on time—a minor miracle, she knew.

Everything was perfect. Exactly right. Nothing wrong in her life.

Riiiiiigggggghhhhhhttttt.

Professionally, things were fine. Personally, it was a mess.

She'd had another fight with Nicole about the father of her baby. Since the evening Claudia had discovered her daughter's feelings, she'd dithered about whether to encourage Nicole once again to let the man know he was going to be a dad. She'd finally taken the plunge last night, and it had not gone well.

"I will *not* be in a relationship built on pity," Nicole had said, her expression stony.

"You don't have to be in a relationship," Claudia had tried to explain. "That's not what I'm saying. But someday your baby is going to ask about her father, and what are you going to tell her?"

"Why does it matter so much to you?" Nicole had shouted. "I didn't grow up with a dad. You made sure of that. So why are you insisting my baby have one?"

Shocked speechless, Claudia could do nothing but watch her daughter storm out of the apartment. She'd never hidden the reason she'd left Saul from her children, and had assumed, the infrequent times she'd thought about it, that they'd understood her decision. It had never crossed her mind that Nicole might blame her for her lack of a parent. Obviously, they had to talk again, but first she'd have to figure out what to say. For now, she was at a complete loss.

Then there was Titus.

They hadn't seen each other since Monday night, when he'd asked her to stay and she'd practically sprinted out the door. She hoped he hadn't noticed how uncomfortable his suggestion had made her. She'd been with Frederick for years and *he* had never suggested she leave personal items at his home.

Unlike Titus, who brought it up two days after they'd started sleeping together.

Not seeing him didn't mean they hadn't talked. He'd called to tell her that Nadia had connected him with someone at the McCord Museum and to ask her to ask Mae for permission to send the original painting out east. "It's a necessary step toward authentication," he'd explained. "We can't expect them to decide one way or another from a photo."

They had shared all the information they'd gleaned from Nadia with Mae, who was excited to learn more of her family history. But she'd been reluctant to send the painting away, unwilling to risk the ire of her father if it were damaged or lost. The back and forth on that subject had required several conversations. They'd also discussed Titus' progress with the auction painting. He'd been terse with her, but she had tried not to take that to heart. He'd promised he'd have it done, and she trusted he would, so hounding him was counterproductive.

Now it was early Sunday afternoon, and she had decided to pull on her big girl panties and beard the lion in his den. Her metaphors might be mixed but her intentions were not. He deserved an explanation of her recent actions, and it was time to give it.

On the drive out, a low, clenching ache set up in Claudia's belly. *Fabulous,* she thought, recognizing the warning sign of the onset of her period. She'd never had a very regular cycle, and the older she got the more unpredictable it was, which was to be expected, but very inconvenient.

She parked next to Titus' SUV and double-checked she had the necessities in her purse before getting out, vaguely aware of music blaring outside. As soon as she opened her door, Mick Jagger lamenting he couldn't get no satisfaction resonated through the usual calm stillness. Determining Titus wouldn't hear either a knock or a bell if she tried to gain entrance through the front, she followed a slate stone path around the corner of the house through a neat shrubbery to the deck overlooking the lake. The music grew louder, but there was still no sign of Titus. As the French doors to the living room were open, she stepped inside. A glance was all it took to determine he wasn't on the lower floor, either.

The Stones were replaced by Bon Jovi as Claudia climbed the stairs to the second level. The volume of the music remained constant, and she realized it must be playing through an in-house speaker system. On the landing, she had a clear view down the hall into Titus' studio.

He was scowling at the easel in front of him, of which she could only see the tripod supports and the back of the canvas propped on it. As she approached, he made several delicate swiping motions, the graceful movements at odds to the rock music splitting the air like an ax.

She was pretty certain he saw her—he was facing her way, after all—but he gave no indication he was aware of her presence. Until she was two steps into the room, when he barked, "Far enough!"

She froze, teetering on one high-heel clad foot before planting the other at its side.

"You're not seeing this before it's done," he said, his focus still on the canvas, "so that's as far as you go."

"Is it the auction piece?" she asked, stepping back to the door and leaning against the frame.

"No."

She waited for further explanation, but he said nothing more. Pulsing beats filled the space between them, echoing the throbbing in her stomach as it spread to her hips.

He dabbed at the canvas a few minutes longer, and then tossed his brush to the side. "Looks like I won't get any more work done today," he said with a glare in her direction. As fierce as his lowered brows made him appear, Claudia felt no fear. In fact, a spark of aggravation flared. Maybe it was PMS, but she was in no mood to take any crap from him.

"Alexa, music off," he said. Silence fell instantly. Turning his back, he gathered up his paints and brushes and moved to the island counter where he began to clean them.

Shrugging away her irritation—after all, she *was* interrupting him—she did what she'd come to do. "I'm sorry I didn't stay," she said. "Last week. When you asked."

His hands stilled, and then resumed their motion. "It's your prerogative. No rule says you have to."

"I should have explained, though. Not just rushed out."

"That would have been polite."

She almost smiled at the thought of Titus giving an etiquette lesson. The man was a walking contradiction.

"It wasn't the fact you wanted me to stay," she said, determined to clear the air, no matter how odd it made her seem. "Well, it was. But it was also your offer to leave some of my things here."

His gaze slid toward her then back to his chore. "It was a suggestion, not a demand."

"And a very reasonable idea. But it was a step I had to think about."

He tossed the last brush upright into a jar to dry and turned to face her. "You had to think about bringing a toothbrush here?"

"I know. It sounds insane." She drew in a breath. "I'm going to tell you something that is going to make you insufferably smug. Try not to let it show."

His eyebrows raised.

"Frederick was the only man I had any sort of long-term...arrangement...with since my divorce," she said, "and I never brought anything to his place. I never even stayed the night with him." She drew in a breath and added in a rush, "But I am thinking about accepting your suggestion. To bring stuff here. So I can stay overnight. If I want. If *you* want."

Instead of the smirk she'd expected, he ignored her final disjointed statements and homed in on her first words. "Never?"

"Never." She realized she was twisting her fingers together and stopped. "And he only stayed at my place a few times."

"You don't do sleepovers."

"Well, that sounds rather juvenile, but in essence, yes. Or maybe no. You know what I mean." Had he even noticed what she was really saying—that she might be willing to change a long-held vow for him? If he hadn't, she wasn't going to repeat herself. She'd felt a little sick just saying the words. But maybe that had been her hormones flaring. "I know it ties in with my marriage somehow, but I haven't worked my way past it yet." She doubted she ever would.

He took the four steps necessary to reach her. She squared her shoulders and lifted her chin.

"I would *never* insist you do anything you are not comfortable with," he said. "But I learned long ago if you don't ask, you don't get. If you don't want to stay the night, I'm fine with that. But now you know that I want you to. You also know I'm willing to clear out a couple drawers for you—if *you* want that. But we'll take this at your pace, Claudia. I'm not saying I won't make any more suggestions"—he took one of her hands in his and played with her fingers—"but that's all they will be. Suggestions. Not demands, not requirements."

The coiled spring wrapped tightly around her spine relaxed. If only the one in her uterus would do the same. "Thank you."

"I do have one question."

In her relief at his acceptance, she blithely said, "Of course. Ask anything."

"If Frederick was your sole long-term *arrangement*"—he'd obviously noted her hesitation when she'd used the word herself—"how many *short*-term arrangements did you have?"

His grip on her fingers tightened before she could yank her hand out of his hold. "I don't think that's any of your business."

"It's not," he said cheerfully. "How many?"

"I didn't keep track."

"That many?"

"No! That's not what I meant." She narrowed her gaze and berated herself for not noticing the mischievous gleam in his eye sooner. "I'll tell you if you tell me."

His lips curved in a grin. "Touché." Then those lips lowered to hers.

His kiss was warm and firm and promising. "I don't care about your past, Claudia," he said, lifting his mouth enough to speak. "Not unless it affects the future. I meant what I said about going at your pace. Never be afraid to tell me what you need." He pressed his lips between her brows in a tender gesture that had her knees weakening.

"Now that's out of the way, how about a drink?" he said. "Also, I have something to show you. Something I found in Mae's painting."

CHAPTER TWENTY-ONE

"I sent the original off on Friday," Titus said as he and Claudia headed to the main floor. "While I was in town getting it shipped, I had the digital file I'd taken blown up to three times the size."

"What on earth for?" she asked.

Today she was wearing another of those long, sexy dresses that floated around her legs and left her arms and shoulders bare. He would paint her in one of those, he promised himself. Standing at the end of a dock with the breeze blowing the material tight against her body and the sun setting...

"Titus? Why did you enlarge the photo?"

Claudia waited for him at the lower landing. It seemed he'd stopped descending the stairs when his vision had hit him. Clearing his throat, he continued down. "I'd stared at it for so long I was certain I'd seen everything there was to see. But I realized that enlarging it might reveal something new. Some detail that could point to where the creek is, for example. If it even is a real location, and not a place created from the painter's imagination."

She looked skeptical, and rightly so. But he didn't care whether she thought he was crazy or not. She was here, and that was all the mattered.

When he'd first spied her coming down the hall, his chest had squeezed in ludicrous delight. Determined not to show it, he'd glowered and grumbled, and his delight had doubled when she'd held her ground. He'd never feared hard work, and in his heart, he knew Claudia would be worth the effort.

"Take a look, let me know if you see anything," he said, pointing at the glossy sheet laid out on the wide dining room table.

Instead of moving to the table, a wince creased her brow and one hand went to her stomach. "Just need to make a pit stop first," she said, and headed to a bathroom down the hall from the living room.

When she returned a few minutes later, he asked her what she'd like to drink, all the while studying her face. She looked pale but no longer as if she was in pain, moving easily to the table and the blown-up print lying there.

His protectiveness was no longer a surprise. As he poured the white wine she'd asked for and popped a beer for himself, he admitted it was one more symptom of the emotions that had led him to create the painting he'd been working on when she'd arrived today.

The one he wasn't ready to show her.

The one she wasn't ready to see.

Claudia gave him an absent nod when he placed her drink on the table to the side of the print. "It's impressive, in this size," she said, "but I don't see anything out of the ordinary."

"I didn't either. At first." The beer slid down his throat, cool and hoppy.

"Did you find something?" Claudia pulled one of the dining chairs out of the way so she could get closer to the print and leaned over eagerly. "What? What did you see?"

"I don't want to tell you, in case I'm imagining things. Maybe I'm trying so hard I'm seeing what's not there."

"Fair enough. Give me a hint, at least, or we might be here forever."

"Look at the water."

She lay one neatly rounded nail—polished in a deep, glittery magenta today—at the lowest edge of the painting and methodically began her scrutiny. Titus drank his beer, keeping his stance relaxed to avoid influencing her, and distracted himself by thinking of the technical aspects of the painting.

Studying it in such minute detail as he had, he'd been struck anew at the expertise of the painter. His talent and skill were revealed in the way he depicted water tumbling over stones, light filtering through leaves, flames licking up from burning logs. If Titus' new contact at the McCord Museum refuted his belief the painting was done by William George Richardson Hind, whoever *had* done it deserved recognition.

When Claudia's slow inspection brought her to where the water narrowed into nothing about two-thirds of the way up the picture, she straightened her back and reached for her wine. She sipped thoughtfully, her eyes still glued to the print, and then placed the glass back on the table.

"Here," she said, tapping her finger upstream of the miner panning for gold. "There's something here."

Titus let out a long breath. "Maybe I'm not crazy, then. What do you see?"

"Letters?" Claudia's voice was tentative. "Numbers?"

"It's like one of those captcha things you need to decipher when logging in to certain websites," he said, excitement building now that Claudia had confirmed his own suspicions. "But I swear you're right."

Blue eyes bright with a thrill that matched his own stared at him. "Could Mae be right? Could there be buried treasure? And does the painting give a clue?"

"One way to find out," he said. He pulled out a chair and took a seat, and then slid the print closer. Claudia remained standing, and she placed a hand on his shoulder so she could lean over him for a better view. He refused to let the warmth of her breasts distract him.

"I think one of the letters could be either an *M* or a *W,*" she said. "It has a few extra flourishes, but it's pretty distinct."

"Okay, I saw that one, too. Remember, if this was painted in the 1860s, the letters may not be formed the way we're expecting. Those flourishes would make them easier to camouflage, too." He pointed upstream a centimetre. "Does this look like an *A* to you?"

After long minutes of concentrated study, Titus sat back and reached for his now room-temperature beer. Claudia had taken a seat next to him at one point. She had made notes on her phone and read them to him now.

"We have two characters that can be read either direction—the *M/W* and an *L* or a *7*. For now, I say we keep things simple and assume those are read the same way as the rest of the characters. That means we have a *W, A, L, K,* and two *S*'s. We also have something that looks like an eight or a cursive *E*, and two characters that are either *T*'s or *I*'s, or one of each. Then there's what I think is a *C* and you think is an *O*."

He swallowed the last of his beer and frowned. "I need to see that written out," he said. In a drawer in the kitchen, he found a notepad and a couple of pens and brought them back to the table. "Say all that again?" In large block print he wrote:

W
A
L
K
S (two)
8 or E
T or I (two characters, either/or)
C or O

"Well, at least there's a word," Claudia said. "WALK makes sense. Sort of. Maybe it's directions like *walk south eight* somethings."

"That doesn't leave very many characters for detailed instructions. And if the first word is WALK, where do you walk *from?*"

She shook her head. "You're right. It can't be that."

Titus stared at the sheet, his brain scrabbling for ideas. Claudia sat taut beside him, her elbow on the table and hand pressed against her temple. He jolted when her fist pounded the wooden surface.

"I'm an idiot," she said with disgust. "I gave the letters to you in the order we deciphered them. Let's put them in the order they appear in the creek."

Again, he wrote as she read.

W
A
T or I (either/or)
T or I (either/or)
L
8 or E
S
S
C or O
K

"I'm not sure that helped any," Claudia said, brows creased.

"Everything helps," Titus said. "Even a negative result is a result."

"That sounds very Zen."

"Actually, it's something my dad says. Thirty years doing investigations as a cop has to give you some insight."

Claudia rubbed her eyes. "Everything is starting to go blurry. I think I need a break." She looked at her phone and gave a start. "It's almost four o'clock! I should get going. I didn't mean to stay this long."

"Do you have something to do? I didn't have lunch, so I don't mind an early dinner. We could take that break, have something to eat, and then work on it more after. If you want."

Claudia was not a dumb woman. She understood this was a gentle challenge, especially given her confession earlier. He might not be asking her to stay the night, but he was asking her to show some commitment to him by accepting his invitation.

She tilted her head to the side and regarded him thoughtfully. "You know how much I enjoy your cooking," she said. "I'd love to stay."

This time, Titus put Claudia to work while he prepared dinner. She was glad for the chance to help, even if it was as elementary as chopping vegetables for the stir-fry he had decided to prepare.

The ache in her belly had subsided now that her flow had started. It screwed up the reconciliation plans she'd had for the evening, but those were the breaks. *More time to focus on the painting,* she thought in resignation.

"Is it at all possible that gibberish will lead us to buried treasure?" she asked as she ripped the stem out of a red pepper.

"If I'm being realistic, then no. But if I let my imagination fly..."—he shot her a quick grin as he deftly peeled a carrot—"then damn right I do."

"Should we tell Mae what we've found? She knows you sent the painting away for study, and that Nadia at Barkerville is looking into the photo and document. But this is different."

"I think we keep it between us for now. Why get her hopes up only to dash them if we don't get any further?"

Claudia's phone, which she'd left on the dining room table, began to ring. She wiped her hands and went to answer.

"Speak of the devil. It's Mae," she said cheerfully to Titus and connected the call. "Hello, there!"

"Hi, Claudia."

It took just those two words to know something was wrong. "What happened? Is Jasmine okay?"

"Yes, she's fine." Mae's words were clogged and hoarse. "It's not that."

"What is it then? Tell me." Claudia pulled out a chair and sat. In the kitchen, Titus raised an eyebrow. She shook her head and pulled her lips into a grimace in answer to his wordless inquiry.

"I found out on Friday. I didn't want to tell you, because I know you'll be disappointed in me."

"You're starting to scare me, Mae. What is going on?" She could picture the young woman, face pale, eyes red from the tears Claudia could hear in her voice.

A long, shuddering sigh came through the speaker. "I was turned down for my grant."

The worse of the tension left Claudia's shoulders. *Thank god it is only money problems,* she thought, and then felt guilty for dismissing Mae's concerns so hastily. She knew how much the young woman had been depending on that money to start her business. "Oh, honey. I'm so sorry. But why would you think I'd be disappointed in you because of that? It's not your fault." Her brain was already racing with what could be done. She was the one that had pushed Mae to apply for the Single Parent's Assistance Grant. It would have given her the funds she needed to set up her daycare. Without it, she had nothing—no savings, no income. "Did they give you a reason why?"

"I don't qualify as a single parent because my divorce isn't official yet. And now that Jamie is contesting it, who knows when that will be?"

"He's contesting it? When did that happen? You didn't tell me." The mention of Mae's husband had Claudia's free hand clenching in preparation for a fight.

"You've been busy with the gallery. I didn't want to bother you. My lawyer tells me he hasn't got a chance, because of the—well, the abuse. But for now, it's stuck in the courts."

"I'm so sorry," Claudia repeated helplessly. "I'll try to think of something else. There has to be other funding. A bank or credit union maybe."

"I've tried everything. This grant was my last chance. I mean, who's going to lend funds to an unemployed woman with a three-month-old baby?" It was impossible to miss the despair in Mae's waterlogged tones.

"What about your family?" Mae's mother had died last year, and her relationship with her father was shaky. But maybe there was an aunt or uncle or—

Mae cut down that hopeful thought. "Dad's on a disability pension because of his back. He has barely enough to live on himself. And there's no one else I'd be comfortable asking."

Claudia spent a few more minutes doing her best to comfort the younger woman. She disconnected feeling she'd had little success.

Titus was standing at the stove, tossing the stir-fry, when she rejoined him in the kitchen.

"That didn't sound good," he said. "Problems with her ex?"

"Yes and no." Needing to do something to wear off the anxious energy buzzing through her, she cleared the counter of vegetable parings as she summarized the phone call for Titus. "Don't tell Mae I told you, okay? She's embarrassed and I don't want her to feel worse."

"I won't." He plated the stir-fry and carried the dishes to the table. "Silverware is in the second drawer on the left."

Her mind still searching for financing options for Mae, Claudia chose two forks and took the chair Titus pulled out for her.

"How much money does she need?" Titus asked. "If

she operates the daycare out of her home there should be all sorts of efficiencies and tax breaks." He offered Claudia the bottle of wine, but she shook her head.

"She and Jasmine are moving to an apartment at the end of next month, one where the rent is supplemented by the Elizabeth Fry Society. Even if she wanted to set up there, it is so small it would severely limit the number of children she could take. Besides, she has bigger plans. She has her Early Childhood Educator diploma and before she married, she worked for one of the largest childcare services in town. Her husband made her quit when she got pregnant." Claudia bit back her opinion of *that* assholism-couched-in-caring move. "She wants to start a multi-age daycare, one that's fully licensed, which means it has to be in a community-based facility. Which in turn means rent and the purchase of a full complement of toys and supplies. Childcare spaces are highly sought after, so she shouldn't have trouble finding applicants, but it all adds up, and she needs financing to bridge between now and when revenue starts coming in."

"I can see why she was so upset, then," Titus said. He nodded at her plate. "There's still stir-fry left if you want more."

She looked down and realized she'd eaten every scrap. "I'm sorry," she said contritely. "You went to the trouble of making something delicious and I barely noticed what I was eating."

"Don't worry about it. It is fascinating to watch how single-minded you are." He rose and stacked her dish on his. "Let's clean up and get to work."

"Work?"

"We have buried treasure to find," he said.

CHAPTER TWENTY-TWO

Despite a couple more hours of intense review and discussion, neither Claudia nor Titus was able to come up with a possible solution to the code they'd found in the painting.

"My brain is mush," Claudia said. "It's probably time for me to get going." She stood, pressed her hands into her lower back, and arched her spine. Titus could sympathize with the action. His vertebrae felt fused with iron after all the time spent hunched in the hard, upright dining chair.

He rose with her. "It's not that late," he said. "I'm all for a break, but why don't we relax for a bit?" He trailed a fingertip suggestively over her collarbone to the swell of her breast. It occurred to him that Claudia had been the instigator of most of their sensuous encounters. He leaned forward with the intention of changing that statistic, but she pressed a hand to his chest. He stopped immediately.

"I can't," she said. "But don't think I'm running away again. I'm not." As if to prove it, she closed the distance between them and gave him the deep, searching kiss he'd intended for her. When she let him come up for air, his heart was beating hard in his throat and his hands gripped her biceps tightly. She didn't seem to mind.

"What were you saying?" he managed to articulate.

Her grin revealed she knew exactly what state she'd left him in. "I can stay if you want. But I just got my period, and I don't enjoy sex when I'm menstruating. So that would not be on the agenda tonight."

"Ah, I see." He was disappointed—what man wouldn't be when told he wasn't going to be having sex with Claudia?—but maybe this was an opportunity. "I won't lie. I want to have sex with you again. And again." He loosened his hold on her arms and swept his palms up and down, savouring the smoothness of her skin. "But there is more to our relationship than that."

"Is there?" She tilted her head questioningly.

"You know there is." It might not support his argument, but he couldn't help kissing her again. This time she was the one gasping and flushed when he released her mouth. "We can turn on the TV or go for a walk. Watch the sunset from the deck. Talk about things other than the gallery or the exhibition or Mae's mystery."

For a few moments she stood there, her eyes searching his face. Then in an unexpected move, she sidled nearer and laid her head on his shoulder. Her hair brushed his cheek, the scent of rosemary and citrus teasing his nose. "I would like that," she said. "I would like that very much."

In the frantic rush to get the gallery ready for Thursday's opening, Claudia had little time to think about the cryptogram Titus had found. Last minute hitches—like an electrical circuit that kept blowing the breaker every time they plugged in the portable panels—ate up her attention.

By eight o'clock Wednesday evening, it was as good as it was going to get. She stood at the front entrance, flanked by Bernadette, Tanya, and Karina, and surveyed the main gallery, trying to see it with fresh eyes, searching for flaws and finding none. A surge of satisfaction warmed her chest.

"Thank you all for working late tonight," she said, looking left and right to encompass them all in a grateful smile.

"It looks fantastic," Karina said. "You'd never guess we were in Prince George."

Claudia's smile widened, taking the compliment as it was meant and ignoring the slight to her hometown.

"I'm sort of sad I have tomorrow off," Tanya said. "I'd like to be here for the first day."

"Nothing stopping you from coming by on your own time," Bernadette replied. She had assumed an unofficial leadership role among the three women. Since neither Tanya nor Karina seemed to mind, Claudia was willing to let the dynamic develop, but would be careful to keep an eye on it. None of the three had been hired to a senior position, and she didn't need or want rivalries within the team.

"Tomorrow will probably be pretty slow, anyway," she said. "Which is fine, that's what I've planned for." That didn't mean she couldn't dream, though. Wouldn't it be wonderful if tomorrow surprised them all by being busy and profitable? She reminded herself to be realistic. She'd done no formal marketing to promote she was unlocking the doors, although she had updated all of Fauna's social media feeds frequently, and Four Winds had been distributing promotional postcards that mentioned both the soft and grand opening. "We need these next two weeks to make sure any bugs are worked out to avoid a disaster during Titus' exhibition."

A breath of movement behind her gave Claudia enough warning that she didn't jump when a deep voice said, "We certainly wouldn't want that, would we?"

As if choreographed, Claudia and the other three women spun to face Titus. Or face what they could of him, hidden as he was behind an enormous flower arrangement.

"Oh, my goodness," Bernadette said with a gasp.

"Congratulations on your opening, Claudia." He peered past the fronds. "Where should I put this?"

"Let me make room on the desk." Tanya darted to the curvy-legged antique Claudia had chosen to use as a reception table.

"You didn't have to do this," she said, not disguising her pleasure that he had. "It's beautiful."

"I told the florist to stalk your Instagram and make sure it would suit." Tanya waved him over. Passing Karina and Bernadette without a glance, he lowered the heavy glass vase onto the glossy surface.

"It's perfect." And it was. The array of white lilies, peonies, and gerbera daisies was offset with twisting twigs and sprays of evergreen foliage. It was both elegant and rustic, exactly the atmosphere she wanted for Fauna. "Thank you."

"You're welcome." His gaze was warm and inviting and Claudia felt a sensual thrill slide through her. They'd spoken every evening since Sunday, usually after Claudia was in bed. Even when the conversation had centred around business, there had been something deliciously sexy about lying cocooned in silky sheets and plush pillows and listening to his voice rumble in her ear.

"Care to give me a tour?" he said.

"Of course." She couldn't help the swell of pride blossoming in her chest. Bernadette called from the door and Claudia waggled her hand in a request to wait a moment. "Let me say goodnight to the women, first."

As she ushered them out, Tanya gave her a friendly elbow nudge. "That's a yummy piece of man candy," she said with a wink. "A friend of yours?"

"That's Titus Wilcox," Claudia replied, realizing the other women had never been introduced to him.

Tanya slapped a hand to her mouth, eyes wide and appalled. "I'm so sorry," she said. "I didn't mean to be unprofessional. I had no idea."

"That's okay." Although something in the teasing comment rubbed Claudia the wrong way. Titus *was* yummy, and she *did* want another taste, but during the last few days he had become something...more. Something she wasn't ready to examine.

Karina, who had been characteristically silent since his arrival, muttered something Claudia didn't catch. "Sorry?" she said. "What was that?"

The redheaded woman flushed, her scattered freckles fading as her skin coloured. "Nothing. It doesn't matter." Claudia raised an eyebrow and waited. Karina squirmed, and then said quietly, "He acted like we weren't even here. He didn't say hello or thank Tanya for helping find a place to put the flowers."

Claudia shot a look over her shoulder. Titus had wandered a few steps deeper into the gallery to study a print hanging on one of the movable walls.

Keeping her voice low, she said, "I'm sure he didn't mean anything by it. He's just a little..." She spread her palms out helplessly.

"He only had eyes for you, is what it was," Bernadette said. "Nothing to worry about. Come on ladies, let's head out." She shepherded the other women ahead of her and the door swung shut.

Claudia took a deep breath and joined Titus, who was standing in front of a gorgeous rendering of a bull moose in a mountain swamp. "So, what do you think?" She clasped her hands behind her back and twisted her fingers together.

Without looking at her, he said, "I think I *am* a yummy piece of man candy."

Claudia choked. "I was really hoping you hadn't heard that. I'm sure she didn't mean to be inappropriate." What else had he heard? Karina had been practically whispering but—

"I'm not insulted. In fact, I'm flattered. I'm old enough to be her father." He shot Claudia a grin that had her stomach somersaulting. "Speaking of which, how's Nicole doing? She hasn't made you a gramma yet?"

Unutterably relieved he had changed the subject away from her employees, Claudia stuttered, "She—she still has a month to go, so no, not yet. And I'm fine with that. I don't know if I'm ready."

"Not much choice in the matter," he said in blunt comfort.

"True." She hadn't told Titus about her battles with Nicole regarding the baby's father, and now was not the time. Needing to get back onto familiar footing and away from the recent barrage of uncomfortable thoughts and topics, she said, "Let's take that tour."

They ended up in Claudia's apartment. Titus settled onto her sofa while she hovered over him, her face calm and open, but her nerves betrayed in her constantly twisting fingers.

"I am very impressed," he said with sincerity. Her hands dropped to her sides and a soft whoosh escaped her lips. "I trusted you to do a great job, but this goes beyond my expectations. I'm glad I didn't come by during the last couple of weeks so I could get the full effect."

The smile that bloomed on her face outshone the beauty of the bouquet he'd brought by one-hundredfold. "You really think so?"

"When have I ever lied to you?"

She laughed and dropped next to him on the sofa. "Either never, or you're so good at it I can't tell. Right now, I don't care which it is."

He bumped her shoulder with his. "I'm giving you my honest opinion. The layout is organic and welcoming, the art high quality yet accessible. You celebrate rural Canada, especially Northern British Columbia, without that air of condescension I've sometimes felt in urban galleries."

"It's hard to walk that line," she acknowledged. "The art has to be true to its inspiration, and the gallery true to its art."

"You've nailed it." He patted her knee, and then let his palm slide up to rest on her thigh. The sleek muscles quivered and she bit her lip, but he could tell she was still thinking of the gallery.

"I hope the customers agree," she said. "And I really hope the Bateman exhibition doesn't screw up yours."

"Bateman? *The* Bateman?" Titus wondered if he sounded as awestruck as he felt.

"Yes." She sighed. "One of my competitors is bringing him in. The day before our official grand opening."

"Crap." He could understand her concern, but there wasn't much he could do about it. Offering platitudes was pointless, as she knew as well as he did how precarious any new business venture was. All she could do was work hard, treat her customers right, and her artists fairly. The rest was out of her control.

He squeezed her leg reassuringly, and then started when she sprang off the couch and turned to face him. "Enough soul searching. Thank you," she said and leaned down to plant her hands on his shoulders. "It's so great to have someone who knows what he's talking about say I've done a good job." She kissed him enthusiastically. It had been days since he'd tasted her. He savoured the hint of coffee and dark chocolate, the luscious wetness of her lips and tongue. His hands rose automatically to grasp her waist, but as he tugged to pull her into his lap, she lifted her head away.

"How about a drink? Tonight is for celebrating. Wine? Whiskey? I deserve to get a bit tipsy."

The thought of Claudia uninhibited by alcohol, loose and pliant, made Titus' body react in direct opposition. Swallowing back a groan, he said what he knew he should, not what he wanted to. "I'd better not. It's late, you've had a busy week and will have a stressful day tomorrow. I should head home."

Her blue eyes, dark and serious, stared into his. She still leaned over him, propped on his shoulders, and her face was so close he could see the tiny lines fanning out from the corners of her eyes. "Stay," she said.

His gut contracted. Was she talking about the evening or something more? "What do you mean?"

"Stay the night," she said, her tone firm and confident.

His fingers tightened on her waist. Not certain he could bear it if she changed her mind, he asked once more, "Are you sure?"

She nodded, a lock of hair falling onto her forehead. "I'm sure. I want what we had at Bowron Lake Lodge. A whole night with you, together in bed."

He knew Frederick had stayed here before, that he wasn't the first man she'd allowed to spend the night, but he still realized it wasn't a suggestion she made lightly. Unaccountably overwhelmed, he tried to lighten the mood by saying, "Tell me it's bigger than the one at the cabin."

"King size," she said, letting her eyes drop briefly to his groin. He hardened even more. "Plenty of room for sleeping. Or whatever else we might get up to."

"Well, if you're sure." He pressed up and kissed her, sealing his decision. "Is that offer of a drink still open?"

"Maybe later," she said, and then straddled him, took his face in her hands, and proceeded to get him drunk on her mouth alone.

CHAPTER TWENTY-THREE

Claudia poured two mugs of coffee and carried them to the bedroom. Titus lay sprawled on his stomach, taking up much of the bed. The sheet was tangled around his hips, leaving bare his broad back and one long, heavily muscled, darkly haired leg. She couldn't help a grin from spreading across her face, though a warning bell rang in her head, reminding her not to get accustomed to the sight. After all, one of the reasons she felt comfortable with Titus was his gypsy habits. Having an end-date in sight meant not worrying about things getting serious. Just the way she liked them.

She pushed away the niggling voice that said *this* time, when *this* man left, things might be different.

Sitting next to him, she put his mug on the bedside table and bounced lightly on the mattress. "I brought coffee," she said when his eyelids fluttered open.

"Thanks." His voice was deeper than usual, rough with sleep. He rolled to one side and propped himself up on his elbow. "You're dressed."

Sipping from her own mug, she smoothed her free hand over her navy-blue skirt. "I woke up before the alarm and was too excited to go back to sleep. I figured

I might as well shower and get ready, but there was no need to wake you."

"We still haven't done that." He scrubbed a hand over his skull then reached for his mug.

"Done what?"

"Showered together."

"Have to save something for later, right?" Considering all they'd gotten up to the night before, there couldn't be much they had left to explore. Titus made her feel safe and adventurous all at the same time. She almost blushed thinking of some of the things they'd done.

"I don't know about that. I want to do everything with you, Claudia. And then do it again and again." His heavy-lidded eyes were no longer slumberous but hot and challenging. A flush prickled up her chest and neck.

"I've got to get to the gallery," she said hurriedly, before she could succumb to his wordless invitation. "Help yourself to anything in the kitchen. I'll talk to you later." Gripping her mug as if it was a lifeline, she stepped out of the bedroom, along the hall and down the stairs, taking a deep breath when she reached the sanctuary of the main floor.

It wasn't the lure of Titus' sexy invitation she was fleeing. It was the wish, growing ever stronger, that every morning could be spent this way for the rest of her life.

Baby steps, **Titus thought** as he watched Claudia vanish out of the bedroom door. She'd asked him to stay the night. That was enough for now.

Hitching himself up so he could lean against the padded headboard, he sipped his coffee thoughtfully. In a minute he'd run down to his SUV and get the overnight bag he always kept on hand. In his early days as an artist, he'd often started driving in the morning and simply kept on going until he found a place he wanted to paint. Sometimes that meant an unexpected overnight stay, and it had become habit to make sure he had a change of clothes and spare grooming supplies packed and ready.

His thoughts circled back, inevitably, to Claudia. Her invitation to stay was obviously a declaration of some kind, but he didn't believe it signalled a change in her basic belief in their relationship. She had been clear from the first that she wasn't looking for permanence. He knew his lifestyle of frequent moves and few ties was what had attracted her in the first place, and that she didn't believe him when he said he was ready to change that.

It didn't matter. Patience was not one of his strongest traits, but for Claudia he was willing to do his best.

Of course, he wasn't yet one hundred percent comfortable with his own feelings for her, either. He kept stuttering over the *love* word. But it was getting easier. Maybe by the time she was ready to hear it, he'd be ready to say it.

Half an hour later, caffeinated, showered, and dressed, he rummaged through Claudia's fridge searching for something breakfast-like. She hadn't been kidding when she'd said she didn't do much cooking. Except for the condiments in the door, the fridge was practically empty.

He discovered two eggs rattling around in the crisper drawer. From the black marker on the shell, he assumed they were hard-boiled. Half a loaf of rustic bread had pride of place on the top shelf, and the mayonnaise wasn't too far past its best before date, so he made himself a simple sandwich. He wondered if she would be pleased or pissed if he brought her groceries. If he was going to spend more time here, she'd have to stock at least a few fresh edibles.

And he *was* going to spend more time here. If Claudia wouldn't—couldn't—yet stay with him, he would stay with her, as often as she'd let him.

After washing up the dishes he'd used that morning as well as the glasses from last night, he packed his kit bag and picked up his coat, ready to head home to get some work done. Something in his pocket crackled, and he fished out a crumpled piece of paper.

He'd taken to carrying around the sheet on which he'd written the cryptic letters he and Claudia had discovered in Mae's painting and studying it at odd intervals, hoping for that Eureka moment when all would become clear.

Nothing jumped out at him this morning. With a frustrated sigh he tucked it back into his pocket and made his way out of the apartment to his SUV.

It was lucky that Claudia had prepared herself for a quiet first day of operations. That meant she wasn't as disappointed as she could have been when she and Bernadette locked up at seven o'clock and they hadn't taken one piece of art off the walls to send to a new home. She'd kept a running tally of customer traffic, and it had been positive given the limited advertising she'd done, but until cash started flowing, she wouldn't be able to relax.

"I think that young couple will be back tomorrow," Bernadette said as she joined Claudia at the back door, nose buried in her capacious handbag as she searched through it.

"The one looking at the Joe Ferrante?"

"Yes. They love the painting but want to make sure it will fit where they intend to put it. I gave them the measurements." She pulled out her keys and shook them so they jangled like bells. "I told them we can reframe it to their specifications if needed."

"Good suggestion. Do you have their name and number so we can follow up?"

"In the computer in the spreadsheet under *Leads*, like you told us to do."

Claudia stopped at the bottom of the stairs leading to her apartment and Bernadette opened the door leading to the rear parking lot. She paused, and then switched her gaze from outside back to Claudia with a knowing grin. "You've got company."

She peered past the other woman and saw Titus climbing out of his SUV. Her heart gave a disconcerting flop in her chest at the same time her lips curved into a smile. He hadn't said goodbye when he'd left that morning and she'd told herself she wasn't bothered by that.

But if she'd truly been unconcerned, why was she so happy to see him now?

She cut off her mental blathering. "He probably wants to talk about his exhibition." It was a weak excuse and she wasn't even sure why she made it. It was none of Bernadette's business whether Titus was here for personal or professional reasons.

"Uh-huh. Sure." The other woman pursed her lips. "It's lucky I'm happily married or—"

"Goodnight, Bernadette," Claudia said firmly. She really had to talk to her staff about objectifying men.

Bernadette chuckled. "Goodnight." She sent Titus a friendly wave, jumped into her tiny yellow compact car, and zipped away.

Titus reached into the back of his SUV and hauled out several large reusable bags. They sagged heavily in his grip. "So, how was your first day?" he said as he approached.

"No sales, but decent traffic. Much as I expected." Not hoped for, but expected. "Here, let me take one of those." She transferred one of the bags into her own hand. "What is all this stuff?"

"There are these stores where you can go and buy what people call groceries." He planted a vigorous kiss on her lips as he went past and started up the interior stairs.

"I am familiar with the concept," she said defensively

as she followed him. "I just haven't had a lot of time lately."

"Which is totally understandable. And since I had to pick up some things for myself, it was simple enough to get a few more for you."

She couldn't suppress an uncomfortable qualm, and she scolded herself for it. He was being nice, not making a snide statement about her life skills.

Together they unloaded the bags, and she had to admit it was satisfying to see a fridge full of fresh food. "Thank you," she said. "Sincerely. This was a lovely gesture."

"Well, I figured if I was going to be spending more time here, the least you could do was feed me."

Claudia froze in the act of folding one of the now empty bags. "Excuse me?"

Titus' eyes widened comically. He looked aghast, an expression she'd never expected to see on his face. "I mean...this morning...I used the last of your eggs and bread...it only seemed..."

Now she recognized the source of her unease. It wasn't because Titus had bought her food—it was what the food represented.

"I let you spend the night once, and that gives you the right to assume it will happen again?"

"No, that's not..." His hands gripped his skull, as if searching for hair to pull. "Damn it, Claudia. I didn't mean it like that. Well, I did, but not the way you think."

"What exactly does *that* mean?" she demanded.

Titus lowered his hands and bumped the knuckles together like a boxer preparing for a round. "I *do* want to spend more time with you. If it's here, great. But that is totally your call. If you want me to go, I'll go. Whenever you ask. Right now, if you like."

Did she want him to go? She pressed the folded edges of the bag flat as she thought.

She couldn't really blame Titus for assuming last night had indicated a change in their relationship. He knew it showed a commitment from her, knew she hadn't made the offer lightly. It was logical he might expect it to reoccur.

And her fridge had been embarrassingly empty...

And she had been very pleased when she'd seen him this evening...

She sighed. "How much do I owe you?"

Titus drew a receipt out of his hip pocket and she e-transferred him the total.

"Does this mean I'm forgiven?" he asked.

"I may have overreacted," she admitted grudgingly.

"And I may have overstepped." He brushed her chin with one blunt finger. "I'm not taking last night for granted. Don't get me wrong, I'm thrilled you asked me. But I can wait until I'm asked again."

She took his hand and kissed the knuckles, eliciting another surprised expression. She discovered she liked her ability to shock this man.

"Have you eaten?" she asked.

"No."

"Well, then, the least I can do is make you dinner."

"You don't like to cook. That's not what I meant when I said you should feed me."

"I can stand it on the odd occasion. And I know." She took out a whole barbequed chicken. It hadn't escaped her notice that he'd made sure to buy easy to prepare foods. It seemed he did know her well. "How does chicken pizza sound?"

"I'm up for anything. Why don't I pour us some wine?"

"I would love a glass." She took a pizza crust—one she'd bought weeks ago—from the freezer and set it out to thaw. The meal was a standby favourite of her daughters, one she'd made so many times she didn't need a recipe.

The atmosphere between them slowly smoothed out as she gathered her ingredients, and he poured their wine.

Titus leaned a hip against the counter and watched her shred enough chicken to cover the crust, which she'd dressed with a premade Szechuan sauce she always had in her pantry. "So today went well? I'm glad," he said.

"It would have been nice to actually sell something, but that will come." She chopped a red pepper with brisk movements. "Let's talk about something else. I need a distraction, or I'll keep obsessing about it."

"Maybe it is just switching from one obsession to another, but I had a couple thoughts about the letters in Mae's painting." Titus went to his coat, which he tossed on the back of the sofa, and returned with a piece of paper. He spread it out on the counter.

Claudia stole glances at it as she cut up a couple green onions and peeled and shredded a carrot.

"I'm coming around to your belief that what I thought was an *O* is actually a *C*," he said. "And it doesn't make sense that there would be only one number in the mix, so I'm going with an *E*, not an *8.*"

"But we still don't know whether the other letter is an *I* or a *T* or one of each," she said. She frowned in thought while her hands automatically scattered toppings on the crust. "The letters weren't written vertically in the creek. They were lying on their sides, so to speak, which is why we've assumed they form a word or words starting from the *W* at the bottom."

"Why don't we write out all the options, based on that hypothesis. At least it gives us a place to start." Titus patted his pockets. "Got a pen?"

"On the coffee table, next to my laptop."

He fetched the pen and returned to her side. "For now, let's say the letters we can't confirm are both *I's.* That means we have *W, A, I, I, L, E, S, S, C, K.*"

"That's too many vowels in a row if it is one word. *Less* is in there, but the letters on either side don't make sense." She finished preparing the pizza with pre-shredded mozzarella, also a staple in her freezer, ignoring Titus' faintly horrified look, and then slid it into the heated oven.

"All right." He added a horizontal line to both *I*'s. "How about *W, A, T, T, L, E, S, S, C, K?*"

"Isn't a wattle that loose skin beneath a turkey's beak?" She washed and dried her hands. "I can't see how that fits anything, and it still leaves us with two *S*'s, the *C* and the *K*." Picking up her as yet untouched wine glass, she gestured to the couch. "Let's sit while the pizza cooks."

Titus sat close beside her and they both stared silently at the paper he held. "This would be a lot easier if we knew what the letters were trying to imply," he said. "Are they directions? The name of a person or place? Right now, the possibilities are limitless."

The leap in logic Claudia's brain made at that moment was so strong her head jerked. "The letters were painted into the water of the creek, right? And we now think the last two letters are *C* and *K*." She sat bolt upright and turned to Titus, her eyes wide. "What if *CK* is an abbreviation for *creek*, and the other letters spell out *which* creek?"

CHAPTER TWENTY-FOUR

Titus _knew_ Claudia was right. "Oh, my god," he said. "That has to be it. It makes perfect sense."

She snatched her laptop from the coffee table and opened it on her knees. "What are the options for the name, if we go with that?"

He scribbled on the paper as he spoke. "Two _T_'s, an _I_ and a _T_, and a _T_ and an _I_—if we can agree two _I_'s in a row doesn't make any sense."

"I do agree, but we'll check that last." Claudia opened Google Maps and typed rapidly in the search bar. "Nothing for Wattless." The keys rattled again. "Or Watiless." Once more her nails clicked on the keyboard. "_Waitless_," she breathed softly, as if afraid she might scare the words off the screen.

He looked over her shoulder and saw _Waitless Creek Road, Wells, BC_ auto-filled in the search results. "Why does Waitless sound familiar?"

Claudia shot him a puzzled look. He was so close their noses almost brushed, and he drew back to see her better just as her expression transformed into one of trepidatious awe. With a few quick clicks on the mouse pad, she brought up the translation of the Chinese poem he'd found on the back of the painting.

It was right there. The key to the whole mystery, if only they'd known how to read it.

Knowledge is weightless, a treasure easily carried.

"There's a treasure buried near Waitless Creek," he said.

"Now who's the romantic?" Claudia said, her cheeks flushed with victory. "If you're right, and there is a stash of gold hidden there, how on earth can we find it? The creek might be miles long."

"We need to get in touch with Nadia and get the exact location of Leung Ah's claim so we can find it on a map."

"You think Waitless Creek runs through it?"

"Either his or the one owned by the two other men. What were their names again?"

"Franklyn and Bilsland."

"Yes, them." He couldn't sit any longer and rose to pace the room. As he did, a beeping sounded shrilly.

"The pizza!" Claudia jumped to her feet and hurried to the kitchen. "Thank god I put the timer on." She slid the baking sheet out of the oven and placed it on the trivet she'd left ready. "Even if the creek does run through one or the other of the claims, we're still talking acres of land to search."

"What we need is a metal detector or someone obsessed by buried treasure." He snapped his fingers. "I might know where to find both."

Friday at Fauna was a cautious success. The young couple Bernadette had wooed the day before came back and bought the wolf print they'd been looking at, and Claudia sold one of the few sculptures she'd decided to stock as well.

While she was thrilled by these results, she found it hard to focus, her thoughts frequently drifting from the discovery she and Titus had made to the evening ahead. She had arranged for Mae to come to the apartment and coordinated with Nadia in Barkerville to be available by video call. Titus had gone back to his house this morning to do some work but would return in time for the meeting, bringing the enlarged print of the painting with him.

Buried treasure! In her mind's eye she kept seeing a pirate's chest heaped with coins and precious gems, which she knew was ridiculous. "There's probably nothing there," she muttered to her laptop screen. She was sitting in her office on the main floor, supposedly answering a few final emails before closing, but her musings kept derailing her from her task, as had happened all day. "Or if there is something, we won't be able to find it."

"Find what?" Tanya said from the doorway.

"Oh, nothing," Claudia said, flustered at being caught talking to herself. "All done out there?"

"Front door is locked, grills are down." The young woman took one step into the office, her expression hesitant. "I know we just opened, and you'll probably want to wait until things are more settled, but I was wondering—" She stopped, biting her lip.

Despite her own distraction, Claudia had no trouble interpreting Tanya's unspoken thoughts. "I would love to consider your work for the gallery," she said.

Tanya's face lit up. "Really? I felt awkward asking, especially so soon, but my girlfriend keeps telling me I have to be more forceful about promoting myself. You have some excellent Indigenous work available, so I'll understand if you don't want to add more. But since you *do,* I thought you'd be open to the suggestion. And I'm babbling. I'll stop now." The smile didn't leave her face, though.

"Didn't I tell you one of the reasons I hired you?" Claudia rose, circled her desk, and leaned a hip against it.

Tanya shook her head.

"Because you included a portfolio with your resume. That was a very daring thing to do. Not only did it show me you are serious about art, could understand what I want this gallery to be, it gave me insight into you as a person, like all great art should."

"Thank you. That means a lot, to have you say that. Sharon pushed me to do that, too. I wasn't sure if I should."

"Sharon has good ideas, and it sounds like she has your best interests at heart."

"She does." She pushed a lock of long, black hair behind her ear. "We haven't known each other long, but I respect what you've done here, and I've really enjoyed these last couple of weeks."

"I'm glad. Now go home, put together a few of your best pieces, and we'll meet next week to see what Fauna can do for you."

"You've made my day," Tanya said, eyes glowing. "Thanks again." Her footsteps raced lightly down the hall and even the slam of the outer door sounded cheerful to Claudia's ears.

Grinning, she climbed the stairs to her apartment and changed into casual after-work clothes. She made and ate a salad from the fresh produce Titus had provided and then headed outside, climbed into her SUV, and set off to collect Mae.

Claudia's SUV was missing when Titus pulled into what he was starting to think of as *his* spot in the parking area at the base of the stairs leading to her apartment. He assumed she was picking up Mae as planned and settled in to wait. Nadia was expected to call in less than half an hour, so they should be arriving soon.

He checked his phone for any new emails, something he'd done compulsively since talking with his father that morning.

"You're looking for Kate Rice?" his dad had asked.

"Rice! That was her last name," Titus said with

satisfaction. "I couldn't remember, but I knew you would."

"Dawson is full of characters, and she is definitely one of them. Why do you want to talk to her?"

He'd filled his father in on the search for buried treasure. Being the calm, logical person he was, he'd done his best to tamp down Titus' excitement, but had also promised to help find Kate Rice.

Nothing waited in his inbox and he tucked his phone back in his pocket impatiently.

At least he'd had a productive day in the studio. It wasn't the first time he'd noticed that the resolution of a puzzle or problem in one part of his life had opened the floodgates in another. But it was less usual for him to use the puzzle to inspire his work, which is what he'd done today. He wasn't entirely sure where the buried treasure motif in this newest painting was going, but it had been fun and freeing to let his brush take control.

It had also been fun and freeing to be with Claudia last night. After his stupid comment, he'd been prepared to be sent home. Two nights in a row would have been a strain on her comfort level even without his presumption. But they'd been so elated after their discovery that one thing had led to another and both those things had led to the bedroom. This morning, Claudia hadn't seemed to mind he was still there, given the enthusiastic way she'd startled him from sleep, but he wasn't going to push it tonight. The next time he stayed, it would have to be a direct invitation.

Her SUV turned into the alley. He got out of his vehicle, bringing the enlarged print rolled into a tube with him, and waited on the lower landing as she parked next to him.

"Hello, there," he called as the two women emerged, along with the sound of angry squawking. Claudia waved and Mae smiled, still reserved but much steadier than the first time he'd seen her. She opened the rear passenger door and ducked in, reappearing with a baby carrier from which the furious wails issued.

"I'm sorry," she said, darting a glance at him. "She hates the car seat."

"Let me carry her for you," he said. Mae hesitated and he added, "I promise not to drop her."

"Titus!" Claudia scolded, but amusement gleamed faintly in Mae's eye. She transferred the handle to him and took the rolled print he held out in exchange.

"What's this?" she asked, rotating the cylinder, which showed the blank back of the paper.

"*That* is what this evening is all about." He held the carrier at chest height and peered in. The tiny being was fastened in using a harness with enough straps and latches she looked like an astronaut launching into space. Her face was red, her toothless mouth gaping, as she squalled her fury. "Hey, now," he said, brushing his forefinger in a barely-there caress against her angel-smooth cheek. "That's enough of that."

Her scrunched up eyes opened, whether at the sound of his voice or his touch he couldn't know. Her bottom lip quivering, she stared up at him as her sobs subsided. "Good girl. Now let's go upstairs."

He looked up to see Mae and Claudia staring at him with wide-eyed surprise. "What?" he said.

Mae shook her head. Claudia said "Nothing," in an odd tone. He shrugged and headed up the stairs, and after a moment two sets of footsteps followed him.

On the upper landing, he made way for Claudia to unlock the door and the three of them—four, counting the baby—went inside.

"I'll get Jasmine out of the seat." Mae took the carrier from Titus and headed to the living area. From the sizable bag slung on her shoulder she took a small blanket and spread it on the floor. As she unbuckled her daughter, Claudia nudged Titus.

"I've never asked," she said quietly, "simply assumed. But I hope you would have told me by now if you did."

He didn't pretend to misunderstand. "Of course I would have," he said. "I would have enjoyed having children, with the right woman. But as you know, I didn't meet her soon enough." He turned to her and let his commitment and intentions show in his direct gaze. "Maybe she'll let me be an honorary grandfather instead."

Heat flushed Claudia's cheeks. How on earth was she supposed to deal with a man who simply refused to accept that she was not interested in a long-term relationship? The odd thing was, his insistence didn't frighten her or make her feel pressured. It was probably because he'd be leaving Prince George in less than a month. Despite his repeated statements that she was *that woman*, he had said nothing about extending his stay, so her escape route was still open.

"I should get ready for Nadia's call," she said, breathing a small sigh of relief as she moved away from his side.

"I wish you'd give me a hint," Mae said as she dangled a rattle over Jasmine, causing the baby to kick her legs and gurgle. "It's been driving me crazy all day, not knowing."

"Soon," Claudia promised. "We don't mean to be mysterious, but we're hoping Nadia has more information that will help us explain."

As she powered up her laptop, spread out the enlarged print, and laid out copies of the Chinese document and photo of the three men, Titus took on the role of host, offering Mae a drink and bringing her the plain water she requested. Maybe it should have bothered Claudia that he was so comfortable in her apartment, but it didn't. Besides, it was wonderful to see Mae so relaxed around him, and Claudia felt a glow of pride. She nodded when he waggled a bottle of white wine in her direction and couldn't prevent a smile of true affection from curving her lips. His gaze immediately sharpened, and she felt an answering tug in her belly before dragging her attention back to her computer.

The three of them were settled with a good view of the laptop in time for Nadia's call to alert on the screen. After introducing Mae and Nadia to each other, Claudia took a deep breath and got to the meat of the call.

"Did you have a chance to look up the geography around Ah's claim?" she asked, crossing her fingers while hiding her hands between her knees.

"Yes," Nadia said. "It was near a small mountain called Smith's Point and bordered on a stream called Muddy Creek."

Claudia's excitement leaked away as suddenly as air from a pricked balloon. She'd been so certain the creek would be Waitless that for a moment she could only sit in stunned silence.

After a beat, Titus asked, "What about Franklyn and Bilsland's claim?"

"As it was right next to Ah's, it also bordered Muddy Creek and included the slope of Smith's Point," Nadia said.

"I don't believe it," Claudia said. She stared at Titus. "We're not crazy, I know we're not."

"Maybe it's not near the claims." His face reflected her own disappointment. "If we expand the search..."

"If it's not near either of the claims, it could be anywhere," she said in despair.

"What could be anywhere?" Mae demanded.

Before Claudia could explain, Nadia went on. "It sounds like you were expecting to hear something different. Does this help? The Franklyn/Bilsland claim was much bigger than Ah's. A second creek ran through it, one that joined Muddy Creek." She looked down, as if consulting notes. "It is an odd name. Waitless. Waitless Creek."

CHAPTER TWENTY-FIVE

"Oh, my god." Claudia's eyes felt like they might bug out of her head.

Titus' mouth opened and closed a couple of times before he found his voice. "We were right. It's there. The creek is there."

"If someone doesn't explain what's going on," Mae said in a voice louder than Claudia had ever heard her use before, "I am going to scream like Jasmine in her car seat."

"And I'll join you," Nadia said from the screen. "What is so exciting about Waitless Creek?"

It took some time and frequent calls for clarity, as Claudia and Titus continually talked over top of one another, but they finally managed to explain what they'd deciphered in the painting and how Waitless Creek Road had led them to hope for further connections. Mae couldn't stop tracing the letters in the print that Titus had brought, and now she knew where to look, Nadia was able to see them in her original-sized print as well.

"This is astounding," she said, awe in her voice, "and I agree it must have been done on purpose. But why? Why hide the name this way? Was the painter in on the secret or did he just do what he was told?"

Claudia shrugged helplessly. "Those are things we might never know."

"We only discovered this last night," Titus said, "so we haven't exactly had a lot of time to think about it. But it *must* have something to do with Ah, Franklyn, and Bilsland. Otherwise, why hide the photo and the document with the painting?"

"And gold," Mae said, eyes shining. "It has to do with gold, right? Remember what I told you when I first brought you the painting? Family legend says it is the key to great treasure. Maybe you've found the key. Maybe we can find the gold!"

"I just realized something." Horror had Claudia's palms suddenly sweating. "Waitless Creek runs through Franklyn and Bilsland's claim, not Ah's. We have no evidence there was an agreement between the three men. If we find the gold, is it Mae's? Or does it belong to their families?"

The jubilant atmosphere bled out as if stabbed in the heart. The glow in Mae's face flickered off like a burnt bulb, and even Titus looked like he'd lost something precious.

Into the silence, Nadia's voice sounded loud and tinny from the computer speaker. "I offered before to look into who owns Ah's claim now. Maybe I should do that sooner rather than later—and while I'm at it, I'll check into the Franklyn/Bilsland claim, too."

"That's a good idea," Titus said. "Worrying about who owns what is moot unless we find the gold, anyway. In the meantime, I say we continue on and hope for the best." Mae's back straightened and she nodded, a trace of her earlier excitement lightening her expression. Claudia's initial dismay faded as Titus continued. "I'm trying to track down a prospector I used to know. She's also a detectorist and has used a metal detector to find gold before—lost jewellery and the like. If I can find her, I'll try and convince her to come look. But that doesn't do us any good right now."

"There are so many *what if*s," Claudia said plaintively. "What if the three men teamed up to work both claims and promised to divide whatever they found? What if they decided to hide the gold instead of sending it to the bank? What if the painting is evidence of a pact between them? What if we're all crazy and this is nothing more than a search for fool's gold?"

Nadia held up her hand and patted the air in a calming motion. "Let's slow down for a moment. Forget the unknowns. Let's look at this like a research problem. What do we know for certain? Not what do we guess—what can we *prove*?"

Everyone fell into a thoughtful silence. Mae was the first to speak. "We know the painting has been in my family since 1931. Also, I talked to my dad again. He says his grandfather, the one who was first given the painting, was born in Barkerville sometime around the turn of the century."

"After the majority of prospectors left, companies still mined on an industrial scale, and the population in the area remained relatively high. If your family was there in the 1930s, it's no great stretch to believe Ah never left. Give me a second." Nadia dropped her attention from the camera, and after a moment the feed showing her shrunk to a small inset and the rest of the screen filled with a blank text document. Characters began to appear.

1864 - Leung Ah arrives Barkerville
1866 - Franklyn/Bilsland register claim on Waitless Creek
1869 - Leung Ah registers claim
1870 - Franklyn killed (June). Bilsland sells claim and leaves (July).

The cursor dropped down a few spaces, and Nadia added:

1931 - painting in possession of Leung family

"We also know the photo had to have been taken between September 1868, when the fire destroyed Barkerville, and June 1870, when Franklyn died," Claudia said. Nadia updated the chronology.

After that flurry, there was a long pause. It was rudely broken by a long, juicy noise from the region of Jasmine's diaper, followed by an invisible but noxious cloud. Claudia and Titus burst into laughter, and Mae scrambled to her feet.

"I'm so sorry," she said, her cheeks cherry red as she scooped up her daughter.

"For what?" Titus said. "When you gotta go, you gotta go." If anything, his joking tone made Mae's cheeks even redder.

"That sounds like more than a wet-wipe can handle," Claudia said. "Feel free to use whatever you need in the bathroom."

While mom and daughter disappeared down the hall, Claudia updated a puzzled Nadia and they settled down to concentrate on the mystery once more.

"I can't think of anything else we know for certain," Titus said.

"We know the words Waitless Creek are hidden in the painting," Claudia objected, "and that it is the name of a stream that runs through one of the claims."

"Of course. But we're trying to figure out what that tells us, right?"

"That's a very good point," Nadia said. "What *are* we trying to figure out? How the men and the painting are connected? Or whether the painting is directing us to a hidden hoard? Having a clear question to answer could be helpful."

"We want to find the treasure," Claudia said firmly. "The rest will fall into place, I think."

"What if we start adding best guesses?" Titus said. "I

am certain—but can't prove—the document and the photo were placed on the back of the canvas when it was framed. So, they would have been already hidden there when Mae's great-grandfather was given it as a wedding gift."

"I'll use red font to indicate what are educated guesses." Nadia added *Document/photo included* to the 1931 line she'd typed before.

"And what about this?" He picked up the photo of the three men Claudia had put on the table earlier. "There is no snow in the photo. I know we've agreed it had to be taken between the fire and Franklyn's death. But given the first was in September and the other in June almost two years later, wouldn't it most likely have been taken in the summer of 1869?"

Nadia nodded slowly. "I'll make a note, but I'm not sure how that gets us any further. Although Ah registered his claim August 1869 so maybe it does have meaning."

"What about the painting?" Claudia asked. "Can we estimate a possible date when it was done?"

"I haven't heard back from the McCord Museum, although they did confirm they received the parcel a couple of days ago," Titus said, "so we have no confirmation on its age, or whether it was done by William George Richardson Hind. If we're just brainstorming tonight, why don't we assume it *is* one of his works."

Claudia pulled up the biography of Hind she'd bookmarked in her browser. "It is believed he made his second trip to Barkerville in 1864, so he could have met Ah then, I suppose. But that was well before any of the claims were registered, so if he did do the painting, there would have been no reason to hide the name of a creek in it."

Titus frowned. "He lived in Victoria most of the time he was in British Columbia, didn't he?"

She scanned the biography. "He did. No one seems

to know for sure, but it appears he left there in 1869."

"Hold on," Nadia said. "Let me get those dates in the chronology."

Mae came back into the living room, Jasmine tucked against her shoulder. "Did I miss anything?"

Claudia shook her head. "Not really." She pointed her chin at the baby. "Someone looks tired."

"I fed her a snack after I got her cleaned up, but I'd like to finish at home so I can put her straight to bed. I'm sorry to ask, but do you mind driving us back now?"

"Of course not." She returned her attention to Nadia. "We've probably taken up enough of your time, too. Why don't we call it a night and set up another meeting in a few days?"

"You couldn't pry me away from this with a crowbar," Nadia said cheerfully before saying goodbye and exiting the video chat.

Claudia repacked the diaper bag while Mae tucked a protesting Jasmine into her carrier.

"I think I'll get going, too," Titus said from the kitchen where he was washing up the few dishes they'd used.

Claudia's head jerked up. "You will?" She realized she'd expected him to stay the night again. Which was wrong. She should be glad for the chance to be alone, like she was used to. Afraid her response had communicated her disappointment, she added hurriedly, "Of course. That's fine."

Titus eyed her speculatively but turned to Mae. "If you're comfortable with it, I could drive you and Jasmine home, save Claudia a trip."

On the floor next to the car seat, Mae sat back on her heels, her hand resting lightly on her daughter's scrunched up legs. Her own dismay forgotten, Claudia held her breath, waiting for the young woman's reply.

"That does seem simpler," Mae said. "Thank you for offering."

Claudia's tensed shoulders relaxed and she smiled at

Mae. A minute or two later she was standing at the door waving the young mother down the stairs. Titus stood on the landing, the baby carrier dangling from his big hand, Jasmine's fretful squawks audible from behind a protective cover.

"Goodnight, Claudia." His free hand cupped the back of her neck and drew her in for a searing kiss that weakened her knees and had her clutching his jacket. "Talk to you later," he said, and was gone without a backward glance.

Not sure whether to be irritated or relieved, she stood and watched until the lights of his SUV disappeared down the alley, and then closed herself into her apartment.

Her quiet, empty, lonely apartment.

Titus was determined the next step in his relationship with Claudia had to be initiated by her. Sure, she'd been the one to break the ice on the sexual side—for which he was *very* grateful—but he wanted more. He wanted a commitment and permanence and 'til-death-do-us-part—all those things he thought he'd never have but hadn't really missed until Claudia.

Too bad those were the same things that seemed to make her run screaming for the exit.

Before dinner, while he was brooding on the deck trying to work up the enthusiasm to make himself a meal, Yvette called, providing an unwelcome distraction. Unwelcome not because it kept him from obsessing about Claudia—that might have been a blessing—but because it made him face the fact she was determined to cut him loose.

"I'm coming to the exhibition at Fauna on the twenty-fourth," she said briskly. "But that will be my last appearance as your agent. I'm leaving Vancouver the first of August, and my new job starts the tenth. That will give me some time to get settled in Toronto."

"You're really doing this?" Somehow, he'd clung to the hope it was all an elaborate ruse to teach him a lesson in humility or something equally preposterous.

"I really am." Yvette's tone was firm. "Have you looked at the list of replacements I sent you?"

"No."

"Titus! You've had it a month."

A raven soared by, croaking its doomsday call, and he glared at it. "I was hoping you'd change your mind."

"Well, stop that and get your act together. If you want the transition to go smoothly, I should spend some time with your new agent before I leave."

He resisted the urge to hang up on her and grudgingly promised he would look at the list. Yvette required further assurances, but finally she allowed him to disconnect. For a minute, he toyed with the idea of asking Claudia to be his agent but rejected it. Asking an old lover to work for him was one thing—asking his current lover, and one who was currently *ignoring* him—was a recipe for trouble.

He checked the time on his phone. Fauna was open from nine until five on Saturdays, so it was easier to accept the silence while he knew Claudia was working. But when it remained quiet while he made and ate and cleaned up dinner, he began to wonder if his plan was the right one.

Of course, it had been less than twenty-four hours since he'd left her apartment, so it wasn't like she'd been ignoring him for long. Shaking his head at his sentimental soppiness, he decided to distract himself from both the annoying women in his life with the treasure hunt. He settled in the living room with his laptop on his knees and two fingers of Canadian Club in a squat tumbler at his elbow.

A Google search for Kate Rice returned numerous results, including an Australian actress and a professor in the Faculty of Medicine at McGill University, but nothing about a prospector in the Yukon. Opening

Facebook—which he used for professional reasons but avoided at all cost otherwise—he searched again, getting a page full of profiles but none even remotely promising. Not that he'd *expected* a seventy-ish recluse who lived in the Yukon to have a Facebook presence, but wouldn't that have been nice? Without any hope of success, he typed *Kate Rice* into 411.ca and scanned the results.

Nothing.

He sat back in his chair and thought. The City of Dawson administration offices would be closed for the weekend, but on Monday he could call and see if anyone there knew how to get in touch with—

A pop-up window appeared in the lower right of his laptop screen, alerting him to an email from his father. His heart rate kicked up. Clicking through to the message, he couldn't help uttering an exclamation of triumph into the empty room.

Titus:

Roberta Biernaskie is still stationed in Dawson. She says Kate is alive and well and still searching for gold. Roberta asked Kate if it was okay to give her phone number to you, and she agreed. She has a cell, but coverage is patchy, so her landline is listed here, too.

Your mother sends her love.

Dad

Titus typed a quick thank you then snatched up his phone and entered both numbers into his contacts. Taking a deep breath, he tried the landline first. His fingers beat a restless tattoo on the arm of the sofa as he listened to it ring.

"Hello?"

He sat bolt upright. "Hello. This is Titus Wilcox. Is this Ms. Rice?"

CHAPTER TWENTY-SIX

"For Christ's sake. You didn't call me Ms. Rice when you were a teenager thirty years ago, why would you start now? Especially now you're a big shot artist."

Kate's voice was firm and confident with a clogged gruffness that reminded Titus he'd rarely seen her without a cigarette clamped in her mouth. "You know about my work?"

"I still have that sketch you made of me. Think it's worth anything yet?"

The sudden memory was so vivid he couldn't believe he'd ever forgotten it. He had tagged along with Kate one sunny summer day on her obsessive search for the treasure only she believed in. They'd climbed high into the hills surrounding Dawson, and when they'd stopped for a drink on an open slope, he'd taken out the blank pad that, even then, he rarely left home without.

She'd settled comfortably onto the ground, canteen dangling from her hands as she rested with her elbows on her bent knees. The canvas hat she habitually wore trailed down her back, held there by the strap around her neck, and her hair—a sandy brown that, even to his teenage eyes, looked like she cut herself—flapped raggedly in the ever-present mountain breeze. He'd automatically started sketching.

Sitting alone in his living room now, he could still feel the pencil in his hand, smell the dust and grasses of the high-altitude meadow, hear the keening of a hawk hunting overhead.

"I can't believe you kept it," he said. He'd given it to her the day he'd left Dawson, on his way to his father's next posting.

"I hate photographs. They just show the outside. But that drawing—you made me look like I feel inside. When I die, it's going back to you. Made my lawyer write that in my will." Her words left him gasping. In the pause, she continued, "Don't have any kids, of course. No one else to leave it to. Figure you'd better have it, so it doesn't end up on the scrap heap."

He finally managed a reply. "I'm so glad you like it that much. And I don't anticipate getting the drawing back for decades yet."

Kate cleared her throat. "Enough auld lang syne," she said. "Roberta didn't know why you were looking for me. What's up?"

He wrenched his thoughts back to the reason he'd called. "Are you still detecting? Looking for your treasure?"

"All you non-believers are going to be laughing out of the other side of your mouths the day I find that gold," she said, indignation quivering in her tone.

"No, no, I'm not making fun of you," he said hastily to stop her from hanging up in disgust. "In fact, I need your help. I have another treasure for you to find."

After a relatively positive Friday at Fauna, Saturday was a deep disappointment. Only a couple of looky-loos wandered through, and Claudia debated about sending Karina home early. In the end, she decided against doing so. She needed her staff to feel confident that their hours were secure, especially to start. If things didn't pick up in a couple months, she'd have to make some hard decisions, but she pushed that aside for now.

The quiet gave her far too much time to think about Titus. And no matter how often she told herself she was *glad* he'd gone home last night, she knew she was lying.

Even though he had already slept at the apartment two nights in a row, and Frederick had never been welcomed more than one night at a time, and that rarely, she'd actually *expected* Titus to stay.

She was losing her mind. She'd fought hard for her independence, her self-reliance. She wasn't throwing that all away on a temperamental artist who would be out of her life in a few weeks.

Remember, she said to herself, *the fact he's leaving soon is half the attraction. Once he's gone everything will go back to normal.*

Thinking of a normal without Titus gave her more than a moment's pause, but she assured herself she would just need a few days to get back into her groove after his departure. In the meantime, there was no reason she couldn't give him a call. They'd fallen into that habit before he'd spent even one night in her bed. It wouldn't be unusual if she reached out again.

As she swiped the screen on her phone, an unexpected knock resounded on her apartment door. The last time that happened it had been Titus standing outside, and she hurried to open it, unable to prevent the grin stretching her mouth. A cursory glance out the peephole wiped it off her face and she tore the door wide.

"Nicole!" She reached out and took her daughter's elbow, her evident distress causing a giant fist to clamp both Claudia's lungs in an icy grip. "Is everything okay? Are you all right? The baby?"

"Oh, Momma!" The childish name did nothing to allay her fears, nor did the desperate hug she received. Nicole's distended belly pressed into her as she wrapped her arms around her daughter's shoulders.

The baby kicked and for a disorienting moment it was almost as if the child was in her own womb. The activity eased the worst of her anxiety and she ushered Nicole in and helped her onto the low sofa.

"What is it?" she said, smoothing the hair off Nicole's forehead in an automatic gesture. "What's the matter?"

"I love him, Momma, and he doesn't even know he's going to be a father!" Nicole's gaze was frantic, her eyes pinwheeling, unable to focus. "I can't stop thinking about it. What if I made a mistake, not telling him? What if you're right?"

"Take a breath, Nicole." Claudia made her voice stern, deeply worried at the rapid pace of Nicole's inhalations. "In through the nose, out through the mouth. That's a girl. Now another one. Slowly, slowly."

For a few minutes they simply sat there, breathing in unison. Nicole clutched Claudia's hand so tightly her bones ached, but at least she'd lost the pinched, panicked look around her eyes.

"Better?" Claudia asked, and Nicole nodded, her head wobbly on her neck. "Okay, let's start from the beginning. Tell me about the father. Who is he, where did you meet him. The easy stuff."

"His name is Leo Kaehlert. I met him on a course I did for work last September." Nicole's breathing remained even, though her exhalations were shaky. "I liked him right away, and he seemed to like me. We went out for drinks the day we met, and it was as if we'd known each other forever. He was so easy to talk to."

"How long were you together?" Claudia asked, careful to keep any hint of censure out of her voice.

Nicole stretched her legs out, her feet on the coffee table and rubbed her belly. "Almost two months." She looked at Claudia, misery in her eyes. "I knew almost from the moment I met him, Mom. It was so right. *He* was so right. I waited as long as I could, but I had to tell him I loved him. I couldn't wait for him to say it first. And then—" Her eyelids closed and tears trailed out from underneath. "I told him he didn't have to say it back, that I didn't care if he wasn't in the same place yet. That I could wait for him. But it didn't matter. He said he didn't love me, that he didn't think he ever could, and that it was best if we called it off."

Claudia's heart broke for Nicole, at the same time it lit with a fierce, fiery anger that demanded revenge. Keeping her tone calm, she said, "You haven't spoken to him since?"

"No. Not really." Nicole lowered her chin and laced her fingers under her breasts.

Claudia hadn't been Nicole's mother for twenty-four years without learning the signals she sent when telling half-truths. "What does *not really* mean?"

"He called me, a couple of times, right after. And texted. But I didn't reply."

"Why on earth not?" Claudia said. "What if he wanted to apologize, or to try and work things out?"

"He hurt me, Mom. I didn't know it could hurt so bad. And I remembered how you always told us that we were better off without our dad, that you were better off without a husband. So why should I be different? Why can't I be as strong as you?"

Claudia wondered how her well-meaning advice could have gone so awry. She'd hoped to make her daughters self-reliant, confident—not scare them away from all life's wonderful possibilities.

"I never meant you should deny yourself love." She spoke slowly, working the words out before she uttered them. "I only wanted you to know you were complete as you were, that you didn't need a man to make you whole. But I never wanted you to deny yourself what many women have—a partner, companion, lover. Someone who would treat you with respect and honesty and passion. And I *certainly* never wanted you to think you were weaker because you found someone who could give you that."

An image of Titus, grey eyes intent and serious,

cheeks flushed with passion, holding himself above her as he moved inside her, flashed vividly to mind. Holy hell. Was it possible she was denying herself the same thing? Had she unintentionally passed on her own fear to her daughters? Should she take her own advice? Suddenly she had trouble swallowing around the clutch of agitation in her throat.

Nicole's belly rippled as the baby moved inside her. Claudia remembered the joy of being pregnant. The dread when she'd realized Saul might turn his anger on his daughters. The terror when she decided to escape him.

"I'm having a baby, Momma," Nicole said, with such sadness that Claudia felt tears prickle in her eyes. "I want her to have a dad. I know you did the best you could for Jill and me. But sometimes a girl needs a dad."

She had no idea Nicole had felt the lack of a father so strongly. It ripped a hole in her heart and dimmed many of the memories she treasured.

Not wanting to make it worse, but wanting to offer some sort of apology, she said, "There were days I didn't think I could make it one more hour on my own. More often than not, those were the days your grampa would happen to come by, offer to babysit, bring me a small bag of groceries, do a handyman repair I hadn't got around to yet. I don't know how he did it, but he always seemed to know when I needed him. I'm sorry you didn't have that...won't ever have that."

"I don't want you to think I blame you for leaving my dad. You'd never lie to us, and I believe what you've told us about the way he treated you. You made the right decision. But now I have to make the right decision for my baby, and I don't know what it is." She laid her head against Claudia's shoulder with a shuddering sigh.

"Whatever you decide, you know I'll support you, right?" She rubbed her cheek against Nicole's silky hair.

"I know." She fell silent, and Claudia felt her body relax deeper into the cushions. She was quiet so long

Claudia thought she might have fallen asleep. Then she said, so softly Claudia almost didn't hear, "The thing is, I still love him, even after all these months. I'm not sure if telling him about the baby is for *her* or for *me*."

Titus woke with a jolt, heart pounding at the unexpected shrilling of his cell phone. Sprawled on his stomach, he fumbled for where it lay on his bedside table and raised himself on his elbows to answer. "Hello?"

"I'm sorry. It's late. I shouldn't have called."

Disoriented and sleep-fogged, he said blearily, "Claudia? What time is it?"

"Almost midnight. I'm sorry," she repeated. "Go back to sleep. I'll call tomorrow at a reasonable hour."

"No. Don't hang up." Holding the phone to his ear, he rolled over and blinked at the ceiling while scrubbing his forehead. "I'm awake now. Is everything okay?"

"Yes, it's fine."

He supposed using the speaker on his phone would be more comfortable, but he loved how her voice sounded low and sexy in his ear. Tonight, he heard a new, uncertain tone. "Are you sure?"

"Yes." A sigh. "Probably."

"Want to tell me about it?"

"Well, since you're awake..." she said, the hint of a smile colouring her voice.

CHAPTER TWENTY-SEVEN

Titus chuckled. "I'm glad you called me," he said, with an emphasis on *me*. And he was. The fact that Claudia seemed disturbed and had reached out for comfort gave him hope that the decision he'd made tonight would be a welcome surprise. Not that he was ready to tell her he had decided to stay in Prince George permanently. He needed to wait until everything was confirmed before mentioning anything. "Is it the gallery?"

"No. It's Nicole."

"Is the baby okay?" The words popped out before he'd even thought them, surprising him with their intensity. As he'd told Claudia, he would have been pleased to be a father if life had worked out that way, but it hadn't, and he was fine with that. Having met Claudia's daughter and spent time with Mae and her baby, he realized he was experiencing a small taste of the joys and anxieties involved in being a parent. It was one more unexpected layer that knowing Claudia had woven into his life.

"Physically, she and the baby are fine. She's distraught and confused, but it's not my story to tell, and not why I called. Well, I guess it is, indirectly."

Another sigh. "I'm not making much sense, am I?"

"Just tell me what you can. When you picked up the phone to call me, what were you feeling?"

"Do you think I'm a good mother?" The words blurted out. "I know it's absurd to ask. You barely know me and haven't spent any time with my girls."

"I've seen you with Mae," he said gently. "You're supportive and caring with her. How could you be anything less with your daughters?" After a pause he added, "Is that *really* what you wanted to ask?"

Claudia didn't reply right away. He waited patiently, staring sightlessly at the ceiling while seeing her in his mind's eye. She'd be biting her lip as she thought, her blue eyes withdrawn and focused. She was probably in bed, wearing a pair of those satiny, luxurious pajamas that—

"Should I have tried harder to make Saul a part of their lives? Did I do wrong by my girls, taking them so far away from their dad, no matter what he did to me?"

Titus felt no compunction to soften his answer. "That man abused you, Claudia," he said, his tone hard and even. "He has ignored his daughters their entire lives. That was his choice, not yours. They were better off without him. You know that."

"I do. I did. But growing up without a dad wasn't easy for them, either."

"I would guess they had a male role model in your father. A good, strong one. A closer relationship with *their* father could easily have made things worse, not better."

"You're right. I've lost some perspective over the years. Saul was *not* a good man. And if he'd wanted to be a father, he could have. He didn't even try."

"Exactly."

He tucked his free hand behind his head and enjoyed the silence that stretched between them. He liked knowing she was on the other end of the line, thinking her own thoughts, even if she wasn't speaking them aloud.

"I feel better," she said. "Thanks."

"You're welcome. Any time. I mean it, literally in this case."

She laughed softly. "Want to get together tomorrow? Fauna is closed Sunday and Monday." He heard a deep, indrawn breath. "You could stay the night."

Satisfaction—and relief—swept through him. "I'd like that very much," he said.

"I've got good news and bad news." Two days later, Titus came down the hall from Claudia's bedroom and joined her in the kitchen. She handed him a mug of coffee and he smiled his thanks.

"Bad news first, always," she said. From his relaxed stance she knew the news couldn't be earth-shatteringly awful. Her toes curled as she thought of exactly what they'd done last night that might have contributed to his laid-back attitude this morning.

"I told the McCord Museum about the letters painted in the creek. If their conservator knows his stuff, he would have seen them, too, but I didn't want to take that chance. I just got an email back. They haven't even looked at the painting. The person assigned to examine it has been on holidays since it arrived. He won't be back in the office until Monday. A week today."

Claudia made a moue and shrugged. "That's disappointing but not a total disaster. At least they haven't dismissed us out of hand."

"No. I think that's Nadia's doing. She gives us some major credibility." He reached across the counter and stole the top half of her bagel, the slice already slathered with cream cheese, and took a large, crunching bite.

"Hey!"

"We can share another one," he said, but didn't move from his position. With a tolerant shake of her head, Claudia dropped another bagel into the toaster. It was kind of fun, having him here to banter with. When the girls were little, she would have sold her soul for a quiet, bicker-free morning, and once they'd left home she'd enjoyed peaceful, calm starts to her day. Yet having Titus here was...pleasant. She shied away from using the stronger words that came to mind.

"What's the good news, then?" she said as she retrieved the cream cheese from the fridge for the second bagel.

"I also got an email from Kate Rice. She's flying down from Dawson on Saturday. Once she's in Vancouver, she'll fly direct to Quesnel then drive to Wells. She's booked a place to stay for five nights. If she can't find the treasure by then—always supposing there is one to find—we'll have to come up with another plan."

Titus had updated her on his conversation with the prospector and detectorist when he'd arrived at the apartment yesterday. It made the whole buried treasure fantasy seem *real*, knowing someone was actually going to search for it.

"Did you mention our worries about ownership of the claim?" she asked. "I know Nadia said she would look into that, but we haven't heard anything, and she's already done so much, I don't feel right badgering her."

Titus talked around another mouthful of bagel. "Kate said she'd look into it before she gets here." He swallowed. "She also didn't seem too concerned. I don't know if that's because she doesn't believe we'll find anything, or if she's always wanted to be a claim jumper. We can ask again when we meet her in Wells Sunday morning."

"*We* meet her? I'd love to come, but I can't afford to be away from the gallery, not with the exhibition on Friday."

"Neither can I. But I think we can spare one day. Kate plans to take Waitless Creek Road to a certain point and then find her way from there. She's guessing it will be a two-hour hike into the claim site. If we leave Prince

George bright and early, we'll have several hours there before we have to head home. I got the distinct impression Kate would be happier on her own, but she says she can stand us for one day."

Claudia shifted on her feet, conscious of the high heels of the black pumps she'd donned for the day in the gallery. And the fact she'd been letting her usual visits to the gym slide in recent months. "I can't remember the last time I went hiking. Do we even know how rough the trail is, getting in?"

"I doubt there *is* a trail. We'll be bushwhacking most of the time, I'm sure." He grinned, eyes gleaming. "It's been a long time since I've done this kind of exploring. I can't wait."

Claudia had *never* done this kind of wilderness walking. She didn't consider herself a city girl, but her outdoor activities usually took place on well-maintained trails, and if there had been no plumbing or electricity in the cabins she'd occasionally rented with her daughters, at least there'd been outhouses and propane stoves. But there was no way she was getting left behind, not if Mae's buried treasure could be found.

"Neither can I," she said, grinning back.

During the next few days Claudia focused with grim determination on Titus' exhibition and the official opening of Fauna, now less than two weeks away. She met with caterers to decide on the appetizers to be offered, a local winery regarding which of their varieties would best match the menu, and a marketing company to finalize the campaign that would kick off after the invite-only event.

Thursday morning, she brought her staff of three in an hour early so she could fill them in on her expectations for the event. Seated in the comfortably upholstered chairs that now graced the client lounge, they discussed dress code, confirmed who would meet and greet when, decided what areas each would monitor for interest from potential buyers, and reviewed how to counter Robert Bateman's appearance at Fauna's rival the night before.

"There's nothing we can do about the event at River's Edge," Claudia said. "All we *can* do is be prepared and professional at our own. There is no doubt some people will be attending both, and those clients who spent money the night before may be reluctant to spend more at Fauna. It is up to us to be encouraging, to offer options and solutions. I have some information that might be helpful." She handed out a page of selling techniques she'd prepared. "Study these and let me know if you have any questions."

"What about the auction?" Bernadette said. "Aren't we asking too much of our clients? Who's going to buy a Bateman, a Wilcox, *and* bid on a fundraiser?"

Claudia couldn't let them see how worried she was about exactly that point. "I've arranged a celebrity master of ceremonies through one of the local radio stations," Claudia said briskly. "It'll be her job to cajole everyone into a good mood and promote bidding. We'll let people mingle and browse for a short while to start, then call everyone together for the auction. Titus' painting will be highlighted on one of the portable panels with appropriate signage, so no one will be able to miss it."

Karina made a restless movement, opened her mouth, and then closed it.

"What?" Claudia said. "If you've thought of something we should do, please tell me."

"It's just"—Karina's eyes slid from side to side nervously—"never mind, it's too late."

"I'd still like to hear your idea," Claudia encouraged. Karina was the quietest of her employees, and always needed a push to express her opinions. "Even if it is too late for this event, maybe it will be useful for the next."

Karina pushed back in her chair and straightened

her shoulders. "This is a fundraiser for women in need, right?" she said, lifting her chin. Claudia motioned agreement. "Then why are you promoting a *male* artist? Why didn't you ask a woman to do the painting, be the main exhibitor? How can you say you support women when you chose a man, one who isn't even a long-term resident, over the many, many local female artists available?"

Tanya nodded vigorously and Bernadette looked thoughtful. Karina gave Claudia a sidelong glance, her fingers clenching nervously in her lap.

"I—" Claudia paused, taken aback by the younger woman's vehemence and overwhelmed by remorse. "I'm sorry. I don't know what to say. You make an excellent point." Her mouth went dry with shame. "I'm embarrassed to admit I didn't even consider that view. I had Titus on my list of possibilities from the start, as he is the most well-known artist currently living in the city, male or female. The idea to do the auction for Elizabeth Fry came later, and by then I had tunnel vision."

"I told you it was too late," Karina said with a faint frown. "I don't expect you to be able to change anything. But it's been bothering me. *He* bothers me, if you want the whole truth. I mentioned before I thought he was rude. Nothing I've seen since has changed my mind."

Claudia would have wondered if she'd created a monster, encouraging Karina to speak her mind, except that the woman looked like she might throw up.

"Do you feel uncomfortable around him?" she said gently. "I would never ask you to put yourself in a situation where you feel threatened."

Karina shook her head. "No, it's not that. He's just, I don't know, gruff. And oblivious."

That Claudia understood. "I'll talk to him." At Karina's alarmed jolt, she said, "Not about you, specifically. But he's going to be at the exhibition, and the last thing I want is for him to alienate customers because he gives them the same impression. Hopefully, he'll take the hint and treat everyone politely."

Karina looked slightly comforted. "Okay," she said, her tone dubious. "And if I was out of line about your choice of artist—"

"You weren't. It's a valid point, and one I should have thought of myself. I'm glad you mentioned it. You won't be the only one with this opinion, and now I can be prepared, instead of being sideswiped unexpectedly." She paused, an idea taking shape. "Maybe there *is* still something we can do, even with the short notice." She pointed at Tanya. "Do you have your portfolio ready? The one I said I'd look at this week?"

The younger woman's eyes widened. "Yes. I finished it last night. I was going to talk to you about it after this meeting."

"Perfect." Her gaze swept the three women sitting in front of her. "Which other local women can we reach out to? I can't go back on my agreement to Titus, so his work will be showcased in the main gallery as planned. But why don't we use this space and the hall leading here for any artist identifying as female?"

"Anyone?" Bernadette said. "Not that I don't love the idea, but you have a distinct vision for Fauna, remember."

"I do, and you're right. This has to be a curated showing," Claudia said unapologetically. "I promise, I will seriously consider future opportunities for artists of all styles and experience. But for this night, we have to make sure the artwork fits in with Fauna's overall vision. Don't make anyone any promises. Get the word out, with the disclaimer all pieces have to go through me for approval. But I promise to be open to as many artists as I can. And Karina? Thank you for speaking up."

CHAPTER TWENTY-EIGHT

Titus adjusted the final canvas on its easel and stepped back. Most of the pieces Claudia would be displaying at his exhibition were being shipped directly to her gallery from the storage facility he rented in Vancouver. But there were a few here in his studio, including his most recent works, and he'd set them up around the room so he could take one more look before she came to get them. The exhibition was a week tomorrow, and preparations were kicking into gear.

She'd requested the *Mountain Spirit* double exposure, the one she'd seen on her first visit to his house, and he had a couple others in that style, including *The Reaching Tree* and *Hidden Treasures*. Then there was the one he'd done at Bowron Lake, which, though not a double exposure, was still unknown to the public.

For the auction painting, he'd had to walk a fine line between honouring the female and mansplaining, and he really, really hoped he'd managed it. As planned, it was another double exposure, but as he'd warned Claudia, the idea had morphed once he'd set brush to canvas. Instead of a single face, he'd painted a progression travelling across the sky, suns glowing from sunrise to sunset, faces reflecting girlhood to old age. While he'd intended to use Claudia as his model, none of the images reflected her exact features. Her influence was in the colour of the subject's eyes, the tilt of her chin, the curve of her mouth. Today would be the first time she'd see it, and his stomach rolled with nerves.

He had a back up plan. If she hated it, or thought it didn't suit, he'd offer to switch the auction item to *Mountain Spirit*. He knew she liked that one, and it would be appropriate as well.

Strolling from painting to painting, he tried to put himself into the position of disinterested viewer—an impossible task. Finally, he came to the last, one he'd simply title *Claudia*.

He wondered if everyone would be able to see the love he'd painted into each brush stroke. To him, the emotions he'd felt while creating the piece shone like a searchlight, but he knew he was so close to it that he couldn't be subjective.

He'd painted her as she'd looked that night in his studio, with the moonlight glowing above her, her chin tilted toward the sky, her eyes dreamy as she stared into the infiniteness of the universe. He'd transformed the long, filmy skirt she'd worn into star-shot water. It spilled from her shoulders, coursed over her breasts, and pooled around her hips so that she appeared to be rising from a lake so dark blue as to be almost black. The forest green hills surrounding her blended into the midnight sky so that the sole light emanating from the canvas came from Claudia herself.

"Titus?"

He blinked, so lost in the painting that for a moment he thought it had spoken.

"Titus?" Claudia's voice echoed up the stairwell from the main floor. "Are you in your studio?"

Whipping the painting from its easel, he hid it like a tree in the forest—among all the other face-to-the-wall canvases lined up behind him. And just in time, as Claudia appeared at the end of the hall and strode toward him.

"Hi," she said, giving him a quick kiss on the cheek. "Am I interrupting something?"

"No, of course not." His heart pounded lightly. He wasn't ready for her to see her painting. It was a declaration of intent he wasn't prepared to make, not quite yet. "I was checking everything one more time."

She turned from him and planted her hands on her hips, surveying the display. She made no mention of the empty easel but focused on the Elizabeth Fry piece, front and centre.

"That's it?" she said, tilting her head to one side.

"Yes." His lungs locked. He knew she liked his work, had no trouble expressing her appreciation. It was lowering and embarrassing to admit, but if he *didn't* have her approval, he wasn't sure what he'd do. He loved her, and how could he love someone that didn't respect what he created?

Without taking her eyes off the painting before her, she said, "Do you have any idea how talented you are? How amazing your work is?"

Air whooshed out of him. "Do you like it?"

She moved forward, gentle fingers tracing the sun-faces arcing from left to right, hovering just above the canvas. "I love it. It's perfect. Inspiring and thoughtful, and the technique is..." Her voice trailed away and she rolled her shoulders in a helpless gesture. "Thank you."

"Thank *you,* for giving me the opportunity."

She came to him then, wrapping her arms around his waist and laying her head on his shoulder. "I think I might miss you when you go," she said, her voice light and teasing. "We make a good team."

Here was his opportunity to tell her. All he had to do was say, "I'm not leaving. I'm arranging to buy this house, and I'm staying."

He couldn't get the words out. Yes, she was one of the

reasons he'd finally decided to put down roots. But if she rejected him, if she didn't see the same future he saw, he would still stay in Prince George.

He'd tell her after the exhibition. He'd give himself one more week with her, one more week before possibly ruining the best thing that had ever happened to him.

"And that's the last one," Titus said, arranging the carefully wrapped package in the rack Claudia had had custom designed to fit in the back of her SUV specifically for transporting canvases.

"The paintings from your storage unit arrived this morning." She closed the rear door with a firm click. The July sun shone brightly, and she pulled her blouse away from her chest and fanned the fabric in a futile attempt to cool off. "We've put everything in the basement for now, but I have a 3-D walkthrough of the gallery with the way I plan to set things up. I can send you a link if you want to review it."

"Sure, sounds good." He shifted his weight from one foot to the other.

"Is everything okay?" she asked. "You seem...I don't know...*off* today." She'd noticed as soon as she'd arrived, when she'd found him in his studio. Not that she could put her finger on exactly what was wrong. He'd seemed flushed and hurried, but that had faded as they talked. Now his discomfort was back.

"I always get nervous before an exhibition," he said, running his hand over his scalp.

"I can understand that." It was a logical excuse, yet she didn't think it was the whole reason. "Don't be. It's going to be great." If she said it enough times, maybe it would come true. She couldn't let her own nervousness transmit itself to Titus, especially given the way he was acting. That wouldn't be fair. Like any artist, he was putting his soul on display. She couldn't add to his worries by mentioning her own anxiety.

He shrugged and shoved his hands into the pockets of his paint-stained jeans. Seeking to distract him, Claudia said, "Have you heard any more from Kate Rice?"

His expression lightened. "She sent a text, confirming everything is still a go for this weekend."

"Excellent. I can't wait. It's all I think about—other than the gallery, of course."

His eyebrow quirked up and the air of uncertainty around him vanished.

"That's a challenge if I ever heard one," he said, stepping forward. The look he shot her was pure Titus, and the butterflies in her belly regarding the exhibition were replaced by dancing sparks of lust. "What about this?"

He yanked her against his body and pressed his mouth to hers, fiery and fierce, demanding she open hers to allow his tongue in. A thrill of desire flashed through her veins and she wrapped her arms around his neck. She loved that he didn't hold back with her, didn't let her past dull the ferocity of his feelings. Didn't treat her as fragile, as broken.

Her hips ground against his, his erection hot and heavy behind his jeans. With a smooth twist, he had her up against the rear of the SUV, the sun-heated glass and metal at her back a pale reflection of his scorching touch. His hands cupped her ass and she raised her legs, encircling him, bringing him closer, tighter.

"Do you have to leave right away?" He muttered the words along the skin of her neck, nibbling his way to her ear. "Why don't you come back inside?"

"I can't," she moaned, in both frustration and passion. He sucked at her lobe and she squirmed. "There's so much to—" One hand cupped her breast and she forgot the rest of what she was going to say. Thank god the vehicle was supporting her weight—she was boneless and weak.

"Tonight then? Tomorrow?" His breath was hot in

her ear.

"I'm sorry, Titus." And she was. Really, *really* sorry that he couldn't strip her out of her slacks right now and take her under the hot summer sun. "I'm video-chatting with Jill tonight, and tomorrow I going to my parents for dinner. And I really do have so much work at the gallery—"

He lifted his head away slowly, using his hips to keep her pinned to the SUV, his hands gripping her waist. She lowered her feet and when she was steady on the ground he stepped back, grey eyes intent on her face.

"Of course. Family is important," he said.

For the first time since she'd come to know him, his expression was closed and shuttered. As if she'd hurt his feelings...

"Are you sure everything's okay?" she asked again.

"Of course. Why wouldn't it be?" His arm lifted, and then dropped to his side.

It seemed a gesture of helplessness, an emotion she had never before associated with Titus. Her heart twisted. Something *was* wrong, she knew it, but she couldn't force him to share. In fact, she had no right to insist he take her into his confidence. Their relationship would soon be over.

"Saturday, maybe—" he said, and then paused.

The urge to do something to make him smile, to bring back the light to his eyes, swamped her like a rogue wave onto an otherwise calm beach. "We have to get up very early Sunday morning," she said thoughtfully, a pulse pounding in her throat. She knew what he wanted—and she wanted to give it to him. If she could. "What if I stayed the night so we could leave right from here?"

Surprise and delight lit his sombre features. "Here? You'll stay overnight *here?*"

She had known he would recognize the gesture as more than a peace offering. Her heartbeat slowed its panicked pace. He understood her, and was willing to accept what she could give, when she was ready to give it. With a sense of surprise and relief she admitted a night in Titus' bed was no longer the inconceivable, frightening undertaking she'd once thought it. "Yes, I'll stay the night. Here." And sealed the promise with a kiss.

CHAPTER TWENTY-NINE

Despite the fact they had to leave at an ungodly hour in order to meet Kate Rice when arranged, Claudia woke before the alarm sounded on Sunday morning. She rarely used one, able to set an internal clock that had yet to fail her.

A glance at her phone let her know she could snuggle in for a couple more minutes. She settled on her side and pulled the sheet over her shoulders.

Titus lay sprawled on his stomach, his face turned toward her, in what was becoming a very familiar pose. *I'll miss this when he's gone,* she thought. *Waking up with him beside me.*

Her wistfulness was unsettling and unwelcome. And so was her next realization.

Staying the night should have been more...dramatic. Instead, it had simply seemed *right*.

She'd come out after work to find another of Titus' amazing dinners prepared for her. In the fading light they'd clambered down the stairs that scaled the cliff on which the house perched, following them to the rocky beach below, and strolled along the shoreline as the day seeped into night. Returning to the house, Titus had made love to her, sweetly and tenderly. And she'd fallen asleep with her head pillowed on his shoulder.

It would be dangerous to let herself get used to hours like those. The day of his departure was drawing near. Though she no longer felt the relief she used to when she thought of it.

A trilling whistle sounded from the far side of the bed. Between one blink and the next, Titus woke. His eyes were soft and blurry, and then a lazy smile creased his cheeks. "Morning."

"Morning." She couldn't help smiling back.

He shifted to his elbow, tapped off the alarm, and then rolled to his back and stretched. The movement shifted the light sheet they'd slept under, tugging it down to his hips, and she impulsively trailed her hand up his abdomen, tangling her fingers in the springy, greying hairs that covered his chest. Under the sheet his cock jerked, morning hard.

Watching her from under lowered lids, he tucked his hands under his head. "We have a long drive ahead of us," he said.

"I know," she agreed, flipping back the sheet and straddling him. "This won't take long."

Titus would have recognized Kate Rice anywhere. She hadn't changed in thirty years.

She didn't think the same of him.

"What happened to your hair?" she exclaimed as soon as he stepped out of his SUV in the parking lot of the Jack of Clubs General Store in Wells. "You're *bald!* And old!"

From behind, he heard Claudia's snort of laughter. Ignoring her, he said peaceably to Kate, "It happens. It is so good to see you."

Kate dropped the butt of the cigarette she'd been smoking into the gravel and ground it out with the toe of her heavy hiking boot. Her handshake was firm, her palm dry and rough. He considered giving her a hug, but that seemed friendlier than their past warranted, and she pulled away before he had a chance to change his mind.

Claudia rounded the front of the vehicle. "This is Claudia Aronson," he said, and the two women shook hands. "It's Claudia's friend, Mae, who owns the painting I told you about."

"She didn't come?" Kate asked, peering into the empty SUV.

Claudia shook her head. "She has a baby, only a few months old. She decided it would be best to stay home."

Kate shrugged, indifferent. "Not like I need an audience, anyway. It will take a few days to cover the entire claim, and I work better on my own."

Titus caught Claudia's amused glance. He'd warned her tact wasn't high on the list of Kate's skills, and she was living up to his billing. "Well, I can't thank you enough for coming," she said without rancour. "I know this probably seems a wild goose chase."

Eyes gleaming in a way Titus vividly remembered, Kate said, "Even wild geese get caught sometimes."

She had rented a small SUV in Quesnel and come out the night before. After a brief discussion, Kate led them from the General Store to the bed and breakfast she had booked for her stay. There they transferred her equipment into Titus' vehicle, left hers parked, and headed toward Barkerville. Claudia had offered to sit in the back seat so Kate and Titus could talk more easily. She'd crawled into the middle so she had a clear view through the windscreen, and he'd noticed her taking a small pill even before he had pulled onto the highway.

It appeared Claudia suffered from motion sickness. What else would he learn about her today?

Soon they turned off the rustic highway onto Waitless Creek Road. Titus couldn't help a thrill of excitement as they bowled along, dust billowing behind them. Being here, on this road, made their hunt that much more real. As they climbed higher into the mountains, the temperature displayed on the dash screen dropped, even though the sky was blue and clear above them.

"The original prospectors working this area probably followed a completely different route to and from the townsite than we're taking," Kate said. "Muddy Creek, which Waitless Creek feeds into, was popular with miners, and therefore heavily staked out. A hundred and fifty years ago there was probably a decent trail following that creek directly into town. We'll be approaching the claims from pretty much the opposite direction today."

Claudia leaned forward between the seats. "Did you find out if there are current owners we have to worry about?"

"I checked out Mineral Title Online. Looks like Leung's claim, and the one owned by Franklyn and Bilsland, are currently lapsed. We're not planning on doing any actual mining, of course, but it never hurts to know." Kate checked the GPS on her cell phone. She'd done so regularly since they'd turned onto the gravel road, in between fidgeting with an unlit cigarette. "We should be coming up to where I want to start in a few hundred metres."

Titus began looking for a good place to park. The road was winding and twisty and narrow, and while they had yet to see another vehicle that didn't mean he could stop wherever he wanted.

Kate yelped as they passed a long-deserted logging area. "There! That was it," she said, twisting in her seat as if watching the Titanic sink behind her.

"Hold your horses," he grumbled. "There's a pullout ahead." It wasn't much more than a broadening of the shoulder, but it was wide enough to get his vehicle off the main roadway.

Kate lit her cigarette immediately upon exiting the SUV. He didn't remember her being so considerate in the past, but it appeared even old dogs could learn new tricks. Glowing tube bobbing from her lips, she kitted herself up, refusing Titus' offer to carry anything. "I'm so used to it I'd probably fall over if I didn't have it on me," she said. Titus and Claudia shouldered the small day packs filled with essentials each had brought, and as soon as they were ready, Kate killed her cigarette, stowed it in a small plastic container dangling from her belt, and led off.

She set a brisk pace through the overgrown cut block. Fireweed, willows, and various scrubby bushes masked the scars of logging, but a wide track was still easy enough to follow. It was a huge area, and it took fifteen minutes to reach the far side, where the forest again rose in a dark green wall.

Kate checked her phone, and with a grunt and a point led them in. There was no discernible trail, but she moved with confidence under the tall trees, whose heavy over-canopy meant relatively clear going. Claudia, between him and Kate, moved easily, her long, sturdy legs protected by heavy denim trousers. Despite the liberal dose of insect repellent Titus had applied, his sweat soon attracted a variety of annoying beasts and he was thankful for the loose, wide-brimmed hat he'd brought. It made an excellent bug deflector when flapped around his head and shoulders.

At first, the jangle of the bear bells that swayed on their packs and the scuffle of their boots through the grass and underbrush were the only sounds Titus heard. Then he slowly became aware of the wild chatter of ravens and woodpeckers, the rush of breezes through the topmost branches, and, after almost an hour of hiking, the splashing tumble of a creek.

Kate came to a halt and Claudia and Titus pulled up beside her. "Waitless Creek," she said with satisfaction.

Titus wondered if his face echoed Claudia's expression of dismay. "This? But...how..." she stuttered.

The creek was barely two feet wide and almost entirely obscured by shrubs and ferns. There was no bank to speak of, and it disappeared in both directions without ever coming into full view.

"How can you use a metal detector here?" he asked. "Doesn't the flat part have to be against the ground to work?"

Kate shot him a scornful glance. "Didn't say I was going to start looking yet, did I? What we want to find today are the tailings piles." He must have looked blank because she sighed and explained. "The gravel and rocks discarded when the miners dug to bedrock or what washed out of the chutes."

"Uhm..." Titus said. "What should we look for?"

Kate shook her head at his stupidity. "Never mind," she said. "Follow me."

The going was much heavier now. Kate kept close to the creek, which meant clambering over fallen trees, pushing through willows, and occasionally jumping over rivulets. In front of him, the back of Claudia's long-sleeved shirt dampened in a line down her spine. The occasional whisper of muttered curses floated back to him, but he heard not one true complaint.

After what seemed an age but was closer to forty-five minutes, he noticed the underbrush thinning and the creek widening. It was now much easier to imagine it as a source for gold as it raced over its rocky bed. When Kate next halted, they were standing in a wide-open area—relatively speaking. On their side, the brush and forest had given way to a flat space about the size of a tennis court that was a mix of round, unstable rocks and clumps of scrubby grass. On the other side, deep depressions were visible, as well as hillocks taller than himself. While plants had gained precarious rootholds, it was easy to see the jagged rocks and stones that had formed them. The creek made a wide curve around the open area and joined another, larger flow of water, barely visible as it flashed in the distance.

"And here we are," Kate said.

CHAPTER THIRTY

Claudia ached in places she'd forgotten could ache. Mosquito bites itched on the back of her hand and upper arms, and a swelling throb behind her ear was evidence a black fly had taken a chunk from her. Sweat had dried uncomfortably under her breasts and down her back, and the rocks she sat on were lumpy and hard.

She wouldn't have missed this for the world.

Their trek through the forest had been a scary new experience, though there was no way she'd admit that to Titus or Kate. She'd had to trust that the other woman knew what she was doing, and letting go of that control had had Claudia gritting her teeth more than once. Shortly after they'd left the clear-cut behind and entered the forest, she had lost all sense of direction. To have Kate find the creek, and then lead them to this remote and abandoned site, seemed little short of a miracle.

Of course, they still had to get back to the road, but she would worry about that when the time came. For now, she was going to appreciate the chance to relax, pleased to be given the job of guarding the backpacks while Kate and Titus explored the other side of the creek.

She sipped slowly from her water bottle. Kate had insisted they bring enough food and water for an overnight stay, despite the fact that wasn't their intention. "Better safe than sorry," she'd said, and Claudia had taken the outdoorswoman's advice to heart. She'd even bought some water purification tablets, just in case.

A breeze came off the stream, shooing away the worst of the insects, and the sun shone warm and bright. High above, the contrail from a jet was the only indication of modern civilization.

The burbling and chuckling of water over its rocky bed was loud enough Claudia couldn't hear the conversation taking place across from her. Kate was gesticulating in seemingly random directions while Titus nodded like a student listening politely to a professor. As if sensing her attention, he turned his head toward her. He said something to Kate, and then made his way across the stream using the steppingstone path he and Kate had efficiently constructed. The last thing any of them wanted was soaking wet boots on the trek back.

"So, what's her plan?" Claudia said as he lowered himself to the ground next to her. He was wearing his ridiculous hat again, and it should have made him look like a rather intimidating clown, but somehow it gave him the dashing air of an adventurer.

"According to Kate, placer miners like ours would dig down to bedrock using picks and shovels, creating pits and piles like what you see over there." He gestured with his chin. "It isn't uncommon to find traces of gold in those piles, nuggets and dust that was either missed or overlooked." He dragged his pack closer and unhooked the water bottle from its carabiner. As he drank, Claudia watched the muscles in his thick neck flex and stretch and had to subdue the sudden impulse to lick the sweat off his skin. He lowered his chin and caught her gaze, his own eyes heating.

"You're insatiable," he said, and she felt her already flushed cheeks rosy even more. "I like that about you."

Biting her lip, she turned away and focussed again on Kate. "We're not looking for traces of gold," she said, dragging her thoughts back to the matter at hand. "We're looking for jars filled with it."

"I gather it's a matter of searching the easiest places first." Titus shifted and winced, obviously finding the rocks no more accommodating than Claudia. "We don't know *why* Ah and his partners decided to hide the gold—always assuming they did, and we're not reading something into the clues that doesn't exist. Kate thinks it's possible the gold was meant to be buried temporarily. If that's the case, where better to hide it than in a pile of discarded rocks? Like hiding a first edition in a library."

"I suppose," Claudia agreed reluctantly.

"To be honest, I think we'd better hope Kate's right, and she finds something in the tailings. I have no idea how well a metal detector works under trees and in brush. If she has to search both claims, that's more than two kilometres square of rugged terrain, which lowers the odds of discovering anything considerably."

And they were basically nil to start with, Claudia thought, but didn't voice. She'd called this a wild goose chase already, and in her heart, she knew it was. But wouldn't it be a fairy-tale ending to an awful period in Mae's life?

It happened just after lunch and well before any of them were ready to leave. Which turned out to be a blessing, Claudia realized later.

Titus disappeared into the woods to answer a call of nature, and Claudia finally succumbed to the lure of the fresh, cold water. She removed her boots and socks, rolled her pants to her knees, and waded in above her ankles. The shock of the icy water was a painful delight on her overheated, sweaty feet, and for a moment she stood, absently watching Kate.

The prospector was searching her third pile, sweeping the metal detector slowly back and forth with one arm, her free hand raised to the bulky, over-ear headphones she wore. She'd explained what she was doing while they'd eaten their sandwiches. "Since we're looking for a large quantity of gold and I don't want to be distracted by smaller finds, I've reduced the sensitivity on my detector. I may need to go back over everything to search deeper, but this is a start."

Claudia lowered her gaze to the water swirling around her shins, the dark amber ripples sun-shot with gold and bronze. The flow was stronger than it looked from the safety of the bank, and coupled with the round, water-smoothed stones in the streambed, made for unsteady footing. A few feet to her left, a small pile of aged driftwood had created an eddy with calmer water and a gravel bottom that looked easier to stand on. She raised one leg—

—and a stone under her heel rolled and twisted, sending her to her hands and knees in the frigid water.

"Damn it," she hissed, and tried to scramble up. A shooting pain lanced up her right leg and she fell back into the water, biting back a shriek.

"Claudia!" Even the rush of the water couldn't cover Titus' shout. "Are you hurt?"

Her knees and palms pressed bruisingly into the stones, and a stabbing ache set up a thrum in her lower leg. "It's my ankle," she said through gritted teeth as he reached her side. His hands slipped under her arms and he lifted her to her feet. *Or foot, rather,* she thought giddily, afraid to put any weight on her right leg as even the press of water against it caused her to suck in a shaky breath.

"Why aren't you wearing your boots?" he asked in an accusing tone.

"My feet were hot," she shot back. They were cool

enough now. In fact, if she didn't get out of the water soon her teeth would start to chatter.

She yipped and wrapped her arms around Titus' shoulders as he dipped an arm behind her knees and raised her to his chest. It was only a couple of steps to where he could place her on the rocky shore, not that he seemed bothered by her weight. She stretched out her legs and eased into as comfortable a position as she could.

By this time Kate had noticed the commotion. She stepped nimbly across the stone bridge, her equipment draped about her, and knelt at Claudia's side. Titus took a spare T-shirt from his pack and dabbed the water from her feet. Even his light touch set off small explosions in her ankle and she hissed.

"I'm so *stupid*," she said. "All I wanted to do was wade for a bit. *Now* how am I getting home?" She'd never taken the vast wilderness surrounding them lightly but suddenly it was terrifying and threatening in a whole new way.

"It's starting to swell," Kate said. "Is there any numbness or tingling?"

"No," she said. "It just hurts like the devil."

"Where's the pain worse?" Kate touched the knob of Claudia's ankle bone. "Here?" She pressed into the soft part below. "Or here?"

"There. The second." Claudia drew in a deep breath. "I think it's feeling a bit better," she said, more in hope than truth. "I'll rest until it's time to head back. I'm sure I'll be fine by then."

Titus and Kate exchanged a glance over her supine form. Then he dug in his pack again, this time pulling out a small first-aid kit. "We're heading back now. It probably isn't broken, but we're not taking any chances." He removed a roll of elastic compression bandage and a tiny waterproof container. He shook out two pills and handed them to Claudia. "Take these. They're just Tylenol but they should help with the pain.

Then I'll wrap your ankle and we'll try and get your boot back on. Even if you can't put weight on it, that and the bandage will help stabilize the joint."

Kate handed her a water bottle and Claudia swallowed the medication. "No, really. We've come so far. We can't go back yet." She felt near to tears for ruining the day. The pain as Titus began winding the bandage around her ankle didn't help, either, though she knew he was trying to be gentle.

"I was going to have to come back anyway," Kate said matter-of-factly. "It will take us longer to get out now, and the last thing we want to do is delay and end up hiking in the dark." She headed back to the other side of the creek to gather the gear she'd left there.

It was useless to be angry, but Claudia couldn't help silently berating herself. Titus worked deftly, and soon her ankle was neatly wrapped.

"How did you learn to do that?" she asked.

"I box, remember? Plus, I've got a dicky ankle from a fall I took as a kid, so I used to wrap mine all the time." He tucked the first aid kit back into his pack. "How does it feel?"

She wiggled her toes experimentally. "Better," she admitted. "It throbs, but the pain is less."

"Good. While there's nothing I like better than holding you in my arms, carrying you out through the bush might be beyond my capabilities."

If anything, his teasing made her feel worse. "I can't say how sorry I am," she said. "I've ruined everything."

He trailed one finger down her cheek and she tilted her head into his caress. "I don't know about *everything*. You didn't do it on purpose, and like Kate said, she was going to have to come back anyway."

"But she *might* have found the gold today, if she'd had longer."

Titus sat back on his haunches. "You know it's probably not even here, right? If it ever was? It's just an excuse to have an adventure. Planning a future where you present Mae her family's treasure is like planning your retirement by buying lottery tickets."

"I know," Claudia said. "But still…"

"Enough." He leaned forward and kissed her firmly. "Let's get you out of here."

CHAPTER THIRTY-ONE

Claudia wouldn't want to relive the hours it took to get back to the SUV, not for all the gold in the Cariboo. Titus fashioned two makeshift walking sticks out of sturdy branches, and at first, she was able to limp slowly along under her own power. Kate led them on the same route they'd taken to get to the claim, and the section along Waitless Creek that had been difficult to traverse the first time was a battleground this time. Her sticks kept getting tangled in underbrush and deadfalls, and she had to scootch along on her ass in several places, as well as crawl under obstructions that she'd clambered over before. By the time they reached the clear-cut she was leaning heavily on Titus for support, her injured foot no longer capable of touching the ground without pain, and her thigh muscles trembled from the unusual exertion.

"Hang on," Titus said when they stepped onto the rutted path that cut through the clearing. She balanced wearily on one leg as he slung his pack onto his chest. Kate had added Claudia's pack to her own load, and it was humiliating to see how easily the older woman handled it. For someone who smoked so much she was in amazing shape. She waited patiently beside Claudia, her breathing soft and even, and watched Titus.

He squatted in front of Claudia. "Climb on," he said, aiming a smile over his shoulder. A red welt creased his cheek where a supple branch had slapped back on him, and dirt streaked his forehead from adjusting his hat with filthy hands.

She stared. "You're going to piggy-back me? That's not going to work."

"Let's give it a shot," he said. "Even if I can only last for a couple hundred metres, it's better than nothing."

Too tired to argue, she gave her sticks to Kate, put her hands on his shoulders and leaned down until her chest was pressed against his back. Slipping her hands around the pack he now carried in reverse of normal, she clasped them together and carefully crooked her bad leg around his hip, her weight carried awkwardly on her left.

"Ready?" Titus said. "One—two—three—up!"

She gave a push with her good leg and Titus staggered a step. Kate reached out a hand to help him balance. He braced his arms under Claudia's thighs and his hands created a cradle for her buttocks. He jiggled to settle her in place, and she bit her lip, stifling a small cry, as the jostling sent waves of pain up her leg.

"Sorry," he said. "All good now."

She was desperately relieved to be off her feet. She held herself tense, waiting for Titus to tire and tell her he needed to put her down. But he strode along at an even pace, still following Kate even though the track they were on was wide enough for two, and slowly she relaxed.

It was late afternoon and the sun shone unabated. All three of them were hot and sweaty, and the layers of fabric between her chest and Titus' back became even more damp, but there was nothing she could do about that. Lulled by the rhythmic movement, comforted by the flex of the strong muscles supporting her, and exhausted by the unremitting pain, she felt her head bobbing until her cheek came to rest on his head, and she dozed.

Titus had been certain from the moment he'd pulled her from the water that Claudia's injury was not serious. Her ankle had shown no sign of the distortion caused by a broken bone, and she'd managed well for the first part of their trek out of the bush, remaining stoic and uncomplaining even though her pale face and tight expression made it clear she was in severe discomfort.

But that certainty hadn't stopped his stomach from churning at what might have been. She could have hit her head and lain unconscious, face down in the water. She could have suffered a compound fracture and been unable to walk at all. She could have—

He cut off his wandering thoughts. None of that had happened. She was next to him in the SUV, the seat tipped back, and her foot propped on her pack to give it support, sleeping calmly under the influence of the heavier pain meds supplied by the emergency ward doctor.

She was safe. She was cared for. She was with him.

He made himself a pledge. He would protect her—always. If she let him.

They had dropped Kate and her gear off at her bed and breakfast in Wells. Titus had promised to let her know how Claudia was doing, and she in turn had promised to keep them up to date on her search. Claudia had waved gamely from her seat in the back, where she half sat half lay so she could stretch her leg out, and then he had driven in as much haste as he could do safely to the nearest emergency ward, about an hour away in Quesnel.

After an examination and X-rays, the doctor had confirmed it was a sprain. She had rewrapped the ankle, given Claudia another dose of painkillers, and provided a prescription in case she needed something stronger than over-the-counter meds. Three hours after arriving at the hospital and with the rental of a set of crutches arranged, he helped Claudia back to the SUV, and they headed home.

The drive north to Prince George was blessedly uneventful, and by the time he pulled into his driveway, the sun had set. Claudia stirred as soon as he turned off the ignition.

"I'm sorry," she said on a yawn. "I was horrible company. I couldn't keep my eyes open."

"You're forgiven. But just this once. Wait there."

"I can—"

"I said *wait*." He jabbed a finger at her and she subsided with a grimace.

He rounded the vehicle and retrieved her crutches from the rear compartment. When he opened her door, she raised the seat back and removed her safety belt, and then swung her legs out slowly.

"Careful," he said.

"Stop hovering." She took the crutches from him and levered herself out of the vehicle. "I wish you'd take me home," she said, continuing an argument started in Quesnel and only discontinued because she'd fallen asleep. "It's a sprain, nothing serious. I don't need constant supervision. It doesn't even hurt that much anymore."

"That's the medication talking." He was going to make sure she rested if he had to tie her to a bed—an image he filed for future reference. "Besides, your car is here, so you'd have to come out sometime." Not that she should attempt to drive for a week or more, according to the doctor.

Once she was settled in the living area, he returned to the SUV and brought in their backpacks.

"I'm just so angry at myself," Claudia said. "We should have had hours more at the site."

"Let it go, Claudia. What's done is done." He removed the detritus of their lunch from the packs and the reminder of food had his stomach rumbling. "I'm starved. Do you want anything?"

She shook her head. "What I need more than anything else is a shower. I stink."

"No shower. You might slip. But how about a bubble bath in a jetted tub?"

"Really?" Claudia moaned. "I would love you forever."

Titus' stride hitched as he moved from the kitchen to the couch where she sat. She didn't mean it, not *that* way. "Let's get you up the stairs, then," he said.

I would love you forever.

He couldn't keep her casual words out of his thoughts as he ran the bath and rigged a scaffold with an easel and towels so she could keep her bandaged foot out of the water. Once she was up to her chin in bubbles, he showered in the glass and tile stall next to the tub, and then left her with strict instructions not to move an inch until he returned to help.

I would love you forever.

Her words kept repeating as he made up a snack of crackers, meats, cheeses, and dried fruit. He munched as he arranged it on a charcuterie board, taking the edge off his hunger, and then carried it upstairs to the master en suite where Claudia reclined in isolated splendour.

She smiled as he placed it on the vanity. "You read my mind," she said. "Now that I'm clean again, I *am* hungry."

"Be right back," he said, and retrieved a step stool stored in a corner of the studio. Perching on that, he balanced the board on his knees so Claudia could help herself.

"This is heaven," she said, popping a cube of cheese in her mouth as bubbles traced a seductive trail from her wrist to her elbow. "I feel very pampered."

She deserved to be pampered. She constantly amazed him with her strength and resilience, and today had been one more example of what a true Amazon she was. But that didn't mean she couldn't appreciate someone who looked after her, someone who stood by and gave a helping hand when she needed it.

He took great pleasure in feeding her until she was sated, and then helped her out of the tub with care and caution. She insisted she could dry herself, but he kissed her into silence and when she was dazed and limp, proceeded to rub her with a large, luxurious towel. He paid careful attention to her breasts, her hips, the dark gold thatch of hair between her legs, dropping more kisses along his path. When he was done, he swung her into his arms—he'd die before admitting aloud his muscles ached from carrying her the last portion of their hike—and laid her on the bed he'd turned down earlier.

He made love to her, softly, sweetly, gently, and after they'd both reached their peak in a swelling rush, watched her slide into sleep between one breath and the next.

He studied her face in repose. He hadn't had the chance to do so before, as she was the one who woke first each morning and he the one who fell asleep first at night. Lines at the corners of her eyes and mouth bore testament to her age, carved deeper today by pain, no doubt. Fragile lids hid the bright brilliance of her eyes. He mapped the bridge of her nose and the outline of her lips with the faintest of touches. She didn't stir.

I will *love you forever,* he vowed silently. He had no doubt about that.

It was *her* feelings he was uncertain about.

CHAPTER THIRTY-TWO

If people don't stop asking me how my ankle is, Claudia thought Wednesday morning, *I might scream.*

Gritting her teeth, she smiled tightly at Karina. "It's fine," she said. "Feeling better every day."

"Well, if you need me to do anything, let me know." The younger woman lingered in the doorway of Claudia's office as if waiting for immediate instructions.

"I will. Thanks." She made a shooing gesture with her hand. "Go unlock the front. It's time to open."

When she'd woken the morning after injuring her ankle, she had been thankful the gallery was closed on Mondays. It ached heavily, and even her teeth had throbbed in sympathy. But after a day being tended to by Titus with icepacks and heating pads and pain meds, the worst of it had passed. At her insistence, he'd driven her home after dinner.

"I won't be able to drive for a few days yet," she'd said, "and it doesn't make sense for you to ferry me back and forth when I have a perfectly good apartment right where I need to be. What's the point of living so close if I can't take advantage of it in a situation like this?"

He'd put up a half-hearted argument, citing the dangers of stairs, but had eventually given in. Still, he'd stayed with her that night, seemingly unwilling to relinquish his mother hen routine. She should have felt overwhelmed and suffocated but hadn't. When he'd left the next morning, she'd felt a sudden stab of regret, knowing he wouldn't be waiting for her when she returned from work—a bolt of pain that sharpened when she remembered in a couple of weeks he wouldn't even be living in the same city.

Staring blindly at her computer screen, she finally admitted something she'd been avoiding with varied success for a while now.

She was going to miss Titus when he was gone.

No, she thought, shaking her head, *miss isn't the right word.* It was too weak to sum up everything she felt when she contemplated life after he left.

But what was the right word? What was she truly feeling? A pencil lay on her desk and she picked it up to give her hands something to do as she pondered.

When she'd fled her husband with two small daughters, she'd made a vow never to lie to herself again. When he'd told her it was *her* fault he hit her, that if she were a better wife he would treat her with respect, she'd ignored the voice inside that told her he was a lying bastard. Only when she'd finally admitted the truth—that she didn't deserve to be treated that way, that it wasn't her fault, that she'd done nothing wrong—had she found the courage to leave.

Now she had to find the courage to look at her feelings for Titus and be honest once more.

Bracing her elbows on the arms of her chair and clenching the pencil in both hands, she closed her eyes.

When he leaves, she thought with a rolling twist in her stomach, *I will never be the same again. I will ache for him. Which is exactly why he needs to go.* She couldn't allow any man to have that power over her again. The power to make her distrust her instincts, to make her want to be with him to the detriment of her own well-being.

The pencil snapped in two, startling her. She stared

at the jagged edges, and then tossed them in the garbage can, wishing she could discard her feelings for Titus as easily.

"I can't believe you didn't discuss this with me," Yvette said.

"I didn't think you'd care, since you won't be my agent anymore." The words were barely out of his mouth before Titus wished he could recall them. He sounded bitter and petty and childish.

A hiss travelled sibilantly through the speaker. "I don't think I deserved that."

He dropped onto his living room couch with a groan. "I'm sorry. You don't."

"Did you just apologize?" The words were humorous, but he caught a note of true surprise.

"Don't get used to it," he said.

"I won't. But I appreciate it. To get back to the subject at hand—you're really going to buy that house? And why *didn't* you mention it to me?"

"It all came together rather quickly," he said. "I found out last week the owners aren't returning, and they accepted my offer right away." From his seat on the low, hard-stuffed couch the huge, colourful abstract oil that hung above the fireplace loomed over him. "Other than some artwork they left displayed, which I've agreed to put into storage for them, it's mine. Lock, stock and barrel."

"Why Prince George?" Yvette asked. "After years of floating around the country, why there? Why now?"

He wasn't prepared to mention Claudia, not yet. He was certain he'd made the right decision, no matter how their relationship evolved—or didn't, as the case may be. "It might seem like I'm jumping into things, but I've thought very seriously about this. Prince George has everything I need—easy access to wilderness areas, a vibrant art community, excellent transportation options. I want to give longevity a try. In the end, it's only a house. If this doesn't work out, I'll sell and move on." Then, because she was his friend as well as his agent, and knew him better than almost anyone, he added in a burst of honesty, "I'm getting older, Yvette. I'll be fifty soon. I want a home base, something concrete to call mine. I'm sure I'll still get the itch to travel, but the lure of a place of my own has been growing stronger for a while now."

"Well, congratulations, then." She still sounded hesitant to give her full approval, but he had sprung it on her. In the twenty years they'd worked together, this was probably the biggest shock he'd ever given her. It didn't compare to the shock *she'd* given *him*, of course, but he was smart enough—this time—not to complain about that.

"Thank you," he said instead. "You're coming up Friday for the exhibition, right?"

"Of course. And now it's more than a business trip. You can tour me around, show me exactly what finally made you toss out an anchor."

Still feeling apologetic about his earlier outburst, he said by way of a peace offering, "I took a look at the list you sent."

"Of my replacements?" she asked guardedly. "What did you think?"

"Alecia Masters looks like she might not be too terrible."

"Coming from you, that's a rousing endorsement. Does it help that she is the one I would have chosen, too?"

"A little."

"Do you want me to contact her?"

"No," he said, puffing out a long-suffering breath. "I'll call, explain what's going on. If we seem a good fit, I'll put her in touch with you."

"You'll like her," Yvette said confidently. "Give her a chance. Don't go into this with a closed mind."

"I'm not like that," he protested. "I'm open to change."

"Uh huh." Yvette's inelegant grunt expressed enormous disbelief. "Whatever you say. You still picking me up at the airport?"

"Yes." A beep sounded in his ear. "I've got another call coming in. Anything else?"

"Nothing that can't wait. See you in a couple of days."

He pressed the buttons that connected him to the incoming call. "Hello?"

"Titus Wilcox?" The man's accented voice was unfamiliar. "This is Denis Bourgeois from the McCord Museum."

The conservator. Titus' grip tightened on his phone. "Thank you for calling. Have you any news?"

"I appreciate your patience on this project." Only a slight harshness on the *th* in *this* betrayed English was likely not his first language. "I have had a chance to review the painting you sent, and I want to thank you. It is proving a pretty puzzle."

"It is?"

"I cannot yet confirm that it is a lost work of William George Richardson Hind. Further study must be made, as well as investigations into the documents we have surrounding his life. But I thought you might be interested in an anomaly we have discovered."

"Is there something wrong with the painting?"

"No, not wrong. But the letters you drew our attention to. The letters hidden in the waters of the creek."

Titus' mouth dried. Had they been so anxious to find a message in the painting that they'd suffered some sort of mass hypnosis and seen something that wasn't there? "Yes?" he asked.

"We are of the confirmed conclusion," Denis said, "after detailed study and consultation, that whoever the original painter was—he or she did *not* paint those letters."

CHAPTER THIRTY-THREE

I have news about the painting. Can I come over tonight after close?

A surge of pleasure swept through Claudia when she saw the text from Titus.

Of course, she had typed back. *Good news?*

Not sure? I'll explain later.

Curiosity over his vague answer buzzed at the back of her mind through the rest of the day and while she hurriedly ate the spinach salad she made for dinner. When a knock sounded, she hobbled to the apartment door as quick as her injured ankle would allow.

Something both relaxed and tightened within her when she saw Titus on the landing. It was foolish to be jittery about a person she was happy to see. She didn't know how to handle it.

"Come in," she said formally, wishing she could recapture the ease she used to feel around him. When it didn't matter so much.

"Where are your crutches?" he said in an accusing tone. "You shouldn't be putting weight on your ankle yet."

"It's *fine*," she said for what felt like the hundredth time that day. "Honestly, it's feeling much better."

With a narrowed look, he stepped through the door. She preceded him to the living room, and he was apparently appeased by the way she walked, as he sat on the couch without further censure.

"So, the McCord Museum got a hold of you?" she said. Instead of sitting next to him as she usually would, she took a seat in the armchair opposite. It was ludicrous being this uncertain around him, but she couldn't seem to help herself.

"Yes. Denis Bourgeois is the conservator who called. They're still investigating the possibility it was done by Hind, but he wanted to let me know something they'd already discovered."

Claudia waved her hands encouragingly. "Which was..."

"One of the first steps in authenticating a painting is using an X-ray to see what is under the surface. It can help determine the type of paper and paint used, preliminary sketches, changes to the composition—all sorts of things. Including where touch-ups have been made or where places were painted over." Titus paused and the hairs on the back of Claudia's neck rose in anticipation. "The letters we found in the creek were not part of the original artwork. They were painted onto the varnish, then the painting was re-varnished to protect them."

Claudia blinked as bewilderment replaced expectation. "What does that mean? I mean, I understand what it means, but what does it *mean?*"

Titus' mouth curved. "It means that, even if Hind did do the painting while he lived in British Columbia, he had nothing to do with the Waitless Creek clue. At best guess, Denis thinks that was done sometime after 1900, maybe even later than 1920. Something to do with the pigments used. That part was too technical for me."

"But the photo on the back. It had to have been taken before Franklyn died in 1870. So how do letters painted at least thirty years later tie in with buried treasure?"

"Your guess is as good as mine."

They sat in silence, Claudia's brain whirling.

"We probably should have an expert look at the document," she said. "They can tell the age of paper somehow, right? We've been assuming the document and the photo were put on the canvas at the same time. We could be wrong about that."

He nodded. "As it's still attached to the canvas, it's with the painting in Montreal. They could probably test it there."

"Of course. I didn't think of that. I'm still gasping, trying to make sense of it all."

"I'll send a note to Denis right now. He knows about those artifacts, but I'll make sure he understands we want him to study them, too." He pulled out his phone and tapped quietly as Claudia sat and thought.

The search for hidden gold, she mused, had always been a long, long, *long* shot. It seemed even less likely now. The painting, photo and document were connected in someway—but how? Since the clue had been added decades after the painting was finished, what was its link to the gold in the photograph of the three men? By the time the letters had been painted, one man was long dead, the other gone home to England. Only Leung Ah had remained in Barkerville, apparently raising a family there, if their conjectures were correct.

"What about this?" she said when Titus lowered his phone. "Someone, let's say Hind, paints the picture in the mid to late 1860s. It comes into Ah's possession. He puts the document and the photo on the back and seals it up. The painting is passed down to his son, who gives it to *his* son—Mae's father's grandfather—as a wedding gift. It could have been someone in one of those later generations who added the letters. Mae said it was family legend the painting led to a great treasure. What if there was an *oral* clue that went along with the painting, and someone was afraid it would get forgotten? So they added that hint—Waitless Creek—into the painting."

Titus frowned. "I suppose that makes some sense. It seems very convoluted."

"This whole quest has been convoluted," Claudia agreed. "At first, I thought this development made the idea of buried treasure *less* likely. Now I think it might be *more* likely. Why go to the trouble of hiding a clue decades later if the treasure wasn't still waiting to be found?"

"We should tell Mae about this. It is her family, after all."

Claudia twisted in her seat to look at the clock on the wall above her head. "I'll let her know tomorrow. I've contracted her to help with the exhibition, so she'll be coming to the gallery. It will be easier to explain in person."

He grunted agreement. Another silence fell between them. Now the conversation had lapsed, Claudia's oversensitivity returned, and she had to stop herself from fidgeting. Titus kept shooting her short glances, his gaze abstracted as if his thoughts were elsewhere, despite his seeming awareness of her.

"Is there something else?" she said suddenly, incapable of suffering the quiet any longer. "You look like you have more to say."

He'd been staring at his hands, picking at the paint she could see rimming one fingernail. After a moment, he lifted his gaze and met her eyes directly.

Titus had no idea why he was so nervous, and it pissed him off. Telling Claudia he'd bought his house should be simple. He didn't have to mention how his reasoning had involved her—even though it had.

But he wanted to tell her. He wanted to tell her how he felt, why he wanted to stay, how much she'd come to mean to him.

He wanted to tell her he loved her but feared her reaction. Over the last few days, he thought he'd seen signs of her softening to the idea of having him as a permanent fixture in her life, but he wasn't certain enough to lay money on it.

"Titus?" she said. "What's going on?"

It was probably best to hedge his bets. He had to tell her *something*, though, now that she'd asked. Sucking in a breath, he said in a rush, "I do have other news. Personal news. I'm staying in Prince George. I bought the house."

Her eyes widened, matching the O of her mouth. "What?"

"I'm staying, Claudia. I'm not leaving after the exhibition. Prince George is home now."

She remained sitting, but he could see the energy vibrating off her.

"Why?" she asked.

Her monosyllabic questions gave him the answers he needed. Deeply disappointed—and worse, not surprised—he thanked the stars he hadn't bared more of his soul. He replied with a partial truth, the same reason he'd given Yvette. "This city suits me. I've enjoyed living here. It has everything I need, and anything it doesn't is easy to access."

"You're breaking the pattern of a lifetime because it's convenient?" Claudia looked doubtful, as well she might. It sounded logical, but unusually cold and analytical, even to his own ears.

Up until now, he hadn't been ashamed to tell Claudia exactly what he felt, what he wanted in their relationship. He was the one that had pushed for something deeper than an affair. The more he thought of it, the angrier he grew. He had put himself out there, had made himself vulnerable. No matter how often he told himself it was Claudia's turn to step up, it always seemed to fall on him.

Well, not this time.

"Yes," he said. "That's exactly why. Because it's convenient."

"No other reason?"

Despite himself, his spirits lifted. Was that disappointment shadowing her face? Had she been expecting a different answer? She'd been upfront from the beginning that the fact he was leaving soon was one of his attractions. Had she changed her mind, as he'd been beginning to hope?

He hardened his heart. If she had, then *she* could tell *him*. He wasn't going to play at guessing games. "No," he said casually. "No other reason."

"I see." She spoke with poise and control, and he heard no hint of wistfulness. The spark flickering in his chest snuffed out. "Well, thanks for coming over," she continued. "But you're right, my ankle is hurting a bit. I think I should have an early night."

It was impossible to misunderstand. He was being dismissed. "Claudia—" he started, and then stopped, wordless. A man could only take so much rejection. She'd made her choice, and he would have to live with it.

If only it didn't hurt so much.

She stood and limped to the door, and then turned and waited for him to join her. "Congratulations on your new home. I wish you all the best."

Ice clamped his lungs. Had he made a horrible mistake, not admitting *she* was the real reason he was staying? She was looking at him now with none of the fire, none of the joy, that had lit her face recently.

"Claudia—" he repeated. And stopped again.

She opened the door. He stepped outside. "Goodnight, Titus," she said, shoulders straight, chin lifted, cold dignity personified. She closed the door.

He stared at the blank panel. Why did he have the feeling she'd just said goodbye? Forever?

Claudia's heart pounded and her skin prickled. She didn't think Titus had noticed anything different after he'd dropped his atomic news but couldn't be sure.

She locked and bolted the door, and then dropped onto the couch. The cushion was still warm from his body, and she shuddered with longing.

Despite the fact she'd practically shoved him out of the apartment, it had been the last thing she'd wanted to do. She'd *wanted* to fling herself into his arms and tell him how happy she was while kissing him crazily.

The force of her own reaction had terrified her, and it had taken all her control to stay rooted in her seat.

Hugging a pillow to her chest, she rocked back and forth. Other women were cut out for marriage and long-term relationships. Not her. The only time she'd tried, she'd lost herself, let Saul chip away at her very soul until she could barely recognize herself.

But hadn't things felt different with Titus? He had never denigrated her concerns or pouted when she'd pushed back. He'd compromised, offered her space to come to terms with her own feelings, in her own time. Even tonight, he hadn't put any pressure on her, had given her no indication that she had played a role in his decision to stay.

If he had, would she have been brave enough to show him how she felt? Or would she have done exactly the same thing and pushed him away?

He cared for her. The dinners he'd made. The way he'd pitched in after the flood at the gallery. And never mind how he'd insisted she rest after hurting her ankle. She wouldn't have made it out of the bush in the first place without his support, both mental and physical.

He wanted her, as she was. He'd never once said or done anything to make her feel less attractive, despite her height and size. In fact, he'd gone out of his way to show her exactly how *much* he wanted every inch of her.

Maybe it wasn't his fault she felt so torn and alone. Maybe it was her inability to trust *herself*, not him.

CHAPTER THIRTY-FOUR

Claudia had been overwhelmed by the response to their eleventh-hour appeal to local female artists to join the exhibition. Over the last few days, she had reviewed and appraised numerous pieces, and the quality had been so high across the board that she'd had to make tough decisions about which to include.

By Thursday evening, she was thankful for the foresight that had prompted her to close Fauna on Friday to prepare for the exhibition. It would be a huge amount of work to transform the gallery, and with the additional displays, that work had almost doubled.

The extra set up was also why her team—including Mae, who she'd hired for the event—was already bustling about the gallery, although that hadn't been the initial plan. Originally, she'd expected only she and Titus would be here during the evening hours...and before his announcement, she'd been plotting ways of christening the gallery she now blushed to think of.

When he'd arrived earlier this evening, she'd greeted him calmly and professionally—and with a touch of queasiness. The problem was, the more she replayed that evening in her head, the more she realized Titus wasn't to blame for her current distress. It wasn't his fault she was a coward.

"Okay, Karina and I have got the lounge and the hall prepped," Bernadette said, popping her head into Claudia's office, where she'd hidden herself under the guise of reviewing the display plan on her computer.

"Great. Here's the printout." She handed over a few sheets of paper, one for each wall in the back display area, showing what pieces were to be placed where. "You'll find the plinths for the sculptures in the basement storage."

"Got it. Oh, and I am supposed to tell you Titus wants to talk to you."

Claudia smiled. At least, she hoped she smiled. Her cheeks felt stiff and frozen. "Of course. I'll be there in a minute."

She scrolled through the plan one more time, and then printed off the pages pertaining to the main gallery. Taking a few deep breaths, she rose from her chair and made her way to the front. In all the furor of recent days, she hadn't found the right time to broach Karina's concerns with Titus, and it was too late now. She had done what she could to lessen the chance of a personality clash by assigning Tanya and Mae to work with him in the main showroom. They had already removed all existing artwork from the portable panels, but instead of taking down the pieces currently hanging on the exterior walls, which was the next step, they were standing with Titus in the middle of the room.

"I'm sorry not to have better news," he was saying. Mae's expression was resigned disappointment, while Tanya stared at them both, open-mouthed.

"You were looking for buried gold?" she asked. "How cool is that!"

"It would have been cooler if Kate had found something," Titus replied.

"It's not your fault," Mae said. "You've done more than enough, and it was a silly fairy tale anyway. Thank you for trying."

Mae and Tanya returned to their duties. Claudia lifted her chin and crossed the room, trying not to limp too obviously. After a full day of work her ankle was aching, but she didn't have time to coddle herself.

"You needed me?" she said as she approached Titus, and then winced. He didn't seem to notice her suggestive word choice, his grey gaze remaining steady on her face.

"Kate called. She found nothing."

"Yes. I heard you talking to Mae." He was more than an arm-length away, yet Claudia swore she could feel his heat encircling her, warming the frozen, scared bits of her heart. Hurriedly she said, "How much was she able to search?"

"Not everything, of course. The two claims take up a lot of acreage. Kate is positive, however, that there is nothing in any of the tailings piles. She checked as well as she could in other likely places, such as the wide-open spaces that may have been where the men set up camp. But it would take weeks, if not months, to search the entire area, and we know that isn't feasible."

His tone was flat and unemotional, yet his piercing eyes scanned her face with intensity. Afraid her expression might give away more than she was ready to admit, she pivoted to stand beside him and focussed on Mae and Tanya. Mae was smiling at something the other woman had said, but her movements seemed heavy and burdened.

"I shouldn't have let her pin her hopes on this foolish hunt," Claudia said. "I know she needs the money, but I should have made her face reality, not encouraged her."

"You have nothing to feel guilty for. I think you were very upfront and honest," Titus said quietly. "Dreams are what make life worth living, even when they don't turn out the way we hoped."

She kept her head averted, too unnerved to look him in the face. He wasn't just talking about the gold. He was talking about *her*, about *his* dreams.

If only she had the courage to give him what she knew he wanted.

Somehow Claudia made it through Thursday evening, a sleepless and solitary night, and Friday morning without losing her poise. Every minute made it more and more difficult to be around Titus. It was as if he were a planet and she was a satellite caught in his gravity—despite her continued resolutions to stay as far away as possible while still doing the necessary work, she constantly found herself in the same room, hovering nearby, initiating conversations.

She desperately missed the closeness and intimacy they'd shared. But it was as if his decision to stay had closed off her escape route, and she was locked in a doorless room, frantic to get out yet terrified to leave.

Titus left shortly after one o'clock, returning to the gallery less than an hour later with his agent—and ex-lover, Claudia thought morosely. Yvette was a slim, elegant woman whose stylish appearance lived up to the promise of her French name. Her face was carefully made up, her artificially silver hair cut in a classic pixie that hugged the curves of her skull. Even in stiletto heels she barely reached Claudia's chin. It didn't help that Yvette looked cool and chic in a pale pink silk wrap dress, while she was wearing grubby jeans and a wrinkled T-shirt.

"Thanks so much for coming," she said, shaking the other woman's delicate hand, feeling clumsy and awkward, as if her arms and legs weren't quite under control. "We're finished setting up, if you'd like to take a look around."

Claudia donned her professional persona with relief and regained some of her composure as she and Titus escorted Yvette through the gallery. Yvette seemed appreciative and pleased, and Claudia relaxed further. Back in the main gallery, Titus excused himself to check his emails and disappeared into the back, leaving the two women alone.

Yvette faced Claudia, one artistically pencilled eyebrow rising. "Now I understand," she said. "It all becomes clear."

"What becomes clear?" Claudia said politely, though her thoughts were distracted. The caterers should be arriving any moment, along with the florist with the decorative arrangements.

"Why Titus has chosen to stay in this city."

Claudia snapped into focus. "What do you mean?"

Yvette patted her arm, amusement glinting in her silvery-blue eyes. "I've been Titus' agent for more than twenty years," she said, "and my main role involves his professional career. But we are friends, too. And I've never seen him look at a woman the way he looks at you."

"He told me about you," Claudia said abruptly, the words bursting out. "About your personal...history."

Yvette's eyebrow climbed higher. "Did he now. That's surprising...and yet not."

"What do you mean?" A shiver raced down Claudia's spine and curled into a lick of flame low in her belly. "What has he told you?"

"Nothing. And that also is surprising." Yvette tilted her head, studying Claudia from head to foot. She resisted the urge to squirm. "Not that he's ever been one to kiss and tell. But he's never hidden his girlfriends from me. You, he's only mentioned in a business sense."

"Maybe that's all there is between us," Claudia said, floundering under confusing sensations. She was hurt—yes, honestly *hurt*—that Titus wouldn't have mentioned her to someone who was so integral in his life. But Yvette seemed to think that omission meant he had *strong* feelings, not weak ones.

The other woman shook her head. "Possibly from your point of view," she said. "I don't know you well enough to guess. But not from his. He looks at you like he looks at his favourite pieces of art—hungry, demanding, tender."

Claudia actively wished for Titus to return. Anything was better than this kind yet excruciating analysis. The cell phone tucked into her back pocket vibrated and she snatched it with a gasp of relief. "It's my daughter," she said to Yvette. "Please excuse me."

Taking two steps away, she held the phone to her ear. "Nicole?"

"Mom?" Her daughter's voice was shaky and tearful. "My water just broke."

Titus hadn't wanted to leave Yvette and Claudia alone together. But he'd seen the speculation in his soon-to-be-ex-agent's expression as her gaze swung between Titus and Claudia during the tour. He'd tried to hide his complicated emotions but had a feeling he hadn't been completely successful. Needing some time alone to rebuild his mask, he had uttered a white lie about emails and gone to ground in Claudia's office.

He hoped he hadn't made a grave tactical error by giving Yvette—never one to pull her punches—time to speak her mind to Claudia.

The last couple of days had been unexpected agony mixed with a slightly frenetic optimism. Claudia had treated him with such oppressive politeness it put his teeth on edge. But instead of avoiding him like he'd expected her to, she was almost constantly nearby. He wasn't sure if she had simply reset their relationship back to its earliest days, or if she was working up her courage to take the next step—whatever that next step might be.

The uncertainty was killing him, and he would have to deal with it soon. But not this weekend. The exhibition was taking up everyone's energy and effort. His personal life would have to wait.

After checking his inbox—he didn't want to be a total

liar—he returned to the main gallery. Yvette was at the far wall, studying one of his older pieces, one she was familiar with, apparently giving Claudia privacy as she talked on the phone.

He instantly forgot his own frustrations and worries at his first glance of her wide eyes and pale face. He strode toward her, hand outstretched, thankful when she accepted his wordless comfort and gripped his palm.

"Everything's going to be fine," she said into the phone. Her gaze was turned inward, as if she could see the person she was talking to. "I'll be there in ten minutes. Just breathe. I'll be right there."

Her hand dropped to her side like a marionette with the string cut, still staring into the distance.

"What's going on?" Titus asked. "Can I help?" She didn't reply. "Claudia?" he said, sharpening his tone to catch her attention.

She blinked and fastened her gaze on him. Red spots of colour bloomed on her cheeks. "Nicole is in labour. It's early. She's not due for a few weeks yet. I've got to get her to the hospital."

CHAPTER THIRTY-FIVE

Yvette turned on her heel and took a step forward. Titus jerked his head and she stopped. He'd fill her in later. Right now, Claudia needed him. He had absolutely no experience with pregnancy, but her distress told him enough. "Should you call an ambulance?"

"She's not having contractions yet. It's early, but not dangerously so. She doesn't live far away, and it's on the route to the hospital. But I have to go." Her eyes darted about the gallery, unable to settle. "The caterers will be here soon. And the florist." She moved toward the rear of the gallery, steps shambling and loose, and then stopped. "Where's Bernadette? I need to tell her what's going on. There's a folder on my desk with all the contact information, the agenda, everything. I don't know if I'll be back. I need to go over a few updated details with the master of ceremonies. And Mae wanted me to review her speech."

"Claudia." Titus gripped her shoulders and gave her a tiny, gentle shake. "Your daughter needs you, so take your own advice. Deep breath in and out."

The skin around her eyes tightened and her chin quivered, but she did as he said, inhaling deeply through her nose, exhaling slowly from pursed lips.

"Again."

She shot him an annoyed look—*She's coming back,* he thought in relief—but obeyed. Without prompting she took two more breaths. "Thank you," she said. "I'm good now."

"Are you okay to drive? I can go with you if you want." She'd lost the absent, lost look that had frightened him so much, but he could still feel a faint tremor in her body.

She shook her head. "No. I need you here." She raised her hands to his wrists and urged him to let go of her shoulders. "I know this is a lot to ask—you're supposed to be the star and get all the fancy treatment tonight—but there's no one else I trust more. You know how much tonight means to me. I need you to take care of things here. My team is good, but they've never run an event like this. You have experience, you've seen how things are done." She laid her palm on his cheek. "You owe me *nothing.* But I'm asking you. Please."

His heart swelled with pride and love. She was so strong, so loyal, knew exactly what was important in life. He wanted to kiss her, but she'd wasted enough time already, and if he started he might not be able to stop. "Go," he said. "I've got this."

Claudia dashed down the back hall and up the stairs to her apartment to grab her keys and wallet. By the time she descended the stairs, Bernadette, Karina, Tanya, and Mae were gathered at the door of the client lounge, faces inquisitive and concerned.

"I've got to go," Claudia said. "Titus will tell you what's going on. Listen to him." Bernadette said something but she didn't hear as the door banged shut behind her.

She didn't remember the drive to Nicole's house, her thoughts flying ahead of her body to her daughter.

She'd been understandably distraught on the phone, and she'd transmitted her fright to Claudia. Thank god Titus had been there to snap her back into herself. Her normal competence and efficiency vanished when her daughters were in crisis.

Nicole must have been watching from the front window of her tiny bungalow as she was out the door before the SUV rolled to a stop. She walked stiffly down the path, one hand pressed to her back, a small bag dangling from the other. Claudia bolted to her side and wrapped an arm around her waist.

"How are you doing?" she asked as she opened the passenger door.

Nicole's face was streaked with tears, but she was no longer crying. "Still no contractions," she said, grunting as she lowered herself into the seat. "But my back is aching something fierce."

Claudia decided not to remind her that back labour was a thing. "Remember what we learned in birthing classes," she said. "Stay calm, stay focussed. Do you have your ID?" At Nicole's terse nod, she hustled around the hood of the SUV and back behind the steering wheel. "We'll be there in five minutes."

Parking was always at a premium near Prince George's only hospital, so she was forced to drop Nicole off at the main entrance and find a spot a block away. Rushing back, she found Nicole sitting uncomfortably on the edge of a seat in the three-storey tall atrium. They made their way to the Maternity Ward, pausing once for Nicole to breathe as pain clutched her back. There, Nicole was assigned a birthing room.

"Momma? Are you coming?" Blue eyes wide, Nicole looked over her shoulder as a nurse led her down the hall.

"I'll be right there," she said.

As soon as Nicole was out of sight, Claudia collapsed into a seat, blue vinyl and chrome, one of many in a linked row lining the hall. She leaned forward, elbows pressed into her knees, palms on her forehead.

"Are you all right?" White sneakers came into the limited circle of her view. Claudia noted absently the bright orange laces were patterned with safety-pink elephants.

She straightened and gave the nurse a weak smile. "Just taking a minute. My daughter just came in. Her water broke."

The nurse—short, round, dark-skinned, with a mass of bushy hair tied back in a ponytail—nodded.

"It's too early." Claudia concentrated. "She's not due for a couple of weeks yet."

"Ah." The nurse smiled and waved a hand as if brushing away Claudia's worries. It was a comforting gesture. "We'll take good care of her and her baby. Let me see what's going on. I'll come back and get you in a minute."

Titus was honoured by Claudia's faith in him.

He was beginning to believe it was misplaced.

"Can't you bring a different appetizer?" he asked in what he considered a perfectly reasonable tone.

The caterer, a dark-haired man almost as tall as Titus but half his width, gazed at him with troubled, wary eyes. Maybe his tone wasn't quite as reasonable as he'd thought.

"Ms. Aronson has designed a very precise menu," he said. According to the detailed sheets she'd left, Claudia had designated her office for the use of the caterer, so that's where they were now, the man several feet away from Titus and standing behind Claudia's desk. Still, he rocked back on his heels as if eager to put more distance between them. "Replacing the Beer Brined Chicken Salad Sliders with something else will unbalance her selection."

"But you can't provide the Beer Brined Chicken Salad Sliders, can you?" Titus tried a smile. From the caterer's wince, it was no more successful than his reasonable tone.

"No." His Adam's apple, prominent in his thin neck, bobbed as he swallowed. "Due to an unfortunate delivery disaster."

"Then you'll have to provide something else."

"I need direction from Ms. Aronson. I can't simply pick *anything*. She might not approve."

Titus gritted his teeth. "I will deal with any concerns Ms. Aronson may have. Later. Right now, I don't have time to deal with this. *You're* the caterer. Pick something!"

"Umm..." A hesitant voice came from behind Titus.

He whirled on his heel, ready to snarl at whoever it was. At the sight of Mae, however, he bit his tongue. "Yes, Mae?" he said, grimly pleased when the words came out a dull rumble, not a roar.

"I was wondering..." She paused again, but her eyes flicked from Titus to the caterer and back. "I mean, I couldn't help but overhear..."

"I am open to any suggestions," he said, sweeping one hand in a welcoming gesture.

Mae looked at the caterer. "I am sure Ms. Aronson's main concern is that her guests are suitably provided for. If she hadn't chosen the chicken sliders, what would your follow up suggestion have been?"

The caterer looked thoughtful. "I suppose the Smoked Turkey Club Sliders would have been a reasonable second choice."

Mae tilted her head at Titus.

"Perfect. Smoked Turkey it is." He pointed at Mae. "You are now officially the main contact for the caterers for the rest of the evening." He slipped by, ignoring her astonished face, and escaped to the main gallery. He applauded Claudia for taking such intense interest in what to serve at his exhibition, but if Mae hadn't stepped in, he would have cut a dozen fast food hamburgers into quarters and handed those around.

The doors were set to open in ten minutes. Through the glass wall looking onto the street he could already see the parking spaces filling up.

Despite the exhaustive instructions Claudia had left—and thank god she'd written them down, not just had them in her head—little glitches had popped up continually through the hours since she had left. Nothing as drastic as the slider emergency—he did understand how important good food was, after all—but enough to keep him hopping. Her team had been well-prepped and were eager to do anything necessary, but they were all new to the art world and couldn't be expected to handle things without her leadership. They'd managed to keep close to the original plan, though. He hoped.

He'd been so busy attempting to handle things that he'd had no time to go home and change. Yvette had offered to get his suit, and then he had used Claudia's apartment to shower and dress, thankful she hadn't locked it when she left and hoping she wouldn't be upset he'd taken advantage of that fact. He'd returned downstairs minutes ago and been immediately accosted by the caterer.

Throughout the recent hours, worry about Nicole had buzzed under the surface. Claudia wasn't one to panic at nothing, and the look on her face had jolted Titus. As he was wondering, yet again, when she might get in touch with an update, his phone buzzed. He hooked it out of the inside breast pocket of his suit jacket and read Claudia's text.

I won't be back. Nicole has started having contractions. Usually first labours last a while, but the nurse tells me things seem to be moving quickly.

He typed back. *All good here. Concentrate on becoming a gramma.*

The message came back right away. *Oh my god, I'm going to be a gramma. I still don't know how I feel about that.*

You're going to be the sexiest gramma ever, he sent. *Give my best to Nicole. Will be thinking of you.*

He waited. There was no reply. It made him uneasy, but he could do nothing about it now.

Five minutes to open.

Focus, he told himself. *Claudia is trusting you.*

"How are you doing?" Yvette appeared at his side.

"I can't wait for this to be over."

She laughed quietly. "For someone who hates exhibitions, you've worked hard to make this one a success."

"Claudia asked for my help. What else was I supposed to do?"

Yvette slipped her hand in the crook of his elbow. "You love her, don't you?"

Why bother to deny it? "Yes. For all my sins."

"And Claudia? How does she feel about you?"

"I have no idea."

"It might do you good to suffer an unrequited love."

He looked down at her with irritated affection. "I thought *you* were my unrequited love."

"You loved me, but not as much as you love Claudia," she said serenely. "Oh, by the way, Alecia Masters called me. We're meeting Monday."

He grunted, pleased they were no longer discussing his failed love life, but no happier the conversation had swung to his new agent. "Great. Now leave me alone. I need to psych myself up."

Yvette laughed again and tugged his arm. He bent down to let her kiss his cheek, and then she wandered away to join Karina at her post near the front door. The younger woman eyed Titus with dislike, as she had done all day. He had no idea what he'd done to deserve it, and he didn't care, as long as it didn't get in the way of how she did her job.

While he knew Claudia was hoping—maybe even depending—on sizable sales tonight, it was the success of the auction she was most worried about. Her anxiety had woven a tight thread through the last few days, and today she'd been even more concerned after learning that Robert Bateman's appearance at the rival gallery had been heavily attended. Not that she'd said so in so many words, but he'd been able to read between the lines of what she *hadn't* said.

As far as he was concerned, the auction shouldn't be a problem. Earlier, Mae had asked him to listen to her speech as she did a final practice run. It was stirring and heartfelt, and if anyone could avoid bidding on the Elizabeth Fry painting after listening to it, they weren't human. So at least he was feeling confident about that part of the evening.

He wasn't nearly as confident about his decision to add *Claudia* at the last minute.

Acting on impulse, he'd asked Yvette to bring it with her when she went to get his suit, and before he could talk himself out of it he'd hung it on the reverse of the portable panel that held the auction painting. Yvette hadn't said anything, but the look she'd levelled at him had been pregnant with understanding. Given her recent comments, the painting revealed exactly what he thought it did.

He stifled the urge to run over and rip it off the wall before anyone else could see it. Having it in public view made him feel naked and flayed—and at the same time free and unfettered. It was the most personal piece he'd ever done, and he was both proud and petrified to show it.

One minute to open.

CHAPTER THIRTY-SIX

"Any more bids?" The master of ceremonies, a local radio personality, scanned the room. "Remember, this is all in support of women's programs administered by the Elizabeth Fry Society. You heard Mae Leung's story earlier. You can give more women a chance for a new life by bidding on this wonderful piece of art."

She scanned the room expectantly, her wrist cocked, ready to drop the gavel that would signal the end of the auction. Silence filled the room, as if everyone was holding their breath. Titus, standing at the back of the crowd, felt his own lungs tighten with sympathetic anticipation.

"Going once," she said warningly. "Going twice. Sold!" The room burst into applause and the winning bidder, the owner of a local car dealership, rose and held her hands over her head like a champion prize fighter.

Air whooshed out of his mouth in delighted relief. He wasn't sure exactly what Claudia had been hoping to raise, but the painting had gone for well over what he would have priced it to sell in a gallery. And though his contract had been very clear the piece wasn't a donation, that he'd get a percentage of the proceeds, he had no intention of accepting the money, and never had, even before he'd heard Claudia's story or gotten to know Mae.

He snagged a glass of wine off a tray as a circulating waiter passed him. The worst part of the evening was over. He could relax now.

The knot of people that had gathered during the auction loosened as clients spread out into all corners of the gallery. It was a good sign few people left now the purported main event was over. He'd have to do some more abhorred mingling soon, but for the moment he stood quietly.

"Congratulations on the auction. Claudia should be pleased."

An older man had fetched up beside him, the crown of his head barely reaching Titus' bicep. The skin on his skull was pale and freckled, thin strands of colourless hair combed neatly across it. He looked up at Titus and smiled, brown eyes twinkling but shrewd.

"Elwin Nyfield," the man said, holding out his hand.

That explained why he seemed familiar. "We've met." Titus shook the offered hand carefully, Nyfield's bones brittle in his grip. "At the Elizabeth Fry fundraiser about a month ago."

"Yes, I know." Nyfield's mouth quirked mischievously, and Titus remembered his bidding battle with Frederick. Obviously, the older man did, too.

Recalling his duties as host, he said, "Thanks for bidding. I hope you weren't too disappointed not to win it." Nyfield had been second bidder throughout the auction, pushing up the price nicely.

"I would have liked it, of course. It's a wonderful piece." He motioned with his hand, an invitation to stroll, and Titus fell into place, matching his long stride to the other man's shorter paces. "But I actually have my eye on something else."

He stopped in front of *Claudia*. Titus' gut squeezed.

With a grin that took decades from his wrinkled face,

Nyfield said, "I know it is an extremely poor negotiation tactic to reveal how much you want something, but I don't care. I want *Claudia*, and I want to take her home tonight."

"Over my dead body," Titus said.

"You're doing great, honey." Claudia rubbed Nicole's lower back as her daughter curled forward and panted through a contraction.

"Mom's right," the nurse said. The woman Claudia had met in the corridor had been assigned to Nicole, and through the long hours between then and now she had learned her name was Amoy, she was originally from Jamaica, and she loved winter. "You're fully dilated. Baby is on her way."

She fussed efficiently around Nicole, getting her settled as comfortably as possible in the birthing bed. "Here comes another one," Nicole moaned.

"Breathe through it," Claudia encouraged, helpless to do anything else, yet oddly reassured by her own memories of labour. They were blurred and faded, but she could still recall how her entire being had been focussed on the job at hand. A bomb could have gone off next to her and she wouldn't have blinked. She could see the same intensity on her daughter's face.

Nicole collapsed back against the mattress. "I can't do this," she gasped, her cheeks flushed, sweat beading her temples. "I can't have a baby. I'm not ready."

"I'm afraid it's too late to change your mind," Claudia said, smiling. She flinched when Nicole bared her teeth and growled.

"I know that! I'm not stupid." Her head dropped onto the pillow and her sudden rage vanished. "I want Leo. He should be here. I made a mistake not telling him." Tear-drenched eyes stared into Claudia's and she grabbed her hand in a crushing grip. "His number is still on my phone. I kept planning to delete it, but I couldn't. Will you call him? Oh, god." Another contraction had her drawing her legs up to her distended belly. "I need to push."

"You go ahead," Amoy urged. "Do what feels right. Your body knows."

Nicole let out a low, rolling groan, squeezing Claudia's fingers painfully. When the contraction eased, she opened her eyes and glared at Claudia. "Call him!" she shouted, nodding her head frantically. "Call him now!"

Claudia scrambled for the phone and searched the contact list. "Are you sure?" she asked, her finger hovering over the screen.

"I want him here," Nicole sobbed. "I don't care if he doesn't love me. I need him."

This is a bad idea. Claudia moved into the farthest corner of the room so Nicole couldn't hear the conversation. There was no doubt in her mind that Leo would refuse to come. How could he be expected to do anything else? He was about to be broadsided by the news he was going to be a father—tonight. And as much as Claudia wanted Nicole to get her wish, she wasn't sure she could blame him if he didn't rush to her side.

The phone rang twice, and then Claudia heard a clattering sound, as if it had been dropped.

"Hello? Nicole? What's wrong?"

Startled at the use of her daughter's name and the concern in the man's voice, Claudia said, "Is this Leo? Leo Kaehlert?"

"Yes, of course. Who is this, and why do you have Nicole's phone? It's two in the morning. Is she okay?"

Claudia's eyes shot to the wall clock over the hospital room door. "I'm so sorry to wake you. I didn't realize what time it was."

"Who is this?" he repeated, sharp and demanding.

"This is Claudia, Nicole's mother. She's okay, she's fine"—a long howl of effort echoed through the room as another contraction hit Nicole—"but she wanted me to call."

"What was *that?*"

"That was Nicole. She's having your baby." Probably not the best way to break the news, Claudia thought, but in too much of a hurry to get back to her daughter's side to worry about Leo's sensibilities.

"Excuse me?"

"Look, I don't have time to go into details. Before you two broke up, Nicole got pregnant. She didn't want to tell you, but she's changed her mind. She's in labour right now. If you want to be here for the birth of your baby, you better get to the hospital. Soon."

"I don't...what are you...she didn't..."

Another shriek split the air.

"Look, I have to go," Claudia said. "If you're coming, use the Emergency entrance. They'll direct you to the Maternity Ward." She hung up the phone and hurried back to her daughter's side.

Dizzy with fatigue and joy, Claudia parked at the base of the steps leading to her apartment and then simply sat.

She had a grandson. She'd kissed his downy head, inhaled his innocent, pure scent, and fallen in love.

Shortly after she'd gotten off the phone with Leo, a doctor and a second nurse had swept into the room, and the birth had happened with bewildering speed. It was only after Nicole's tiny, perfect son had been delivered that Claudia saw the young man standing off to the side, near the door, as if unwilling to come in but unable to leave.

In the euphoria of post-labour, Nicole hadn't noticed Leo right away. "I don't have any boy names picked out. I was so certain I was having a girl," she said, her expression enraptured as she stared into the baby's scrunched up, irritable face. "But now I can't imagine anyone but him."

Claudia nodded at Leo but said nothing until the medical staff had done whatever they needed to do to tidy the room and settle Nicole and baby. Once the four were alone in the room, she touched Nicole's shoulder.

"Leo's here," she said quietly.

The happiness drained from Nicole's face, leaving it blank and frozen. Carefully, as if her neck was made of ice and might shatter if she moved too fast, she turned to the doorway.

No way was Claudia leaving her daughter alone with this stranger, but they did deserve some privacy. She sat in a chair in a far corner, turning it so it faced away from the bed, and tried to make herself invisible as she texted the good news to her parents and Jill.

Soft steps signalled Leo approaching the bed, followed by low, quiet murmurs. Determinedly ignoring what was going on behind her, she also sent a text to Titus, despite the fact it was an ungodly hour of the night. She wouldn't feel complete until she'd shared her wonder with him, too.

The conversation behind her continued. She could distinguish the difference between voices, but not words. After a few minutes, when the tone remained calm and even, she risked a glance toward the bed.

Leo was perched on the edge, staring into the blanketed bundle Nicole held. As Claudia watched, Nicole reached out her arms, and Leo gingerly accepted his son.

The security light blinked out as the pre-dawn glow brightened the sky. Claudia rolled the stiffness of sleeplessness from her shoulders, tears burning her eyes. Who knew what the future would hold for those three, but at least there was one less secret between them.

Wearily, with a sense of unreality, she climbed the stairs and entered her apartment, kicking off her shoes and tossing her purse onto the kitchen counter. In the living room, she stopped short.

Titus sprawled on her couch. It was far too short for him, and his legs draped awkwardly over one end while his neck kinked uncomfortably at the other. He'd covered himself with the throw blanket she kept in a basket, but it barely reached from his shoulders to knees.

Why hadn't he gone home? she wondered, dropping into the chair opposite and staring at him in a daze.

Because he cares about you, she answered herself. *He wants to be a part of your life. And like an idiot, you keep pushing him away. Yet he keeps coming back.*

Silver threads glinted in his beard and his chest rose and fell rhythmically, a light snore ruffling on each inhalation. He was still fully dressed, though a tie lay coiled on the coffee table and he wore no shoes. His arms were crossed at his chest, his cell phone held limply in one hand.

Her gaze traced his face. The stubble on his cheeks and under his chin blurred the usual sharp edge of his beard, and the corners of his eyes were creased and pinched. A lump in her throat caused her breath to catch and her fingers curled with the urge to tuck him in more securely under the inadequate blanket.

She hadn't thought about the auction and exhibition once during the hours of Nicole's labour. She'd left everything in Titus' care, and her gut had obviously agreed with her brain. She could trust him to do his best for her, for what she cared about. She didn't have to do everything on her own anymore.

Now that she *had* thought of the event, she knew she wouldn't get any rest until she'd gone downstairs to check things out. Curiosity dragged her to her feet, and she took the inside stairs down to the main floor.

CHAPTER THIRTY-SEVEN

Her office had a cold, empty feel. In the middle of her desk, placed where Claudia couldn't miss it, was a short note from Bernadette. When she read the results of the auction, she groped for her chair and plopped into it. The total was almost exactly what she'd hoped for. Despite all her anxiety, all her worry—and the fact she hadn't even *been* there to make sure things went well—it had been a huge success.

It wouldn't have happened without the loyalty of her team...and Titus.

Not only had he painted an image that spoke to the heart, he would have wrangled and cajoled and encouraged bids, no matter how much he professed to hate that sort of interaction. He would have done it, because he understood how important it was for her.

Because he wanted her to be happy.

She left the office and wandered across the hall to the client lounge, inspecting the displays highlighting women artists. A satisfying number of pieces had little red stickers on their tags, indicating they'd been sold. She headed for the main gallery, excitement bubbling through her exhaustion. Had Titus been as much of a hit as she'd hoped, too?

All thoughts of red stickers vanished from her mind at the sight confronting her when she stepped into the front room.

Even with the display lights off, the painting glowed magnetically. She recognized herself immediately. Her hair, her eyes, the tilt of her chin. Fascinated and terrified at the same time, she walked slowly toward it.

Titus' eyes shot open, his pulse racing, his heart seizing as it vibrated wildly.

No, wait. The vibrating was his phone, lying on his chest.

Pushing himself up to a sitting position, he rolled his aching neck as he answered. "Titus here."

"This is Denis. Denis Bourgeois, from the McCord Museum?"

Still disoriented from being awoken so suddenly, Titus mumbled a reply.

"Je suis désolé," Denis said. "I've just realized what time it is in British Columbia. My apologies, but I hope my news will make up for my rudeness."

"You have the results on the painting?" Titus said, no longer sleepy.

"This is not one hundred percent confirmed, you understand," Denis said, "but we are confident any further investigation will uphold our conclusion."

Get on with it, man. Titus loosened his clenched jaw. "Yes?"

"Other than the letters added to the creek, as we've already discussed, I am thrilled to tell you the painting shares all the characteristics of known William George Richardson Hind paintings from his time in your province."

Titus collapsed against the sofa's cushioned back. "It's a Hind? You're sure?"

"As certain as we can be. There is some minor investigating still to be done, but according to our chemical and technical inspection, this is an original work by Hind."

"My god."

"Yes, my thoughts precisely," Denis said, his humour apparent. "Do you know how exciting this is, to discover an unknown piece of Canadiana like this?"

"What about the photo and the Chinese document and the over-painted letters? Do you know anything more about them?"

"Not yet, but their presence is not an issue. They add to the mystique of the painting and in no way detract from its value."

"Its value," Titus repeated. In the shock of having his hopes confirmed, he'd rather forgotten the main reason for having the picture appraised. "Do you have an estimate of its worth?"

"I will want to bring in the Art Dealers Association of Canada before I can give you a true evaluation. But I was able to find information on the auction results of his currently known work. The most one of his pieces fetched was in May 1993."

"Which was?" Titus held his breath.

"Nineteen thousand eight-hundred dollars. But that was thirty years ago, and for a work with known provenance. With the story behind your piece"—Titus could hear his shrug over the connection—"who knows what a collector or museum might pay?"

Claudia had no idea how long she stood before her painting.

It wasn't a painting *of* her. It was *her* painting. She'd never felt so seen, so cherished, so *loved*.

She wondered if Titus understood how much he had revealed in his dramatic brush strokes, his bold colour choices, his magical composition.

Even though the painting commanded her full attention, she knew the instant he entered the gallery.

Without looking toward him, she stretched her arm back, hand held out in welcome. Apparently still shoeless, he made almost no sound as he crossed the hardwood floor and gripped her fingers. She drew him close so she could lay her head on his shoulder, her other hand wrapping around his bicep to keep him near.

"How did you know I was here?" she asked softly.

"I woke up, saw your purse on the kitchen counter." He drew in a breath, but she had to speak before he did, before he broke this spell she was under.

"She's beautiful," she said. It didn't feel odd, talking about the Claudia in the painting in the third person. The woman done in oils wasn't herself, she was how Titus saw her.

"*You're* beautiful," Titus replied, confirming her thoughts.

She shook her head. "I'm not. I'm too tall and weigh too much and I'm stubborn and I won't accept help and have unreasonable expectations of people."

"And all of that is what makes you, you. You are more than beautiful, Claudia. You are vibrant and strong. A warrior." With a teasing lilt he added, "And a gramma. Congratulations."

Her smile stretched her face. "He's gorgeous. I can't believe I love him so much already."

He turned her so they stood with the portrait at their side and tipped her chin so she had to look at him. His pupils were liquid silver in the dim light. "I have something to tell you," he said.

"Me, first," she said quickly.

"But you'll want—"

"No," she said, covering his mouth with her hand. "I mean it. Me, first."

She felt his lips curve in a smile and amusement flashed in his eyes. He nodded his agreement, and she lowered her hand and twisted her fingers together.

"First, thank you for last night." He lifted one

shoulder in a negligent move and she glared at him. "Don't act like it was nothing. I know it was out of your comfort zone and it was much, much more than I should have asked of you. But I saw the auction total, and there are red stickers everywhere. It couldn't have been a bigger success. So let me thank you."

"You're welcome, then."

"Second." She pulled in a slow breath and forced herself to meet his gaze. "The painting. *My* painting." Shrugging helplessly, she struggled for words. "I am overwhelmed."

It was his turn to look uncomfortable and embarrassed. "I shouldn't have included it without telling you."

"Don't worry about that. I'm beyond flattered."

"Don't." He spit the word out angrily and she started. "Don't be flattered for being recognized for who you are, Claudia."

He was right—and she was done apologizing to herself and others for who she was. "I didn't mean it that way. I'm still stunned. I'm not explaining myself properly."

His heated expression softened. He cupped her chin in his palm, his gaze searching and vulnerable. "Do you like it?"

"How can you ask that? I love it." She gripped his wrist, the muscles and bones and tendons warm and strong. "I love what I see *in* the painting, too."

His eyes locked on hers. "And what's that?"

"I see how *you* see *me*. I see your pride and understanding and attraction." She swallowed and said the rest. "I see your love."

His eyelids flickered and her heart froze. Had she misread his work? Had she infused it with a meaning he hadn't intended?

Had she seen her own feelings, not his?

She released his wrist and took a step back, breaking contact. Chills flushed her skin and a wave of nausea made her dizzy. "I'm sorry," she said, more and more frantic the longer he was silent. "I shoul—"

His eyes snapped wide and he pulled her into his embrace with a sudden jerk. "For god's sake, stop apologizing," he said, his face buried in the crook of her shoulder.

Without volition, her arms circled his waist. "I didn't mea—"

His arms tightened almost viciously, squeezing the breath from her lungs, choking off her words.

"I did mean it," he said, raising his head so she could see his face. His expression was a confusing mixture of fury and affection, exasperation and satisfaction. "I did paint it with love, Claudia. Other people saw it, too. But I didn't know if *you* would see it. And if you did, I figured you'd fight it, deny it, refuse to admit it."

"I can't," she said. "I don't want to. And it's time to stop denying my own feelings, too."

His hands, which had been sweeping up and down her back, caressing her shoulders, lingering on her neck, froze. Guarded suspicion narrowed his eyes and she almost laughed. Who could blame him? She'd shoved him away so often he probably thought she'd have to lose her mind before she changed it. Maybe she had.

"What are you saying?" His voice echoed into the empty gallery.

"I'm tired. It's been a long night." She shouldn't be teasing him like this. It made light of the depth of the feelings she was finally able to welcome into her soul.

He shook his head. "You won't ruin this, Claudia. I don't care what excuses you give. But I need to hear you say it."

Tenderness pierced her heart. She ran her hands up his chest to his chin, his beard soft, tickling her palms. And she said the words he wanted to hear with lightness, with joy, with fearlessness.

"I love you, Titus."

His eyes blazed. "See? That wasn't so hard."

She urged his head lower and pressed a kiss upon his lips. His mouth instantly opened in welcome as his hands stroked her back, gripped her hips. Claudia let her weight rest against him, confident he wouldn't let her fall.

Heated passion eased into a glowing warmth, urgency replaced by a loving familiarity. "When's the last time you slept?" Titus murmured against her ear.

"I can't remember." The words felt heavy and awkward on her tongue. She wondered if it was possible to be delirious from exhaustion and emotion.

"Let's get you upstairs."

Linked together, arms about each other's waists, Claudia let Titus lead her to the apartment. As she collapsed on the bed, she mumbled, "Didn't you have something to tell me?"

He pulled off her shoes and unzipped her jeans. "It can wait until later. Get some sleep."

"I love you," she said, her eyes already closing, but she struggled to stay awake so she could hear his reply.

"I love you, too."

CHAPTER THIRTY-EIGHT

Two weeks later, Claudia stood in the upper hallway of Titus' house, leaned her arms on the rail, and looked down on the party below.

Her eyes were drawn to her grandson, cradled in his Auntie Jill's arms. Nicole was seated next to her sister, heads close together as they talked without taking their eyes from the baby.

Claudia had told Nicole that Leo was welcome to attend the party, but she didn't know if the invitation had been extended. From the little her daughter had let slip since the birth, it seemed she and Leo were cautiously forging a new relationship, at least where their son was concerned. Claudia had taken the fact that Nicole had agreed to Leo's suggestion to name the baby Noah as a positive sign. Though she hadn't spent any more time with him, his rapid appearance at the hospital and continued willingness to accept his son hinted to Claudia that he was a good man. Even if his parents never committed to each other, Noah would be better off with an honourable father figure, something she hadn't been able to give her daughters.

A burst of laughter drew her attention to the group of women gathered around the dining table, its surface laden with food and drink. Yvette, Tanya, Karina, and Bernadette were obviously finding something amusing in a story being related by Patsy and her partner, Chris.

Claudia's parents were also below, conversing with Nadia Yu who had made the trip from Wells, the three of them on the couch facing the fireplace.

And in front of the fireplace stood Mae and her father, Jasmine asleep on his shoulder, supremely undisturbed by the hubbub around her. Mae and Mr. Leung were listening intently to something Denis Bourgeois was saying as he pointed at the party's guest of honour—William George Richardson Hind's painting.

"Here you are." Two arms bracketed her and the heat of Titus' chest warmed her back. "I wondered where you'd gone."

"Noah spit up on my shirt. I went to change in your bedroom."

"*Our* bedroom," he corrected.

"Right."

The celebration wasn't just for the return of Mae's painting and the exciting news of its value and heritage. It was also a housewarming party, as Titus had taken full ownership the day before. And while the house was in his name, and there'd been no discussion of the future, he was insistent that Claudia look on it as her own.

"Did Mae tell you what she's going to do with the painting?" he asked.

"She hasn't decided yet. Denis is advising her to take it slow. She could probably get a pretty penny for it if they auctioned it off today, but it might be a better long-term investment to hold off for a while. In the meantime, she could see some revenue by loaning it to museums for public exhibits." While Mae had been ecstatic at the news of the painting's value, the discovery had complicated, rather than simplified, her financial situation. If it had been worth less, had a less intriguing story attached to it, the decision to sell would have been less difficult, giving her the funds needed to launch her daycare. Now that selling was in question, she would need to continue exploring other avenues. Luckily, she had received a bursary recently that had added to her savings, and her eloquence the night of the auction had resulted in contract work to present at other Elizabeth Fry events. While it wasn't a lot of money, every bit helped, and hopefully as soon as her divorce was final, she'd have access to other funds.

"Not quite the treasure we were looking for, but a treasure all the same," Titus said, lowering his chin to her shoulder. She tilted her head so they rested temple to temple.

"Do you think the gold is still out there somewhere?" she said.

"Who knows. Kate says she's willing to try again. But maybe it's best if we don't solve that mystery. That's part of the lure of the painting, after all. We don't want to detract from that."

"True." She twisted in the cage of his arms so that her back was to the rail. "The painting's not the only treasure we found."

His teeth gleamed whitely in the frame of his dark beard. "Are you getting sentimental on me?"

"Maybe." She dropped her gaze, toying with a button on his shirt. "I have a housewarming present for you."

A low growl vibrated through his chest, under her fingertips, and she peeked up at him. "Should we go somewhere more private?" he said, his hands slipping from the rail to clutch her hips. She arched her back and was rewarded with a return pressure that told her exactly what he thought her present involved.

"I should have said two presents," she teased. "You'll get that one later. This is the one I was talking about."

She reached into the pocket of her skirt and held up a key. He frowned. "What's that for?"

"My apartment."

His eyes flashed to meet hers, and she knew he understood what a step this was for her. "You don't have to do this."

She dropped it into the breast pocket of his shirt and patted it. "I do. You gave me keys to your house. This seems fair. Besides, I *want* you to have it. I trust you with my heart—how could I not trust you with my home?"

"You know I think of here"—he tipped his head from side to side—"as your home."

"I know. And someday, I will, too." To be honest, she didn't think that day was far off, but for now, she needed the safety net the apartment represented. "I don't want you to think I'm shutting you out. It's not that, not at all. Take the key, Titus." She patted his pocket again. "Take it as it is meant, a pledge to blend our lives, to share our love, in the way that suits us best."

"You are so amazing." He lowered his forehead to hers.

"And you are more patient than I deserve." She tilted her head to brush her lips gently across his.

"You deserve the world, Claudia, and all its riches. And I want to give it to you."

"You *have*," she said, deepening the kiss. "You gave it to me when you gave me your love. And when you let me love you back. You deserve it, too, Titus, every nugget of joy and happiness I can give you."

After saying which, she dragged him to his—*their*—bedroom and gave him his second house-warming present while the party went on without them.

ACKNOWLEDGEMENTS

The more books I write, the braver I am about asking experts for help. I am most often pleasantly surprised by their responses to having their brains picked by a romance author, and this book was no exception to that.

Thanks to James Douglas, Public Programming & Global Media Development for Barkerville Historic Town and Park. In my previous life as a television commercial writer/producer, I worked with James for many years, and was comfortable asking him to read my manuscript to ensure I hadn't made any egregious errors regarding the Cariboo Gold Rush. He had several helpful suggestions and minor corrections which I gladly incorporated. But the biggest surprise was learning that his stepmother also wrote romances, and that he was familiar with the genre. So not only was he able to assist with the historical aspects, but he also assessed the story as a whole. His kind words really made my day!

I would also like to thank Amy Rose, of Library and Archives Canada. She kindly answered my vague email query regarding the value of William George Richardson Hind artwork (more on him below), despite the restrictions of working from home in the early days of the COVID-19 pandemic. Even after her initial response, which included the fact that the most Hind's work fetched in auction was $19,800 in May 1993, she didn't forget me, and provided more information weeks later, for which I was extremely grateful.

As I was dealing with the history of a Chinese-Canadian family (even though fictional), I wanted to ensure the subject was treated properly. Through connections at the University of Northern British Columbia (you know who you are, Zoë!), I was put in touch with Dr. Christine Ho Younghusband, Ed.D. Her reassurances in this area were greatly appreciated—as was her enthusiastic response to the story, even though she doesn't consider herself *a reader*.

British Columbia had two major gold rushes, one on the lower Fraser River in 1858, and the next in the Cariboo, near the centre of the province, starting in 1862. The town of Barkerville was the hub for this second rush, and all facts in this story regarding this site and its Chinese community are accurate. There are numerous online resources where you can find out more about the Cariboo Gold Rush and the Barkerville Town and Park National Historic Site.

I would also like to make note that the Elizabeth Fry Society is a real organization doing important work across Canada.

Finally, while all the main characters in *Richly Deserved* are imaginary, four secondary characters deserve some explanation.

Just in case you've never heard of Robert Bateman, he is a Canadian art icon. Find out more about him at robertbateman.ca.

While wandering down rabbit holes on the internet in the guise of research, I came across the obituary of Julius H. Franklyn. According to the article on the website, Find A Grave, the Cariboo Sentinel newspaper reported he died on June 15, 1870, age 23, due to a fall down the shaft in the Perseverance Mine (of which he was part owner). He was a native of Jersey, but raised in London and came to Victoria, British Columbia in 1862 before moving on to Barkerville. At the request of

Jewish residents, parts of the Old Testament and suitable address were read at his graveside. I paid a small homage to him, and all the others who came in search for the Mother Lode, by using his name for one of the two miners connected with Leung Ah.

My prospector, Kate Rice, has no basis in reality. But I was inspired to give her that name because of Kathleen Creighton Starr Rice. The real Kate Rice was a prospector, adventurer, and writer from Ontario who, in 1912, left her upper-middle class family to homestead in northern Manitoba. She was widely recognized for her adventurous spirit, high intelligence, and her success as a woman in the mining industry.

And last but not least, I want to draw attention to William George Richardson Hind. All details of his life included in this story are a matter of record (including the fact he was kicked out of the Overlanders for being too irritating). Although my long-lost painting and its secret documents are fictitious, at least two of Hind's early pieces are missing. According to experts, the quality of his work varies, but it is generally agreed that his most historically significant pieces are those portraying mining life in the Cariboo in the 1860s. For further information, visit biographi.ca.

THANK YOU!

Thanks for reading *Richly Deserved*. I hope you enjoyed it!

Reviews and ratings are a great way to help other readers discover new authors. Just a line or two is all that's needed—or simply click the number of stars you think it deserves. I encourage you to post your honest opinion at the retailer where you purchased your copy, or on GoodReads. Thank you so much!

I'd love to stay in touch. Subscribe to my newsletter and you'll immediately receive a free read, be able to tag along with my dog-walking adventures, find out what I'm reading when I should be working, and other randomness...along with all my writing news, of course! You'll probably only hear from me once a month—unless I've got something really exciting to share. You can also find me on social media—I'm most active on Facebook and Instagram. You'll find everything on my website, brendamargriet.com.

ABOUT THE AUTHOR

Brenda Margriet writes savvy, slow burn, contemporary romances with ordinarily amazing characters. In her own ordinarily amazing life, she had a successful career in radio and television production before deciding to pilfer from her retirement plan to support her writing compulsion.

Readers have called her stories "poignant," "explicit and steamy," "interesting, intriguing and entertaining," and "unlike any romance you've read before" (she assumes the latter was meant in a good way).

Discover more about Brenda and her books at her website, brendamargriet.com.